GONZO
DAVIES
Caught in Possession

GONZO DAVIES

Caught in Possession

EDDIE BUTLER

Gomer

Published in 2015 by
Gomer Press, Llandysul, Ceredigion, SA44 4JL

ISBN 978 1 78562 032 4
ISBN 978 1 78562 033 1 (EPub)
ISBN 978 1 78562 034 8 (Kindle)

A CIP record for this title is available from the British Library.

This book is published with the financial support of the
Welsh Books Council.

Printed and bound in Wales at
Gomer Press, Llandysul, Ceredigion

1

The four figures on top of the Blorenge stepped off the wide grassy track and entered the bracken. Almost immediately the walkers vanished, consumed by the greenery that covered the sheltered side of the slightly domed top of the mountain. Gonzo Davies was third in the line. Only he stood head and shoulders above the highest fronds and was able to admire the sea of foliage all around them. The bracken swayed from matt to gloss in the breeze beneath a clear blue sky of high summer.

This gentle motion of the landscape was rudely interrupted. At the head of the line, Capper Harris was boring a tunnel and what had been started as a narrow passage by the sheep that grazed on the moorland, then slightly widened by the wild ponies that roamed up here, now gave way to this human excavator. Capper's thick arms flailed at the stems and as they broke or folded, his bald, domed head sometimes came into view. He added a soundtrack of grunting to this process of deforestation.

'Dear God,' said Our Marnie, second in line. 'He's turned into Tarzan.' She stopped, put out a hand, pulled a frond that had managed to stay upright towards her face and examined it. 'Not being funny,' she said. 'But isn't this stuff … like, poisonous?'

Gonzo caught up with her. He took the unfurled, tender frond from her. 'Fiddleheads …'

'Fiddlesticks,' said Our Marnie. 'Are they dangerous?'

'Only when they give off spores,' said Gonzo. 'I think we're a bit early for that.' He peered even more closely at the bracken. 'They're a delicacy, they say …'

'But you're not sure, right?'

Grace, last in the line, arrived. 'I don't think we should eat them,' she said.

'Maybe not,' said Our Marnie. 'But I reckon when it comes to food, you say that about everything. Don't get me wrong, Grace, but what you need is a good three-course meal.'

Gonzo slipped an arm around Grace and put his fingers lengthways down the gaps between her ribs. She was about to protest when Our Marnie continued: 'After what you went through – and it's still only a few months back – you need to get your strength up … and put on a few pounds.'

Our Marnie turned and started to follow the sound of the bulldozer, now fifty yards ahead. 'Unlike somebody else I could mention … somebody who needs a little more exercise like this and a little less food.' She stopped again. 'It'll be a relief when you two …' – and she nodded her head in the direction of Capper and then looked back at Gonzo – 'get back into training for the new season. Won't be long before it starts all over again.'

She turned and listened. The crashing had stopped. 'Right,' she said. 'Better make sure the king of the jungle isn't snacking on these … fiddleheads.' She lifted her hands to the sky. 'A short-cut, he said … I ask you. We'll be lost before you know it. You mark my words.' She set off and was soon out of sight in the bracken.

Gonzo didn't move. He squeezed Grace and sighed. 'She's right, you know.' Grace tensed. 'No, not about you being too skinny. Although you could do …'

'Careful, now,' warned Grace.

'OK. No, she's right about the training. By now we should be hard at it. Kit on and out here, running. Looking forward to the first match.'

'We're not at the end of July yet.'

'Aye, but … I don't know. I seem to have hit the buffers a bit.'

Grace eased herself away from his arm and turned to face him. She took both his hands. 'Is it me? Am I stopping you?'

'Maybe,' said Gonzo. Grace was so dismayed she tried to let go but he held her. 'But it's more that I'm … I've got to face it. I'm not getting any younger. And I spend a lot of time thinking about what comes next. And yes, that includes thinking a lot about you. You and me …'

Grace paused and looked straight ahead, at the lower part of Gonzo's sternum. 'And is that good?' she whispered.

'It's good. Very good.'

At a similar altitude to the Blorenge on the edge of the South Wales coalfield, but at the other end of the world, lay Kakanui Rangers Rugby Club. It was not far from Kyeburn, one of the old gold-rush towns of Central Otago on New Zealand's South Island. The Rangers no longer ran an adult team but were a social hub for seven or eight surrounding communities, and on Sunday mornings children from these hamlets and homesteads came from miles around to play. The youngsters rarely had to play away from home because their parents also fired up the finest barbecue on South Island, and everybody wanted to come to them.

On this Sunday, a cold rain had been falling all morning and the party mood was never quite the same when all the cooking and eating had to be done inside. Some of the visitors might have been tempted to leave early, so drenched had they been on the touchlines. But more or less all of them had decided to stay. There was to be a special guest – or rather, a special homecoming – to keep them interested. The Kakanui Club was also the place where Lachlan 'Tai' McDonald had learned his rugby. And he just happened to be the number 8 and the current captain of the New Zealand All Blacks.

Capper came back down the pathway and almost bowled Our Marnie over. He swerved to the right and dived into the bracken. He emerged with greenery plastered to his sweating brow.

'My Tarzan of the Apes,' she said and climbed into his den.

'You Jane,' said Capper.

'God, you're panting and sticky.'

'D'you want to be as well?'

'Cut it out … the others will be along in a minute.'

Capper crawled back to the track he had beaten and looked back down it. He stood up, the top of his head poking out of the bracken. He jumped up and down but he was not built for leaping high and he couldn't see over the top.

'Oi, Gonzo,' he shouted.

'Shush,' went Our Marnie.

'What?' said Capper. 'We've got the whole mountain to ourselves and you think it's a public library?'

'I'm just saying … show a little …'

'What is it?' shouted Gonzo, not far away.

'Where are you?'

'Where d'you think we are?'

'What can you see?'

'I can see your bald old head.'

'Less of the old …'

'What d'you want?'

'Look ahead, you great useless lighthouse and see which way we go. There's a fork in the path and I want to check …'

'Thought you said you knew this shortcut …'

'Aye, well that was before this fuckin' bracken grew and doubled the height of the mountain. Just tell me what you see.'

'Well, to the left I can see the Cotswolds in England. Over your shining head I can see the Bristol Channel. To the right there's moor and more moor …'

'Very good …'

'And behind me …' Gonzo turned and looked at Grace. 'The best view of all.' He bent down and with one arm picked her effortlessly into the air. Grace began to unbutton his shirt.

'Just tell me what to do at the next fuckin' fork,' yelled Capper.

'Language,' said Our Marnie.

'Go right,' shouted Gonzo at Capper. 'And you,' he said to Grace, whose hands were wandering. 'You should stop.'

'You sure?' shouted Capper. But all had gone quiet on the path behind him and Our Marnie. They waited for half a minute before Capper climbed back into the flattened clearing among the tall stems.

'He can see the Cotswolds, can he?' said Our Marnie.

'Look at the view I've got.' Capper's T-shirt had ridden up to expose a domed moorland of belly. He reached out and pulled her down. 'Not here,' said Our Marnie.

'Oh, so they have all the …'

'I'm not saying it's out of the question. I'm just saying we need to do it our way. Not copycat …'

'OK, OK,' said Capper. 'Anyway, what were you talking about back there?'

'We were talking diets and losing a bit of weight.'

'Please don't go on one. You're fuckin' perfect the way you are.'

'Language. We weren't talking about me.'

'Oh.'

'Diets … and training. As in doing some …'

'Oh.'

'Come on,' said Our Marnie, jumping to her feet. 'At least we can start on the exercise front.' She put her foot to Capper's chest as he struggled into a kneeling position and pushed him to the ground. 'Catch me and you can have your wicked way.' And she ran off down the tunnel through the bracken.

The day before, Tai had captained the All Blacks to victory over South Africa. He had then given an interview on the touchline – as the man of the match was obliged to do –

and he had said as a joke, in response to the suggestion that New Zealand's win had been 'comfortable', that in the first minute his old rival, Corné du Toit, had hit him so hard in the tackle that he had seen stars. And that had triggered a whole series of questions about concussion protocols and Tai's availability for the next round against Australia.

He would have laughed off such concerns, except that in the very last minute of the game his temple had been struck by the knee of his own very large team-mate and second row, Bryce Collins – nicknamed Clumsy for a good reason – and Tai had truly had been dazed for a second. He recognised that he was now in no shape to make any sort of judgement about his own well-being. But in his mind's eye – and he was alert enough to see the irony of relying on his cognitive powers – what he had suffered was no worse than anything he'd been through twenty times before. He hadn't become a legend of the Kiwi game and won 99 caps without putting his body and his head on the line. He wanted to win his 100th cap at his home stadium in Dunedin and if that meant ducking out of a thorough assessment and running a medical risk, then he was prepared to take it.

Long before he had played against South Africa, he had told the coach, George Pai Taihonga, about an engagement at his old club and permission had been granted for him to leave Auckland before the team.

'Go with our blessing,' the veteran Maori coach had said.

But that was before Clumsy struck. Tai had decided to catch the first Sunday-morning flight south to Dunedin and had risen earlier – and not without being conscious of a pain in the side of his head – than strictly necessary.

Having checked for photographers or fans wanting a selfie, he stepped smartly out of the hotel into a car driven by Jimmy O'Hara. Jimmy, originally from Invercargill, had been doing errands for the All Blacks for two decades. He had never played but he knew all the secrets of rugby. He had pulled some – most – of the most famous names in New Zealand from hazardous situations. He had carried them drunken from pubs and police cells, and even naked from bedrooms. Once, when he knew he would not arrive in time to extricate little Anton Gillespie from a certain boudoir in Wellington, he had thrown himself against the windscreen of the returning husband's car as it swung around a street corner four blocks from home.

'It's all quiet,' said Jimmy to Tai now, 'which is what you should have been.'

'Not you too, Jimmy,' said Tai.

'Don't you "Not you, too, Jimmy" me. You should know better than to give them a single scrap to seize on. If I didn't know you, I'd say you'd had a bang on the head.'

'Very funny.'

'And how is it, by the way?'

'How's what?

'The bang on your head.'

'What bang? Du Toit didn't …'

'No, he didn't. But Clumsy did, didn't he?

'Damn.'

'What? You think old Jimmy didn't see it?'

'You old …'

'So how is it?'

Tai rubbed his head. 'Kind of sore.'

'You'd better rest it then.'

They drove in silence. Tai tried not to shut his eyes but he awoke as they pulled up in front of the domestic terminal.

'What day is it?' asked Jimmy.

'Sunday.'

'What was the score yesterday?'

'34-18.'

'What's your father's younger brother's name?'

'Colin.'

'See you later, Tai. Have a good day. It's a great set-up down there.'

Tai slung a bag over his shoulder and walked into the terminal. He sneaked a look back to see if Jimmy was on the phone yet. Jimmy waved at him. Tai turned away and headed for Departures.

'Yep, he's just looked back,' said Jimmy into his hands-free phone. 'He got the score wrong, George.'

Grace and Gonzo lay down in the bracken so gently that not a stem broke. They watched a beetle clamber on to the back of Gonzo's hand and climb up his forearm until it fell off and landed on its back, its legs waving helplessly. Gonzo flicked it over with his forefinger and the beetle walked away into the darkness that surrounded the small clearing.

'I was in the Land Rover the other day,' said Gonzo. 'I was sitting there, outside the club, waiting for Capper. And there was this huge bluebottle, buzzing around the cab …'

'I hope this isn't a passion-killer, this story …' said Grace, undoing his last shirt button. Gonzo shook his head.

'And I was just about to, you know, chase it and swat it

with a load of rolled-up invoices, when it got caught in this web, right down by the corner of the windscreen. Only a couple of strands, it looked like, and when the fly started thrashing around, it looked for sure it'd break free. But it couldn't and it started to tire. And suddenly this tiny spider comes out of the gap by the air vent and pounces on the fly. The fly starts writhing again, but the spider won't be shaken off. Round and round he goes, spinning the fly up in his thread. A minute at most. All over. The spider drags this bundle, twice his size down into the air vent.'

'Could have been a she,' said Grace.

'Who?'

'The spider. You said "he". I'm saying it could have been a "she". We're much better at that kind of thing.'

Sunlight, dappled by the slatted leaves, had been dancing over the couple but now it seemed the leaning stems had righted themselves and the fronds over their heads joined and interwove in the breeze. The hideaway was now softly lit.

'I …' started Gonzo, but Grace interrupted him: 'Stop talking. For a few minutes. First, this.' Gonzo groaned and surrendered. 'I'll soon have you all wrapped up,' whispered Grace. 'Of course, when I'm done with you, I'll have to kill you.'

He was called Tai, short for Taieri, after the river and gorge where his Scottish ancestors had settled 150 years previously. Tai's father had then moved the family from Middlemarch to a farm near Kyeburn and his son had joined the Kakanui Rangers and played and eaten exceptionally well. The club had tried to change his nickname to Kye, swapping an abbreviation of his old home for his new, but he had insisted on the original. And they soon found out that Tai McDonald generally won his arguments. He went back four or five times a year, using the club as a safe haven, where he could talk rugby without having to be careful, or simply to enjoy the grub. As far as the captain of the All Blacks could ever be off-duty, this would be it.

There was another aspect of Kakanui Rangers Rugby Club that set it apart. Rising up out of the plateau was a mound. It wasn't particularly high – from bottom to top had taken a 12-year-old Tai forty-three strides – but it was as much a signature feature of the club as the man-made facilities. The mound ran down one side of the complex, a sort of natural bank on which the spectators could sit on match days, and a source of pain on training nights.

'Pound the mound,' was the shout that greeted generation after generation of players. Well-worn tracks went up and down the slope. The floodlights, powerful enough to illuminate professional games – that were never played here – lit up junior training nights and were angled in such a way that the mound remained in full view whenever the club's youngsters swarmed all over it.

On the Sunday of Tai's visit, the mound was empty. The rain had driven everyone indoors. Back in the early days of the club, water would run off the mound and collect in puddles on the pitch. Those days were long gone. The rain still flowed in rivulets down the training tracks, but once they hit the lush grass of the playing surface, they vanished into the sandy soil. Every square inch of the Kakanui Rangers' pitches was immaculately drained. It was a major topic of conversation in the clubhouse. The growth and upkeep of the grass never ceased to absorb the parents, even if on this day they couldn't admire the fruits of their labour. The windows of the clubhouse were steamed up and the floor was slippery with the water that dripped off the coats of the Sunday lunchtime throng. Youngsters, showered and just as dripping, darted in and out of the legs of the grown-ups.

When Tai entered the clubhouse there was a little surge from the children to greet him, but only because they knew him so well. Four of them were his nephews and nieces and there were at least six cousins in the club. They high-fived him and then ran off again. The adults all shook his hand and they talked of the weather at home and the game up in Auckland, without reference to the concussion. He was handed a cold beer and he held it in his large hand and drank slowly. It would be his only one of the day.

Running away from Gonzo and Grace, Our Marnie reached the fork in the bracken. She stopped and waited for Capper to catch up. He arrived, hotter and stickier than ever.

'All right, all right,' said Our Marnie as he lunged for her. 'Go and find somewhere. He said to go to the right; so go left.'

Capper began to push his way through the vegetation, following the narrowest of sheep tracks. He soon stopped. Despite appearances, this wasn't a trail at all. The tops of the bracken seemed to extend in a flat line, but the ground suddenly fell away under his battered old trainers. 'Bit of a drop here,' he said. 'You hang on there, while I check it out.' He carried on, still noisily sweeping the bracken aside with his arms but taking more cautious steps, peering at the ground in front of him.

Our Marnie stayed at the fork. She flapped at the front of her shirt to let some air in, smiling at the thought of Capper building a little love nest for them. She caught a glimpse of his head at one point, but then he was lost from sight. She heard him curse a couple of times, only for the crashing to resume. Then came a single knock, a sort of muffled crack. And then all went quiet. She waited for him to announce that he had found the perfect spot, but there was no sound up ahead. 'Capper?' she said. 'Come on, no messing now.'

She made her way carefully forward, until she reached the point where the beating of the pathway stopped. A grey rock stood in her way, tight up against a boulder of limestone, covered in patches of lichen. Beyond these obstructions – and all around – stood an untouched wall of bracken. 'Capper?' she said, louder now.

The first tremor was felt as lunch was being laid out on the tables that ran at right angles to the bar. Three trestles collapsed immediately and it was the shock to the food that caused more of a stir than the movement of the ground. Tremors were rare up here but everybody had felt one before. Silence fell and everybody waited. Even the children stopped in their tracks.

The second shock-wave sent a ripple from one end of the clubhouse to the other. Photos fell off the walls and there was a loud crash overhead in the roof space. Again, there was no panic but a murmur went around that it would be safer outside. In the three minutes of stillness that followed, people gathered up their families and left the clubhouse and gathered in clusters on the main pitch.

The third wave was so violent that there was genuine alarm. The pitches visibly buckled and at least twenty people were knocked off their feet. Several children began to scream, and once they began to scatter there was general pandemonium. Parents ran after their offspring, shouting even when the movement stopped and the grinding rumble, emanating from beneath them, died away. Most children were quickly rounded up, but Tai spotted little Doddie Fairbank, one of his cousins, on his own on the pitch, pointing at the mound. Tai ran with his familiar loping gait towards Doddie and swept him up.

'It's Amy, Tai. She ran that way.'

Tai looked at the mound. Little Amy Frazer stood at its base. And then she began to sway. The last shock wave knocked Doddie out of Tai's arms, but the ground moved even more violently under Amy. She was pitched into a crater that opened up under her. Tai swayed drunkenly towards her and he too fell into the hole. He picked her up and threw her as hard as he could. The upward thrust drove him deeper into the crater, where the earth seemed to have turned to watery dust. He looked down. He was up to his calves in this glue. He felt a rush of adrenaline, a surge that seemed to cause a flash of pain in his injured head. But at least he wasn't being sucked down any deeper. Suddenly he was calm. Every thought came to him with absolute clarity. He looked up. The crater wasn't deep. There was a way out. There were children to rescue. He lifted his left foot, just as a slice of the mound split away with a sound that was almost like a sigh, and slid towards the crater. Tai saw it in slow motion. The slide stopped a foot in front of Doddie, who was frozen to the spot. Grass and liquefied soil buried little Amy Frazer up to her waist. And the moving mound totally engulfed the captain of the All Blacks.

Gonzo heard Our Marnie coming back towards them, calling his name. It wasn't the best moment to be interrupted, but he poked his head up, slightly flushed and irritated. 'Over here,' he said. Grace frowned too, and stared to gather up her clothes.

'Sorry,' said Our Marnie, when she saw his head. 'I won't come any closer.' She stopped and then broke into a low wail. 'But it's Capper. Something's happened. He's disappeared.'

2

The Blorenge formed a mighty block at the head of two valleys that twisted and turned for twenty miles down to the Bristol Channel. The village lay to the south of the mountain's summit, lower and overlooked by two sides of high ridges – but still on a high plain of pitted, pockmarked flat grassland, where rainwater gathered before either sinking into the fissures of the mountain itself, or gathering pace from this standing start, running visibly and freely towards Newport. If the Blorenge was the giant head of the terrain, the village was a pimple on its neck. No bracken grew on the exposed moor. The prevailing wind blew up from below and cut down what little grew above the ankle-high grass. In winter the wind could shift to the north and come at the village over the top of the Blorenge; everything exposed to its biting blast wilted. On rare days of stillness, frosts – even in early summer – finished off what was left. Ever since the coal mine had been sunk – and certainly ever since it shut nearly half a century ago – the area around the village had been known as 'the wilderness'.

West Street was the village's highest point and was more exposed than anywhere to the elements. It was a cul-de-sac, a single row of twenty terraced houses, ending at a rusty old gate to the moor. The most worn of the paths that ran over the wilderness from that point went down to the rugby field at the bottom of the village. The pair of houses closest to the wilderness had been converted into a rugby clubhouse – or what remained of it. On the last night of the previous season, a night in late spring of rain followed by starlit clarity across the heavens – the party night of all party nights, thrown to celebrate the village team's victory in the Babcock Cup – the gable end had collapsed. And since then, the clubhouse had sat empty.

In the early hours of that memorable occasion, Gonzo had faced the rubble, now filling the club's pot-holed car park, and the suddenly revealed moor and mountain, and declared that they would rebuild, bigger and better. And although the immediate response had been to carry on singing and drinking, within a few hours of the end of the carousing, Gonzo and Capper were organising bleary-eyed but willing volunteers into working parties. They set about the debris, shovelling with the intensity of those of their mining forebears that had worked the Garw seam deep in the mountain beneath their feet. And that evening, the players and supporters had wrapped their blistered palms around beer glasses and drank again, this time not accompanied by song, but by the plans they were making for their new rugby home.

But since then, nothing had happened. It wasn't through an evaporation of interest, but because of the subsidence that had caused the collapse in the first place. It was spreading, buckling the kerbstones in front of the Williamses at number 18, cracking three panes in the kitchen window of the Evanses in 17. As the Joneses of 16 awaited their turn, the shifting ground beneath their feet did a little side-step and missed them and the empty numbers 15 and 14, but reappeared at the Capaldis, bringing down the low front-garden wall that Giovanni – Job-shy Joe – had only just completed as his project to welcome in the spring.

The council sent up their engineers to examine the advance of the destruction. They arrived in teams to take their measurements and stroke their chins. It didn't take them long to condemn the entire street and order an evacuation of all the residents of West Street, provoking a storm of protest from one end to the other about insurance and compensation. The chief engineering officer only had to point to the rugby club and ask if that was what they were prepared to suffer in their own homes, where their children slept, and most obediently moved out. A few stayed for a month or two, unable to find alternative accommodation quickly, or because they had no children on whom a wall might fall, but they too joined the exodus. Only the Capaldis remained, disinclined by nature to acquiesce to any orders from officialdom.

With the departure of the inhabitants went any possibility that permission to commence reconstruction of the clubhouse would ever be granted. Strangely enough, this shutting-down of a whole row of housing stock in the community coincided with the return of light. For forty years the streetlamps in the uppermost street in the village had been extinguished, but one of the engineers, while conducting a fire assessment, had found a simple disconnection. He made the most straightforward of electrical repairs, the sodium lights came back on and the almost deserted West Street glowed again after dark.

As Capper fell, he had time to think that it was strange that so many thoughts should come to him – he who had never set too much store by thinking – in this brief and helpless surrender to gravity. He sensed his time in space would be brief and he presumed that there would be pain at the end of it. And that he was about to die. This, he thought, was what it was like then. It was different from what he had imagined – in the rare moments when he had ever mused on his mortality – although he had always suspected his would be a roly-poly kind of death, as opposed to an emaciated, bed-bound end, his burliness ravaged. He would miss Our Marnie. That came to him with absolute clarity, bringing with it the first pang of regret. But even that gave way to a flash of ill-judged good humour. This above all was a ridiculous way to go.

All this was going through his mind in the second and a tiny bit more of time he spent in feet-first free fall. Just as a startlingly clear picture formed in his head to accompany the ludicrous circumstances of his demise, Capper's copious backside struck rock and he began to bounce. The rock was smooth, filed by the rush of water over millions of years, and rather than forming a vertical shaft, the tunnel curved from the point of contact towards the horizontal. Capper began to slow, bruised and grazed but not shredded or impaled. He dared to think he might even live to tell this tale when his forehead struck the roof of the tunnel as it contracted on all sides and he lost consciousness. A fraction of a second later his large stomach became wedged and a long wound opened up under a spike of rock. He lay motionless in the pitch black, sixty feet inside the mountain. His legs were left dangling over a void below. Slowly a trickle emerged from the hem of his T-shirt, fabric that could absorb no more of the blood oozing out of the big incision and all the scrapes on the upper part of his body. This rivulet ran under his shorts, down his legs and began to drip off his calves, a movement of fluid that was the only sign that Capper's heart was still beating.

It wasn't strictly true that West Street in the village was empty apart from the Capaldis, or that nothing had happened at the clubhouse. Nothing had happened downstairs, in the communal part of the building. Upstairs lay the steward's flat, converted by Gonzo and Capper in their early days as builders and now occupied by Our Marnie. And of course by Capper, who had fallen head over heels just before the Babcock Cup final for the girl he had known since school. It had been Capper's considered opinion that to abandon the clubhouse would be to invite either vandals or thieves or squatters – or quite possibly all three – to make the club's problems worse. Strictly for the short term, as he swore to

Our Marnie, he began to reinforce the floor of the flat. He said it was important to maintain a presence at the club, if only to protect the memorabilia, of which the shirts Gonzo had worn in his first international against Argentina and in his last against England were the most prized, and to be able to keep an eye on the stocks of beer. He knocked up a wall of waterproofed plywood, cut out a hole, covered it with polythene so that Our Marnie might enjoy the view over the moor, and declared before a slightly unenthusiastic – and now redundant – steward that they were staying put.

'Comrades,' Job-shy would say to them on West Street. 'We're the last on the barricades. Feel the power, brother and sister.'

'Feel the power, my arse,' replied Our Marnie.

Gonzo ran as he had never run before, not even when he was on the charge for Wales in those now-distant days when he was on his way to becoming their player of the season. It had been his one-and-only Six Nations campaign. That was years ago, when he had been in his prime; now, as he set off across the top of the mountain, sprinting for home under a sun that was no longer gloriously warming but harsh and punishing, he feared that his legs would not carry him far at this pace. For less than a quarter-of-a-mile he flew through the trampled bracken and over the springy, cropped grass of the main path, and then he felt a burning in his chest and heaviness in his legs. There were four miles to go. He tried to suck air into his lungs, to find a rhythm in his breathing.

'If he lives I'll get fit, if he lives I'll get fit,' he forced himself to repeat, a mantra to go with his gait. He pushed against the pain, waiting for his second wind, that opening of the tubes that would allow him to continue at pace across the moorland.

It had taken five minutes to work out what had happened to Capper. Our Marnie and he had run to the clearing where the boulder stood, and gone round and round in circles in the clearing, shouting out Capper's name. Gonzo was in nothing but a pair of shorts, that he had hastily pulled on, complete with the odd strand of greenery. By the time Grace joined them, looking dishevelled, they had stopped their aimless circling. The only sound on the mountain came from the swaying of the foliage, the skylarks high over their heads and Our Marnie, giving way to a sobbing panic. Grace rushed to hold her up. Gonzo was trying to recreate Capper's progress, step by step.

'Tell me again, Marnie. Exactly what you saw.'

'I saw nothing,' she cried. 'There was nothing to see. Look. Nothing. Bloody bracken, that's all.'

'What you heard, then. Think.'

'Crashing. Then nothing.'

'There must be more. Come on, Our Marnie.'

'Stop it,' she shouted.

'Think.'

'It's OK,' said Grace.

'It's not OK,' said Our Marnie.

'One more time,' said Gonzo quietly. 'Go through it in your mind's eye.'

Grace took Our Marnie's shaking hand. Our Marnie groaned. 'There's nothing, I'm telling you. He set off, crash, crash … then a clonk and silence.'

'What clonk?' said Gonzo.

'I don't know. A clack.'

Gonzo spun round. 'Like rock on rock?'

'I suppose.'

Gonzo raced to the boulder and the rock leaning against it. He looked at where they met and ran a finger down a slight scratch through the lichen. He climbed up the rock and put his back against the boulder. He placed his feet against the rock and braced himself for the huge push that alone might shift such a weight. Instead, almost at the first application of pressure, the rock tilted back and Gonzo slipped into the gap between the grey masses, narrowly avoiding a hole that opened up in the ground. Grace ran forward and grabbed his arm. The rock stopped suddenly and began to move back towards them. It seemed perfectly weighted to be a pendulum and for a moment they thought it was going to rock back and crush them. Gonzo's back was against the base of the boulder now, and he raised a foot and held it against the rock. It stopped.

'Dear Mother of God,' said Our Marnie and leapt into the space, her legs astride the hole, her shoulders keeping the rock and boulder apart. Gonzo stood up and reached for his mobile phone and turned on its torch.

'Capper,' screamed Our Marnie into the darkness.

The name came echoing back out of the depths, but without accompaniment. Gonzo reached down and shone the torch into the hole but it revealed only a few feet of smooth rock before the blackness overwhelmed the light.

'This has got to be it,' said Gonzo. 'He's down there.' He reached for a stone, thought better of it in case it hit Capper's bald head, and grabbed instead a handful of soil and broken stems. He dropped them into the hole. They floated away and there was no sound of them landing.

Gonzo turned off the torch and checked for a signal on the phone. There was nothing. 'Right,' he said. 'We need a rope. Stay here.' And he started to run.

Three months after the collapse of the gable wall, Our Marnie was still living in the clubhouse. The dereliction of the building and the street began to pull her spirits down. Without ever discussing the matter with Capper or Gonzo, she appointed herself company secretary and set up office in the back room of the house they were renovating in Straight Row. One week before Capper fell down the hole in the mountain, she was faced with her first difficult decision. The house was about to be finished. Where would she go next? By now it was clear that she was a positive force in the company, bringing a sense of order to the boys' projects and a whole load of noise and vitality to the workplace. But there was no other property on the books that could double up as an office.

The morning the deed of sale was completed on the house, Our Marnie was sitting at the table she had borrowed from the clubhouse on West Street. Capper had reminded her that they had to be out in two days' time. She slapped the wooden tabletop, stood and reached up to the row of hooks she had stuck on the wall, a simple solution to one of the many examples of poor workplace practice she had uncovered – Capper was forever mislaying the keys to the vehicles. She selected the old Land Rover, knowing it had the low-loader trailer attached. She shouted a goodbye to the empty house and drove away, down to a salvage yard in Newport Docks. She returned four hours later with a glorified garden shed onboard. Out of the roof poked a stovepipe, dented and leaning at an angle. She summoned Gonzo, Capper and a digger, and showed them where to position her purchase – on the site of the old mine, a stone's throw from the rugby field. When Capper released the lifting chains, the wooden structure slumped a little, bowing in the middle and leaning slightly to one side, exaggerating the tilt in the other direction of the chimney. Just when it seemed it would be down even before it had ever been up, the building settled into place, slightly skewed, but more or less upright.

Gonzo inspected it carefully. He pushed the walls. They did not move. 'Just checking,' he said when Our Marnie put her hands on her hips and stared. 'Don't want any more walls falling down, do we?' He stepped back and put his hands on his hips too. 'So,' he said carefully. 'What is it?'

'This is the new company headquarters,' said Our Marnie.

'It's a shed,' said Capper.

'It's my office. Our office,' insisted Our Marnie.

'Oi, Gonzo,' said Capper. 'What's the name of that bloody great tower in London?'

'The Shard.'

'That's it. It's not a shed, Our Marnie. You've gone and got us a Shard. I fuckin' love it.'

Gonzo's second wind wouldn't come. 'If he lives, I'll get fit,' he repeated, forcing his legs to keep working. His feet were bare but if they struck the occasional stone on the grass path he did not notice. His feet were the least of his concerns. His chest was heaving and white flecks of spittle were flying from his mouth. In agony, he pressed on.

In the old days, watching Gonzo Davies pounding across the mountain had been a ritual. Meg and Annie, stalwart supporters of the rugby club, used to nudge each other and gaze admiringly at the number 8, all sweat and muscle and striding for home. Now he ran without an audience. With the clubhouse closed, the sexagenarian Meg and Annie had nothing to keep them anchored to the sport when there was no action on the field, and they had drifted away from rugby for the summer. Like everybody else in the village on this glorious day, they were stretched out in their gardens, doing nothing. If they had seen Gonzo, however, as he sped towards his cottage, they would have said that there was a surprise; the old boy had never looked better on the move.

He reached the track that led to the cottage and stopped. He doubled over and was violently sick. For a moment he felt a stab of pain in his head and he almost cried out in frustration. 'Not now,' he pleaded quietly. He dared not shout aloud, in case this truly was the return of the pains that had once felled him. Danny Mewson had ended Gonzo's professional playing days with a double stamp to his head and one of the after-effects had been confinement for months in semi-darkness, alone with double vision and blinding headaches.

It was only the briefest of pangs. Or perhaps Gonzo forced the pain away by thinking of Capper, stranded in total blackness. The pain subsided and he set off again on the final sprint for home.

*

Our Marnie and Grace had pulled their men after work into the great outdoors as often as the weather allowed. Capper and Gonzo willingly allowed themselves to be taken on walks. They knew they should be running and training, but this was a far more pleasant – and much less punishing – way to spend their evenings. Sometimes they walked into the village and sat in the café, but at the first sign of clear skies over the moors, they headed for the old dram roads on the mountainside. And when the evenings grew warmer still, they extended their walks to take in the entire mountain range.

From just about any vantage point over the wilderness they could look down on Gonzo's little house. From afar it looked idyllic, a white speck in the green vastness. Close up, it was even more derelict than the rugby clubhouse. When Grace had reappeared in Gonzo's life, on the run from her husband, Martin Guest, her state of near-collapse went with the property to which she managed to stumble. It was a gutted shell, a ruin on a wasteland, but she refused to leave it. Gonzo had offered to move her to any one of the more completed houses in the village, but she had insisted on making this uninhabitable cottage their home.

On her own in the day, while Gonzo and Capper worked on more straightforward renovation projects in the village, she made do without running water and electricity. Gonzo had said he would work on the cottage at the end of his working day, and spent a few evenings in the mini-digger, laying a network of trenches and holes hither and thither across the patch of scrub that had once been a garden, and down the track towards the road that led to the village.

'That should do it,' he said one evening, turning off the machine. 'We're ready to be connected.'

'There's no rush,' said Grace. Gonzo climbed down from the cab and she handed him a cup of tea. 'I like it without contact with the outside world,' she said.

'For the moment,' conceded Gonzo. He took a sip and grimaced.

'I forgot the sugar,' said Grace. 'The Courtneys never took it.'

'No,' said Gonzo. 'See? You can't even make builder's tea.' They walked slowly back towards the cottage. 'Reality will kick in, Grace. You need hot water from a tap, and power. You'll need to be reconnected – for your work. A phone, so you can speak to your brothers.'

'I know. But for just a little longer …' They walked on, both thinking about the same person – Martin. If ever they spoke of the ex, Martin was 'he'.

'If he does come … and I'm only saying if …' said Gonzo, as the cottage and garden came into view, complete with the network of trenches. 'If he comes, well, there's one good thing about being off the grid. He'll never get past the mantraps.'

Our Marnie and Grace were now on their knees, with their heads in the hole, when Gonzo returned. Our Marnie had been talking to the Capper she could not see or hear, speaking into the emptiness, telling him of the old days, of growing up in the village together, of loving him. When she filled up with tears or simply ran out of words, Grace took over, reassuring Capper that Gonzo was on his way. They were all here for him. Hang on in there.

Gonzo was out of breath again. He had driven back, taking the old Land Rover Defender as far through the bracken as he could, but had had to run the final few hundred yards, weighed down by a rucksack and the heavy rope that Capper had once brought back from a chandler's in Milford Haven. A souvenir of the seaside, he had called it. Gonzo now tied one end of it around the boulder, threw the heavy coil into the hole and prepared to lower himself after it. He handed Grace the big torch he had found at the cottage, turned on his trusty head-torch and started to climb down. Grace and Our Marnie bumped heads as they strained to follow his progress. They could see all of him until he reached the point where the tunnel turned away from the vertical.

'This is a good sign,' came a muffled shout. 'It's not so steep from here.'

Gonzo disappeared from view, although the dancing light from his head-torch could still be seen. Soon that faded too, and Grace and Our Marnie could follow him only through the twitching of the rope. After a couple of minutes that stopped and fear gripped them. They dared not speak although both wanted to scream into the hole. They gasped when the dancing light reappeared and the head of Gonzo came into view below them.

'Pull when you hear me shout,' he said and disappeared.

'Is he alive?' said Our Marnie, trembling.

'Save your strength,' said Grace. They both reached for the rope and waited for Gonzo's order.

Gonzo didn't know if Capper was alive or dead. The body he found was inert and didn't move as Gonzo struggled to put the rope under his arms. Only when he shouted, 'Pull,' with his mouth tight against Capper's right ear in the confined space, did his old friend grunt. Gonzo almost hugged him in relief but he knew by the stain on the T-shirt that a lot of blood had been lost and he didn't know what bones might be broken. The journey to the surface was going to be bumpy enough without a rib being broken with an embrace. As the rope went taut Gonzo tried to push and ease Capper out of his wedged position, but in the end he went above the burden and pulled on the rope too. Slowly Capper came unstuck.

Our Marnie took the strain while Grace readjusted her grip on the rope and then vice versa. Inch by inch they pulled Capper up. Gonzo came into view first.

'Is he …?' said Our Marnie.

'He's alive,' said Gonzo.

'If we get through this, I swear to God …' said Our Marnie, quickly wiping the sweat off her hands before grabbing the rope again. Grace said nothing, but concentrated furiously on holding firm. Her arms were starting to shake with the exertion.

'Sorry, you two,' said Gonzo. 'But there's not a lot I can do for the moment. Not until he's passed me. See if you can pull him on your own.'

Our Marnie and Grace pulled and Capper moved, but by the time he was in the vertical part of the tunnel they were spent. They could barely hold Capper in place.

'Right,' said Gonzo, 'Secure the rope around the boulder. I've got him on my shoulder. He won't move.'

Half a minute later Capper could dangle by himself. Gonzo rested for a few seconds, then took a deep breath, and put both shoulders under Capper's backside. He positioned his feet against the wall and began to pull with his arms on the rope, hauling himself and Capper upwards. Capper's legs and feet bumped against the walls, smearing blood over them. Gonzo didn't look up, but stared at the rope and his hands. One small rise and one change of foot. One small lift and one change of grip. 'If he lives I'll get fit.' Just when he thought he could go no further, that his arms would come away his shoulders, that his biceps would explode, that his dripping hands and aching fingers would lose their grip, suddenly arms from the surface began to pull on the rope again. And then hands reached down to grab enough of Capper – by his ears and shirt – and pull him up and over the edge. Gonzo quickly followed and fell in a heap alongside Capper, shutting his eyes against the blinding sun. Capper groaned and opened his eyes. Our Marnie started to examine him, the old nursing training kicking in. Grace lay down alongside Gonzo.

'You're shaking all over,' she said. But so was she, and they lay there, quivering with exhaustion.

Capper groaned again and tried to speak.

'What was that?' said Our Marnie.

'Is this the pla …' mumbled Capper, but had to stop to spit soil and bracken from his mouth. 'The place where I can have my wicked way?'

'This is the place, all right, Capper Harris,' said Our Marnie. 'The place where your diet starts.'

Capper shut his eyes. 'I saw you, Our Marnie,' he said. 'As I was falling.' He tried to move but not a single part of him responded. 'Swear to God, I thought I was going to fuckin' die.'

'Language,' said Our Marnie.

'You were nearly my last thought.'

'Charming. And what was the last thing you saw?'

'Me. What a dull way to go, I said to myself. Falling down a hole like Alice in fuckin' Wonderland.'

3

Kitty Vernon-Evans was sitting at her husband's desk in the back room that looked out at the Sugar Loaf – not the peak of the same name in the Black Mountains to the south, but a smaller mound that her guidebook described as a 'prominent knoll' in Carmarthenshire, near Llanwrtyd Wells. Kitty was not staring through the bay window at her local landmark but was head down, re-reading a letter written in the graceful hand of Vi Protheroe. Kitty's oldest friend was asking her if she would consider having her name 'tossed into the ring, thrown forward as a candidate', phrases written with a typical flourish by Vi and followed by: 'We're on the lookout for a local magistrate.'

Vi had already spoken to Kitty about the undertaking. It all harked back to the early spring and the time of the Welsh Hell, when for a moment it seemed that social disorder was about to sweep the land. The bomb explosion at the Senedd had shaken Cardiff Bay and shocked Wales to its core. In the heart of rural mid Wales, Vi had taken a hard line, admitting without shame that hers was the traditional reaction of the landowning class.

'Round up the lot of them, put them in jail and chuck away the key,' was her solution, expostulated on the Saturday after the 'uprising', as she called it, as she prodded lamb shanks with deep suspicion at the Llandovery Farmers' Market.

'Well, yes, of course,' Kitty had said, placing a restraining hand on Vi's wrist, under the watchful eye of an organic butcher from Llandeilo. 'But perhaps we should be equally mindful that … well, don't you think this trouble may be born of – how might I put it? – justifiable indignation?'

Kitty was married to Horace Vernon-Evans of the National Assembly of Wales, and it was the line of this independent Assembly Member, who had at various stages of his political life been a member of three of the four major parties in Wales – but who had crossed the floor to sit on his own six years earlier – that there was more to the Welsh Hell than met what he called 'the jaundiced eye of the endangered political factions of Labour, the Conservatives, the Liberal Democrats and Plaid Cymru'. Listening to Horace's views at that time, Kitty had been pleased to espouse and repeat them.

'Yobs and looters,' said Vi, not so willing to take a more conciliatory line. But as the months had passed it had become clear that in the lawlessness that briefly wrecked Cardiff and especially through the bomb that strangely and instantaneously brought the day's turbulence to an end, there were symptoms of a greater unease in Wales, a more deep-seated uncertainty about where the nation stood.

In her home town of Llanwrtyd, Vi Protheroe was known as Vi Not, often said with a German accent. 'I'm not afraid to say I'm not without influence in the county,' was how she introduced herself to strangers. For locals who had known her all her life, this was a couple of 'nots' too many in one sentence. It was not uncommon to see people raise an arm in a Nazi salute behind Vi Not's back. But if she never realised what her very neighbours thought of her, she had a canny appreciation of the bigger picture. She quickly felt the shift in the winds of change in Wales. A softer approach was advocated by all parties in the politics of the land. Humility was the key. Vi had invited Kitty to lunch in her large house and bluntly – humility not being Vi Not's own particular strong point – laid it out before the wife of the AM that she possessed every one of the virtues sought in the 'Guide to Becoming a Magistrate': good character; commitment and reliability; social awareness; sound judgement; understanding and communication; maturity and sound temperament.

Kitty was halfway through the list, written out in full again in the letter, when a train tooted on the Heart of Wales line. It meant a rare occurrence – the Shrewsbury to Swansea train was going to stop at Sugar Loaf Halt, one of the quietest stations on the entire British railway network. Kitty looked at her watch and worked out how long after this train she would have before the next to Swansea. A few hours, it seemed.

A magistrate. Justice of the Peace. Once upon a time she would have been pleased to be asked. Now she ripped the letter up into tiny pieces and threw them in the bin. She then picked them out again, walked to the fireplace and burned them instead. Mere weeks ago, she had been proud to promote the views of Horace. It was what any

50-year-old stalwart of a wife would do by way of support for her husband. But then Horace had had his stroke and everything had changed. From the moment he had collapsed into the dresser in the kitchen and brought down half her collection of Denby plates, Kitty's world had fallen apart.

While Grace waited for electricity, a landline telephone and water, she busied herself about the ruin. She raided Capper's stores for salvaged odds and ends, and hammered chipboard over the cellar to make a floor for a downstairs bedroom. She rearranged the other ground-floor room into a kitchen, running on bottled-gas power, and a bathroom. Hot water for the galvanised bathtub that sat in the corner came from an old boiler, powered by a generator that throbbed away outside the cottage. She swept the cottage's two chimneys, covering herself in soot that turned the water of the bathtub dark grey. She lay in it for an hour, before heaving the tub into the garden, emptying it, carrying it back, refilling it and lying in fresh water for another hour, thinking of Gonzo.

She had first seen him as he ran naked into the Keeper's Pond on top of the Blorenge. He was about to leave the village and start his career as a professional rugby player, soon to be immersed in the all-consuming adventure of playing for Wales. They had met again in Cardiff. She had cheated on Martin Guest to be with Gonzo. It hadn't lasted long. When he finished with her, releasing her to be with Martin, he told her that when this adventure – or whatever it was he was on in rugby – was over, he would go back to the village, back to the top of the mountain. And that was no place for Grace, born a Courtney into a grand house down on the banks of the River Usk. Gonzo said he wasn't dumping her; he was letting her down gently.

Now, all these years later, she was back in his life, back on the mountain. Grace was calling herself Courtney again, to shed her married Guest name, but she was not the woman Gonzo thought she was. She did not tell herself as she dragged the bathtub back and forth from the kitchen to the garden and back that she was meant for a better life than this. Every morning as she took out the nails in the board that served as a window and blocked out the light of the changing seasons, she did not admit that she was not cut out for this. She didn't have to because she loved every moment of her life in the wilderness. And every day Gonzo rang the utility companies, pressing them for a connection date, because he suspected that Grace's state of bliss would not last.

After a preliminary examination, the hospital had left Horace Vernon-Evans for five hours in a corridor in Accident and Emergency. Kitty had been so exasperated as he lay, barely breathing on his trolley, that she found a nurse and explained, as humbly as she could, that her husband sat on the all-party Health Committee in the Assembly. He knew all about the problems for doctors and nurses in Wales. He was on their side. The nurse had shrugged and moved on.

Horace now lay in his own home, upstairs in their bed directly overhead. Had he been able to move he could have enjoyed an even better view of the Sugar Loaf. As it was, he could not. He was motionless there, as still now as he had been on his trolley in hospital, his head barely making an indentation in the pillow. The faintest line of dribble ran from the corner of his mouth on to the Egyptian cotton pillow case, part of the set bought as a twentieth anniversary present by Kitty's sister. Horace, silver of hair and grey of face, lay in his bed of crisp whiteness. He had disconcerted Kitty two days after his return home, as she was running her hands over the unruffled bedspread, by opening his eyes. Kitty had stared hard at her husband. Was he trying to open a dialogue by movement of his eyelid; two for a no; one for a yes? Perhaps it was just an involuntary flicker.

When he had eventually been allocated a bed in the acute ward, she had had to fill in all sorts of forms and provide information about him that she did not know off the top of her head. You think you know somebody inside out, she remembered musing with some amusement, and three questions on a sheet of paper reduce you to ignorance of your partner. Perhaps it was his essence that counted, not his life in numbers, enrolments or tax coding. Happy enough then not to be fully acquainted with Horace's numerical minutiae, she had set off in search of what she needed – his National Insurance number, for instance. She had gone into his study and immediately realised that she had very rarely been in this room. It was a place as foreign to her as the adjoining alcove where Horace kept his shotguns and his fishing rods. Field sports were Horace's passion, very much part of his essence, an alternative to the children that he and Kitty did not seem able to make. Their childlessness – the subject they no longer discussed; the elephant, presumably long dead, in the room. Horace would have the gun in his racks, the deadly weapon that would have knocked the elephant stone dead at a thousand paces. Even before she tried to open his desk drawers, it had dawned on Kitty that her husband had always been something of a mystery to her. Perhaps even a stranger.

Four of the drawers had been locked. Kitty had rattled the handles and wondered what could possibly be so important in his home – not his office, but the place he boasted was his retreat from politics – to warrant any form of security. The front doors of mid Wales still went largely unlocked; they would still swing open at the turn of the handle and a push. Robberies were almost unknown. Kitty had stared at the locked drawers, sensing that they were out of place – an affront. She tried to prise one open with Horace's letter knife, a gift from Kitty's late mother. The blade snapped. Kitty walked to the twin garage and found a small crowbar in Horace's toolbox. Back in the comfortable chair that she had bought for him at an antique fair in Knighton, she was suddenly seized by an anger that she barely recognised herself capable of generating. Perhaps it was an expression of her exhaustion, from all the hours of keeping vigil by his bedside. She had sat hour after hour in silence, aware that she had read somewhere that it was good to talk to an unconscious loved one. She had been unable to think of anything to say.

Now she stabbed with the crowbar and levered open the drawers one after another, loudly splintering the antique desk, part of Horace's inheritance – a piece of solid furniture that had come with the solid house. Only when all four drawers gaped beneath her, did Kitty begin to sift through their contents. There was nothing there of interest. No insight into a Horace she did not know. Not even any numbers. Just the record of a local life mundanely led.

There was only so much Grace could do without power or running water to make her living space comfortable. Telling herself she should start to think about taking some pictures, but still nervous about going out on her own, she (slightly reluctantly) packed her camera bag and set off from the cottage towards the village. On their walks she had seen Our Marnie's Shard from a distance, but now wanted to go inside. The boys, not without muttering between themselves about planning permission – or the complete lack of it – had repositioned the office on a concrete base closer to the rugby ground. It still tilted at an angle and they were reluctant to let Our Marnie settle behind her desk until they had done further reinforcing work. She had shooed them away. She liked her workplace the way it was.

Now, two days after Capper's accident, Grace came to the office for the first time. Capper was lying on a red sofa he had 'rescued' from the Miners' Institute. His bald head and legs were encrusted with scabs and it seemed he believed the long wound on his stomach would heal faster if he exposed it fully to fresh air. He was wearing a pair of shorts, heavy-duty work boots and nothing else. Our Marnie hastily threw a tea towel over his midriff: 'Excuse the bleeding Buddha, Grace love,' she said. 'Cuppa?'

The office had water and electricity already. The boys had tapped into the utilities going to the changing rooms under the stand at the rugby ground. Our Marnie had said she would work on a retrospective planning application and inform the necessary utility companies. She was sure the council would be sympathetic to their initiative, what with the club finding itself without a home – but Gonzo and Capper had advised her to wait.

'Hang fire a bit,' Capper had said when she told him she was wary of engaging in anything dishonest. 'It's just while we … what is it we're doing, Gonzo?'

'We're assessing our options.'

'That's it,' agreed Capper. 'And we need electricity and water while we do all this assessing. The club won't mind. We'll make tea for everyone … once we start training, like.'

Our Marnie had reluctantly gone along with the majority view of the board of this joint venture between the building company and the rugby club – that mum was the word. It was a difficult secret to keep. The Shard sat conspicuously in the middle of the scrubland that surrounded the rugby ground, while inside – and just as arrestingly on display – lay Capper, baring himself almost in his entirety to anyone that walked into the company headquarters.

'A tea would be lovely, thank you,' said Grace, taking a picture of Capper.

'Please,' said Our Marnie. 'Don't encourage him.' She took the mug that Capper was holding out. 'No biscuits for you.'

'See, Grace?' said Capper. 'It's like the workhouse here.'

If Kitty found nothing in Horace's desk, a different story began to unfold in the place where he kept his guns, the recess he still called the alcove although it was secured by a sturdy door. The day after her unprecedented fury – and with the splinters of the drawers still lying on the study carpet – Kitty had worked her way through Horace's full key ring until she found the one that let her into his armoury. She was calm but determined. She had lain all night next to her unmoving husband, almost matching him for stillness. Her mind was racing. Perhaps his was, too, behind his paralysed features. She awoke, hiding her impatience, leaving the bedroom without even looking at him. She couldn't explain her mood. Perhaps she now thought Horace's locked drawers were a little too antiseptic to be true. She knew he had danced to a fairly eccentric tune in his political career, first locally, then as Member of the Welsh Assembly, and she knew that his life of inherited wealth on a moderate scale had allowed him to be more diverse than the drawers' archives – consisting of heating receipts and the history of the extension they had built a decade ago – revealed. For a moment she had willed her Horace to be a little less dull.

In the wooden box where he kept his Browning pistol, however, she found a small ledger. Inside there were handwritten notes about monies received. It was clear that Horace, Assembly Member, had never been averse to keeping the company of lobby groups, and being rewarded over the years by them. He had not made a million but he had received regular kickbacks from a whole range of companies and individuals. The most regular paymasters seemed to be A. Davies of RX Agro-Supplies, PG-H of Milford Haven and M. Guest of Steel-Ag. Kitty knew none of them. Her husband was not so dull after all; he was venal, a politician on the make.

Then she found the tin in the ammunition drawer. Beneath a layer of 12-bore cartridges lay a neatly bound collection of letters. Love letters written by Felicity Protheroe, the daughter of Vi. Felicity, she of the downcast eyes and downy cheeks that blushed so easily. She of the broad hips and sturdy calves, so different from the long legs that Horace had always said were Kitty's 'top assets'. Felicity, daughter of Vi Not. Vi no; Felicity yes.

Kitty worked her way quickly through the wad, looking more for dates than detail. It was clear that the affair was long over. The last letter was written fifteen years previously. Felicity had returned home after university – the middle-of-the-road girl had become a middle-of the-class History-of-Art student at Reading – but had left to work in a music archive in Bath. Still close enough to be within striking range of Horace. Perhaps they had transferred to electronic *billets doux*, thought Kitty at first, her state of calm determination not yet giving way to anything volcanic. It seemed, though, that Felicity had ended the affair by hard copy.

'You have taught me so much, and from such a tender age … but now you must let me go,' wrote the daughter of Kitty's best friend.

It was the 'tender age' that made Kitty go down to the start of the affair, to the dates of the letters at the bottom of the pile. Felicity was certainly under 16 years of age when … Kitty could not contemplate it. She felt numb. And in that state of numbness took the tin up to the bedroom where Horace now lay – in their marital bed – and showed him what she had found.

'Is this the man you are?' she asked. The eyes of her husband of twenty-four years stared back. Go on, thought Kitty, two for a no and one for a yes. But Horace's eyes flickered in a rapid burst and then closed. 'I'll take that as neither one thing nor the other,' Kitty said quietly.

Three days later, strangers came to the village. Dario Aspetti had warned Gonzo they were on their way. Dario, despite having to use crutches to swing his twisted body up and down between the village and his caravan just off the Garn-yr-erw road, kept up his patrols and remained a vigilant sentinel. He had seen the newcomers swooping in and out of the quarries on the crest of the high ridge. They had then come into view, racing down the dram roads, dashing back and forth cross the moor, and then climbing back to the top. But now the dozen or so cyclists came into the village for the first time.

The green rectangle of the rugby pitch may have caught their eye, or perhaps the Shard lured them down from the high ridges. Once they pulled up on the site of the old mine, however, it was only the patch of grey – the wasteland in the wilderness – that held their attention. They slowly circled it on their bikes before dismounting and approaching the Shard.

Our Marnie did not hear their knock on the door. She had a pair of headphones on, to keep out the noise of Capper's snoring from the sofa. She was head down, emailing an order to the local builders' merchants. Gonzo was on site in Llanfoist Street, juggling a bit of blockwork there with a kitchen installation in Beaufort Street and a plastering job in James Street. Grace had walked into the village to buy milk for the fridge and biscuits for Capper's stash behind the sofa. Our Marnie looked up to find three mud-splattered men standing in front of her. She gave a little shriek and Capper woke with a start. He was on his feet in a flash and now it was the turn of the strangers to be startled, by this half-naked barrel of scabby menace.

'Down, Capper,' said Our Marnie.

'Sorry to startle you,' said the first cyclist. 'My name is Mike Lewis. And this is Dai Lewis. No relation. And Tom Lewis. No relation. We're from the Graig Cycling Club.' The Lewises each held a safety helmet in one hand. They raised the other as a brief hello, but were not so genial that they tried to shake Capper's hand.

Tom Lewis stepped forward. 'We've got to say – this place is perfect.' The other two Lewises nodded in agreement. 'And we were just wondering if we could talk to the owner of the land.'

'Ah,' said Our Marnie, thinking that these cyclists would be the ones who would expose their trespass. Undone in two days. Barely had she started, her operation was about to be shut down.

'Well,' said Capper. 'That's a very interesting question.' He pointed at the rugby field and stand through the window. 'That's owned by the rugby club.' The three cyclists looked at him with the slightly blank look of listeners not entirely astonished to be informed that the rugby pitch was owned by the rugby club.

'It's more this patch we're on here,' said Tom.

'It'd be perfect for a little circuit,' said Dai.

'We'd like to ask permission …' said Mike.

'Permission …' said Capper. 'See, that's the interesting bit. I suppose it would be the council.'

'And …?' said Mike. There was an awkward pause. Our Marnie shuffled uncomfortably and started to rearrange a few bits of paper on the table. Capper pulled on an old grey T-shirt. Dust and wood shavings floated off him, caught in the late afternoon shaft of light streaming through the window.

'Come and tell me all about it,' said Capper, showing them to the door. 'Cup of tea, lads?'

Once she had finished burning Vi's letter, Kitty returned to the desk and picked up the tin containing Felicity's. She carried it upstairs and very deliberately took the letters out one by one and arranged them over the quilt her sister, Angela, now living in Maine in New England, had made for them.

'Something for the carers to see,' she said. 'They've told me they can manage – that I should take a break.' She picked up a pillow from her side of the bed and held it in front of Horace. He opened his eyes. His blank expression did not change. 'I thought about it for a moment,' whispered Kitty. 'Putting this over your face and pressing the life out of you.' She stood up. 'But no. I shall leave you in a sea of your lover's words. You can breathe her in.'

She went into the en-suite bathroom and ran a bath. Ten minutes later she dried and dressed in front of Horace and then packed a small suitcase, carefully folding some of her favourite clothes and discarding all but two pairs of shoes, one for outdoors, one for in. She returned to the bed.

'I'm going to take that break,' she said. And she walked out of what little was left of Horace's life. She made a last trip to the gun alcove and carefully locked its door, but as she left the house, she deliberately left the front door ajar. She slowly made her way down to the very quiet Sugar Loaf Halt, where she waited patiently for the next train for Swansea.

Half an hour later Gonzo pulled up alongside Grace in the old blue company van. She was walking through the village, carrying a shopping bag. They were both heading for the Shard. They arrived to find Our Marnie going around a circle of cyclists, handing out mugs of tea from the large tray she had brought down from the clubhouse. Capper was standing in the middle of the circle, not so much a frightening sight now as the Graig Cycling Club's tour guide to their new playground.

'I'm just telling the lads all about the village,' he shouted at Gonzo. 'And all about our unique selling point as a sporting centre of excellence.' Our Marnie rolled her eyes. 'And this, everyone …' he continued.

' … is Gonzo Davies,' said Mike Lewis.

'Gonzo Davies …' said Dai Lewis.

At that very moment a convoy of four cars pulled up on the wasteland. In a cloud of dust, six children appeared. This half-dozen of the nine young players of the rugby club – all named after plants by Capper: Daisy, Buttercup, Daff, Tulip, Moss, Ragwort, Blossom, Fungus and Buddleia – came and formed a rough square of rugby players beside the circle of cyclists.

'What's this?' asked Daff, nodding at the Shard.

'And hello to you, too, Daff,' said Capper. 'Graig cyclists, meet the Plant. Children, the Graig Cycling Club. We're going to be neighbours.'

'Are we now?' said Our Marnie.

'Bloody 'ell, Capper,' said Fungus. 'What's happened to you? Have you given him a good wire-brushing, Our Marnie?'

'Whatever turns you on, I suppose,' said Moss.

'Evening, Our Marnie,' said Blossom. 'Is this the new clubhouse then?'

'Now that, Blossom, is the best idea you've ever …' said Capper.

'It's an office,' said Our Marnie.

'But think of it …' said Capper.

'Big enough for a table for me to work at, and a sofa for you to sleep on …' said our Marnie. 'And you can cut out the cheek, Moss. He fell down a hole.' The Children giggled. 'Well,' she said, 'I suppose it's good to see you all. Hello, you lot. What are you up to then?'

'Well,' said Daisy. 'We thought we'd come and have a bit of a kick-around, like.'

'No offence, Gonzo,' said Buttercup. 'But, you know, the season's not far away …'

'And we haven't heard anything …' said Buddleia.

'So, we thought we'd come and see …' said Ragwort.

'If we still had a rugby club,' said Daff. Nobody moved.

'What d'you think?' said Tulip.

'I think I'd better go and get my kit,' said Gonzo and ran to the van.

'Gonzo Davies,' said Tom Lewis.

'The great Gonzo …' said Mike.

4

Early the next morning Grace filled the bath as full as she dared and Gonzo, with great difficulty, lowered himself into it. Water sloshed over the kitchen floor.

'Wasn't even a tough session,' he groaned. 'Look at me. I can hardly move. Grace, I'm too old for this.'

Grace kneaded his shoulders, digging her thumbs in, pushing his head down into his chest and stretching his neck. 'Just a little tight,' she said.

'Seriously,' he said, 'I'm thinking of …'

'Wait,' said Grace, pulling his chin up. 'First thing, did you enjoy it at the time? Putting your kit on, getting out there on the field again.'

'I did. It was good to see everyone. He's going to be good, that Ragwort. He can run.' He lifted his elbows and pulled them back. Water splashed over Grace. 'But if after every session I end up …'

'You're rusty, that's all. A little un-toned. Won't take more than a couple of weeks to get you back into shape. A bit longer for Capper …'

'I suppose.' Gonzo slid down into the water and a wavelet broke over Grace. She looked down at her soaking T-shirt, one of Gonzo's old training tops. She took his head in two hands and turned it as if she was going to ease more stiffness out of it, but held it still and kissed him.

'You will know when the moment comes,' she said, still close to his face. 'It will simply hit you – that the moment has come to stop. Somewhere. Wherever. But not right here and not right now.'

'I suppose,' said Gonzo. 'Thank you, doctor.'

'You're welcome.'

'It was funny, though, without the Professor. I was thinking about why we haven't really got going before now. And it's obvious. The Professor did all the organising. He did everything. He'd have had us out there well before now. Feel we're letting him down a bit.'

'I wonder if we'll ever see him again.'

'The Professor and his secrets. Our mystery man. We may never find out. But we owe it to him to carry on.'

'Well, that's a change of heart.'

'I'm feeling better.' Gonzo reached out and put an arm around Grace's shoulders. 'You're soaking,' he said. 'You couldn't be any wetter if you climbed in here.'

'You're right,' said Grace and was about to do exactly that when there was a loud thump on the chipboard that served as a front door. Gonzo and Grace did not move and all that could be heard was the water going back and forth in the tub. There was a second banging on the door.

'Gonzo,' cried a voice.

'It's Dario,' said Gonzo. He pulled himself out of the tub and wrapped a towel around himself while Grace hurried to open the door. Little Dario nearly fell through it. He managed to right himself on his crutches and sat down heavily on the one armchair in the cottage.

'Don't lean on the …' said Grace and Gonzo together, but it was too late. The left arm of the chair collapsed – it was the reason it had been thrown into the skip from which Capper had liberated it – and Dario ended up in a heap on the floor.

'What's up, Dario,' said Gonzo. 'Who's here?' He thought the village sentinel must have seen 'him' – Martin.

'No, no,' said Dario, rolling up one trouser leg to reveal a livid graze on his twisted and emaciated right shin. 'It's not 'im. It's me. I've done a Capper. I've fallen down an 'ole.'

Kitty knew where she was heading, but she was prepared to stretch out the journey, take a detour, prepare herself. She sat in the first carriage of the train's two, holding the ticket she had just bought from the conductor.

'One-way to Swansea, please,' she had said, the most important direction she had ever given in her life – not the destination, but the no-return element.

The conductor had taken a little interest in this passenger because to pick up anyone who wasn't a tourist with a bicycle at Sugar Loaf Halt was unusual. And this middle-aged woman folded herself into her window seat with the suppleness of a dancer and placed her case beneath her knees with real daintiness. She spoke with calm clarity, but she was obviously lost in her thoughts in a different world. The conductor left her to the company of the only other travellers in the carriage, three students, all listening to music.

Kitty stared out of the window, hardly seeing the passing countryside of mid Wales. She was thinking of Horace's lifetime of treachery and her life of being duped and deceived. She blamed herself for being so satisfied with her lot that she had rarely questioned him about his existence away from their home. She had taken for granted that the politician who made his name out of putting principle before party would be by nature a decent man. He was fraudulent on two fronts – an up-for-sale hypocrite, even before he turned to … Felicity. Kitty had married a multi-headed monster. Briefly she felt colour flooding into her cheeks. She burned for a moment or two with rage, although nothing other than this glow gave her away. To anybody watching from the side of the track, she was the rather elegant Kitty Vernon-Evans on the slow train to Swansea.

By the time she reached her first destination, her anger had faded. Somewhere around Llangadog, between Llandovery and Llandeilo, it had been replaced by the calmness that comes with a difficult decision irreversibly taken. Anger followed by resignation. Kitty had heard Horace's regular carers talking about that. Kitty quite liked Dilys but didn't like Pat so much and she thought Horace might have been in hearing range when the sharp-faced Pat had practically boasted about how good she was at spotting it. That turning point, when the people they cared for – Kitty thought she might have heard Pat referring to them as punters rather than patients – came to accept death. Kitty had wondered if the awful Pat was referring to Horace in particular, or if it was an overview of all the punters of Llanwrtyd approaching their end-of-life experience. If she was talking about spotting any change in Horace, then Pat must be blessed with keener powers of observation than Kitty possessed. Horace hadn't moved more than an eyelid. Well, they were welcome to him, resigned or not, now.

Dario wasn't the only surprise package to turn up in the village that morning. In the summer months little by way of post was delivered to the clubhouse on West Street. Capper had received a provisional list of fixtures, starting on the first Saturday in September, and there were the usual circulars about coaching and refereeing courses provided by the Welsh Rugby Union, minimum requirements for medical facilities at member clubs, offers on clothing at the WRU shop in Cardiff and even a reminder about drinking. Capper thought he was being encouraged to do more of it and made a rare exception to his reading habits – and opened the letter: 'Whilst it is the view of the governing body of the game in Wales that the clubhouse facility is rightly prized for its vital role as a social hub in so many of our rugby communities, it would however be remiss of us not to express our concern at what the recent Singleton medical report has described as a worrying rise in alcohol-related ...' Capper gave up and from that moment viewed every letter that dropped through the letter box – the same gap through which Danny Mewson had once tried to pour petrol with the aim of burning down the club – with suspicion.

This morning, however, one letter held his attention. The envelope was thick, almost downy to the touch. He was about to tear it open with his stubby fingers when he thought better of it and delicately peeled the seal apart. With his fingertips he pulled out an embossed card: 'To the Winners of the Babcock Cup the Presiding Officer cordially extends an invitation to attend a reception on the occasion of the Reconvening of the Welsh Parliament.'

The winners of the Babcock Cup. For the first time since the most momentous day – the only momentous day – in the village rugby club's history, Capper felt a true surge of pride, a real tingle of achievement. He had a brief flashback to the final against the 'Gulag' Academy: his battle to be fit; his hour on the stage; his exit to a standing ovation. Most of all he remembered the moment when Gonzo handed him the silverware, the Babcock Cup itself. While the number 8 embraced the two New Zealanders, Murray Collins and Conrad Thomas, who had been his coaches in his brief professional career and were now guests in the presidential box, he had told Capper to raise the trophy. Capper now felt the sting of a tear running into one of the grazes on his face. He looked down, not wanting anything salty to plop on the card, and read the final part of the invitation: ' … a Night to Celebrate Reconstruction of the Senedd and to Ignite a Spirit of Reconciliation across Our Land.' He wasn't sure he understood the last part, but recognised that this was one postal delivery well worth the read, and hurried as fast as his wounds would allow down to the Shard.

Kitty stood on platform 3 of Swansea station. She waited for the lunchtime Intercity bound for London to pull out and the noise to abate, then found the number for the St Tysul Hotel, which she had read about in the days when to thumb through brochures and magazines was an everyday pleasure for a woman of leisure. She phoned on the mobile that was well overdue an upgrade to see if there were any rooms available. She was put on hold. It was peak season and Kitty was assuming the only chance she had of obtaining a room by the sea was to go straight to the luxury end of the market. A little slice of the high life – in the flesh, as it were, rather than viewed as a glossy page. The voice of the St Tysul returned. They were sorry but they had no rooms, as such, available. The receptionist was however able to offer their finest suite. Might that be of interest? The woman did not sound too hopeful that Kitty would be able to absorb the shock of the high-summer rate.

'That sounds splendid,' said Kitty. 'I'd like to book in for three weeks.' She ended the call, went to the cash dispenser and took out as much money as she could. Horace was paying. She thought briefly about catching a train from Swansea to Saundersfoot, but instead walked out of the station and climbed – elegantly – into the taxi at the head of the line, and placed her case – daintily – by her side and ordered the driver to head for Saundersfoot in Pembrokeshire, fifty miles to the west.

Gonzo, Grace and Dario had already joined Our Marnie in the office. Gonzo was rummaging through the drawer into which Our Marnie had transferred all the keys to the various live building projects. Capper mislaid house keys as well as the vehicles'.

'Why aren't you at work?' said Capper to Gonzo, who ignored him. 'Dario, what are you doing here?' Dario was about to answer, but Capper turned to Grace. 'Morning, Grace. How are you?' Grace was about to speak, but Capper kept going: 'You're a pearl in our shit-heap, Grace. Put the kettle on, my darling.'

Grace laughed and shook her head. She flicked the switch and went to the sink to rinse out the mugs.

'What are you on?' said Our Marnie to Capper.

'What have you done with the keys to …?' said Gonzo, still going through bunches of keys by the handful.

'What I'm on,' said Capper, interrupting him, 'is the A-list. We all are. We're going to the fuckin' Oscars.' He handed Our Marnie the invitation.

'Well, well, well,' she said. 'I feel a frock coming on, Grace.' Grace, Gonzo and Dario gathered round her.

'That's brilliant,' said Dario. 'A treat. You deserve it. A spirit of reconciliation party – I like it. After the bomb, a booze-up. You'll have a great night.'

'Who's "you", Dario? You're us. I mean, we're all "you",' said Capper. 'Fuck it, I mean we're all going.'

'I'll email the Assembly,' said Our Marnie. 'Not a thing I say every day ... but here goes. RSVP to ...' Her fingers flew over her keyboard. ' ... Delighted to accept. Great honour for our club ... generated huge buzz in the village ... may we confirm numbers with you?' She sat back. 'There.'

The kettle began to spew boiling water into the sink. Grace hurried to turn it off at the mains.

'The switch has gone,' explained Our Marnie. 'Now, Capper, where are the keys to the Straight Row job?'

'How should I know?' said Capper. 'I'm on the sick.' He nevertheless patted the pockets of his shorts and pulled out a set of keys. 'Ah,' he said, 'picked them up by mistake yesterday.' He held them out towards Gonzo, but then withdrew them. 'But what d'you want the keys to our four-bedroom prime-location dogs' bollocks of a property for, anyway?'

'Dario needs a place to stay,' said Gonzo.

'I went through the floor of my bathroom,' said Dario. 'It's the caravan. It's had it. Falling apart.'

'No offence, Dario. But there's more money in Our

Marnie's petty cash box – the one Grace emptied yesterday for tea bags – than you've got.'

'I've got more money than you think, Capper Harris,' said Dario, who didn't. 'I can pay rent, no problem. And Ragwort's looking for a place to stay, and all. And he's got a good job at the college. That's rental income times two from a property that's been sitting idle for two months. Do the maths. I could put a deposit down right now.'

Grace handed out tea and went round with a bowl of sugar.

'You know your caravan, Dario …' she said.

'Floor's gone, Grace love,' he said stirring his mug vigorously. 'Thanks for the tea.'

'How about this?' said Grace. 'We'll do a swap. We'll take the caravan off you and you can have the room in Straight Row. Let's say you'll be the nightwatchman. Because you are …'

'Have you seen his caravan?' said Capper. 'It's fifty years old.'

'It's a classic of its kind,' said Grace.

'With Dario-sized holes in the floor every three paces.'

'It's a thing of beauty,' said Grace. 'And I have a plan.'

There was a little ping from Our Marnie's screen.

'The Assembly say … hang on,' she said. 'Here it is: "Please feel free to bring one full busload to the reception".'

Kitty spent all her cash in two days. She took out more. She spent liberally on her credit card and new clothes filled her suite. And she felt nothing. A numbness seemed to have crept over her entire being, ever since her anger faded near

Llangadog, a place in Carmarthenshire she did not know at all, but that she now recognised as the small stop on her railway journey where her life was anaesthetised. No amount of sea air or walking along the Pembrokeshire coastal path seemed to reanimate her. She was glad. The decision had been taken and this was merely killing time. She knew little of the ways of sport, but she found herself thinking this was what it must be like, waiting before the Wimbledon final. My Wimbledon final, she thought. How silly.

Having taken the air in the first week and caught the sun – she hadn't bothered to apply any high-factor cream and was a little scorched of face – she settled down to drink in the second. She was determined to stay in a semi-permanent state of inebriation and topped up from mid-morning until mid-evening on the hotel's finest bubbly. Why should she do such an uncharacteristically disreputable thing? Because she could. She invented the role of a slightly batty widow and sat in the lounge and turned as brown as a berry and a little sloshed. Only early in the morning did her hangover make her dwell on the reality of being a deceived wife and she waited impatiently to pop her first cork. Here's to you, she said by way of a toast, the never-was Justice of the Peace, pissed.

She went to bed before she fell asleep in the lounge. That would have been a lurch too far into misbehaviour. There was only so much loss of dignity she could contemplate and being caught with her mouth open in public was unacceptable, even for a lush. She did toy with the idea of staying up to the death one night and seducing someone behind a closed door – someone, anyone – and taking pictures of herself doing things with that anyone and sending them home. She would have Dilys the carer spread Kitty in her abandon over the bedspread. Show them to Horace. Two blinks for a no. Blink, blink, blink, blink. That's what happens to good character, commitment and reliability, social awareness, sound judgement, understanding and communication, maturity and sound temperament when you are turned numb.

She seduced no one. In the third week she took to the infinity pool and swam back to sobriety. She swam until her eyes burned, the closest she had come to crying since taking to the drawers of Horace's desk with the crowbar. At the end of that last week she paid her enormous bill and told the cleaners to help themselves to all the new clothes she left on the bed. Looking tanned and slim, her elegance and daintiness restored, and carrying nothing more than her handbag, she hailed a taxi and asked to be driven back to Swansea station, where she waited patiently for the next train to Cardiff.

5

The news that training had begun spread fast and twice a week the village evenings of the unseasonably hot August were filled with the efforts of the team to prepare for the new season. The old guard arrived – minus the vanished Professor – and Mystic, Useless and the Twins took up their customary positions and waited for Gonzo to bring order to the forwards and invention to the backs. But before he allowed them to attempt anything more complicated than half an hour of touch rugby, he worked on their fitness – and his. He struggled to keep up with the Children at first, but as the new season approached he found himself stretching out on the long runs for home across the moorland. Daff, the outside-half and something of a fell runner in the summer months, liked to take the lead on these long runs, but he became increasingly aware of a large presence on his shoulder in the closing stages. With each session, Gonzo edged a little closer, until a week before the first game he overtook Daff. He challenged the other youngsters to beat him then on the strides and sprints up the steep dram roads on the mountainside, but only Fungus and Ragwort, the wingers, could occasionally keep up with him.

Even Capper began to lose weight and by mid-August could do the Big Six – the half-dozen sprints of varying distances on the steepest slopes – without stopping. His scabs had dropped off to reveal white splashes of new skin against the rich tan of his head and upper body, the result of a fortnight of sitting in a deckchair outside the Shard. The wound on his stomach had healed into a dark red scar that rose and fell in the sunlit hours of Capper's convalescence. Grace took a picture of him dozing in his chair. She captioned it 'Bulldog on Guard 2' and hung it on the office wall next to the picture of Capper in a tea towel sleeping on the sofa – 'Bulldog on Guard 1'.

If anything drove him out of his seats it was the dust of the cyclists. More and more of the Graig club arrived to sample the joys of going in and out of the quarries and up and down the same dram roads that the rugby players used for fitness. Word spread across South Wales and more and more enthusiasts on all sorts of bikes came to the village for their summer sport. It became their custom of an evening to descend after the high life to the site of the old mine. There, mere feet from the Shard and Capper's deckchair, the cyclists marked out a rough track and men and women, boys and girls sped round and round, creating a storm of dust. Capper was driven by this clogging dry filth to stand in protest and go back to work of sorts. He drove the Land Rover to the yard off Beaufort Street, where the few bits of plant that weren't in use on site were kept, and came back towing an ancient water tanker. It leaked a bit, but was perfect for damping down the track. It became an essential part of the new ritual of pedal-powered speedway to have Capper going round and round in the Bulldog Bowser. And just as the mountainside, with its variety of contours and tracks and its fresh air, appealed to a whole new group of outsiders, so the speedway grew into an informal league and the village became more and more a destination for lovers of bicycles.

These cyclists paid their way. The Graig hierarchy, the unrelated Lewises, did the rounds, using a pannier for a collecting bucket, and gave the proceeds to Capper to cover the costs of the tanker.

'There are no costs,' said Capper.

'Then for your time,' said Tom Lewis. 'You've been good to us.'

'Got to admit,' said Capper, 'it is a fuckin' sight to behold.'

The waste ground that had served as nothing more than a bumpy car park on match days in winter, was now teeming with sport. Laughter and shouting filled the air, drawing a crowd down from the village to see what was going on. The mine had never seen such movement since the days of coal.

This summer crowd grew thirsty in the hot summer days and nights, and here Grace's plan bore fruit. Just before the explosion of interest in CycleCity, as Capper now called the area, Gonzo appeared with Dario's caravan in tow. It was an ancient American Airstream, silver and rounded at its ends. It was also rounded in the middle, with bits of plywood hanging from its bowed underside. Grace and Gonzo walked carefully through Dario's old home, noting that fumigation would be the first order of the day. In the end there was no need, because Gonzo simply gutted the entire interior and threw himself into rebuilding the floor and laying on water and electricity from the same illegal supply that fed the Shard. Within days the work was complete and Grace concentrated on converting the empty shell into a summer clubhouse, complete with a huge awning at the front, should the weather ever break. The awning remained tightly rolled as August remained glorious.

Grace and Gonzo, Capper and Our Marnie stood before the caravan one morning. It was ready to go into service.

'You don't think we need, I don't know, a licence or something?' said Our Marnie.

'I expect we do,' said Capper. 'But who's ever been to check on anything that goes on up here in the wilderness?'

'But it's not, is it?' said Our Marnie, staring at the Airstream. 'It's anything but part of the wilderness. You were right, Grace. It's beautiful. The rounded ends, the silver … I could eat it.'

'We'll soon be able to eat in it,' said Grace. 'But she is lovely, isn't she?'

'What's the name of that thing in London, Gonzo?' said Capper. 'Green, curved ...'

'The Gherkin.'

'Aye, that's it. It's on its side, Grace, but you've built the fuckin' Gherkin next to the Shard.'

As the season approached, Capper grew toned as well as tanned. Once the cyclists' dust had stirred him from his deckchair he was soon back at work full time, joining Gonzo on site by day and down at the Shard and Gherkin in the evening, where Our Marnie and Grace ran a roaring business. The caravan was soon full of refrigeration units and cookers. The Children worked out a rota system and took turns to fire up the barbecues that Gonzo and Capper built to take the pressure off the serving hatch. On the Tuesdays and Thursday evenings of rugby training, the Lewises organised a posse of cyclists to help run the catering.

Old Marlene Jenkins came over from the café in the middle of the village one evening and for a moment Our Marnie thought they were in trouble for stealing trade from the her long-established business. But Marlene was merely curious to know what had caused all these cyclists to come to the village and provide such an upturn in her fortunes.

'Me in the caff, and Gethin at the Colliers next door, we don't know what's hit us,' she said. 'Bloomin' marvellous, got to say.' The pub and the café were prospering. The village had never seen anything like it.

Everything was going well, apart from Capper's scrummaging. At long last, Gonzo on training nights had begun to work less on pure physical fitness and more on ball skills with the backs and collective work with the forwards. They started each session with a game of touch rugby – no heavy contact, Gonzo stressed – but he took the ball away when the hard work started. Now, just at the moment when for three weeks he had been pointing the players back up the mountain, it reappeared. A little cheer went up.

'Right,' said Gonzo, 'I'm off to do a few set-piece moves with the backs. Capper, take the pack and start working on the scrummage.'

'Righto,' said Capper. 'Not before time, you lot. Let's get to real work.' But when he raised his arms and put them in a tight embrace around his props, as he had been doing as a hooker for nigh-on two decades, he felt a sudden unease. And when Blossom and Mystic packed down behind the front row, and the arms of this second row pairing came between the legs of Moss and Daisy and gripped the waistband of their shorts, and when these other four members of the front-five fraternity of the scrum squeezed together to give the formation a togetherness and solidity that would define the team's prospects for the season ahead, Capper felt sick. The wing forwards, Buddleia and Buttercup, took their place on the side of the seven-man pack and they waited for Capper's instruction to lower themselves forcefully into position against the ancient scrummaging machine he had built from salvaged steel from the mine.

Capper couldn't speak. Without thinking, Buddleia, who normally gave the order to drive when the opposition were putting the ball into the scrum, took over: 'Crouch … bind … set,' he shouted. And Capper just had time to duck his head and be carried down and forward with a lunge and a thud into position against the cushioned pads that represented the enemy front row. He was doubled over, as he had been thousands of times, in his crucifix position, ready to add to the drive with his legs and shoulders, but suddenly all he wanted to do was free his arms, to save him from falling. He couldn't move.

'Ready … ready …' shouted Buddleia. One more order of 'Now' and the pack would push as one. But Capper was being crushed in a tunnel and he was tumbling towards a rock that would split him open.

'No, no … please,' he mumbled.

'Now,' shouted Buddleia and the scrummaging machine was jolted backwards.

'Good first scrum,' shouted Buttercup from the other side of the pack. But when they disengaged, Capper fell to his knees and dipped his forehead against the grass.

'You OK, Capper?' asked Mystic. 'Is it the scars?'

'Must be,' Capper managed to say. 'That's it, I'm scarred … no, I'm fuckin' scared.'

The season began on the first Saturday of September. The good weather held and the team left for their first game, away from home, a dozen miles down the valley in a small convoy of cars that stirred the dust outside the Shard and Gherkin, now condensed by name to the Sherkin. The Owain Owens bus was reserved for longer trips. It had been trundling the team – often in a cloud of exhaust smoke every bit as thick as the dust cloud now billowing – up and down the valleys, or east and west along the Heads of the Valleys road, for as long as even the Widowers, the longest-serving supporters, could remember, but was given this day off. The players' convoy of cars was soon followed by a handful of vehicles driven by the supporters, including Meg and Annie, devotees of the team and companions of the Widowers.

Capper travelled with the supporters. He was in no condition to play. The Children had managed to draft in one of the security guards at Coleg Gwent, Billy Dodds, to make up the numbers, but Billy was no Capper. He was a gentle soul who conscientiously did his rounds of the college after dark, but who lived in mortal fear of ever discovering anything or anybody untoward. Billy was happy to play anywhere in any position, from 1 to 15, and readily accepted his role of stand-in on permanent stand-by. Capper, classifying him as too old to be a Child of the Plant, called him Standpipe.

Today, Standpipe made the starting XV for the first game of the new season. Capper had ceded him his place, acknowledging himself to be a liability. Every scrum gave him the heebie-jeebies. His most basic duty, to strike for the ball on the field of play, complete with all the rough and tumble that so appealed to his essentially aggressive nature, was beyond him. His dark little underworld in rugby had become a no-go area. Every time he surrendered his arms to his props and stooped into position in the middle of the scrum, he had a panic attack.

The team lost – not heavily, but to much jeering from the opposition supporters: 'Aye, that's them … the Babcock Hotshots …' Gonzo did everything he could, but it was a game of many errors all around him, and therefore of many scrums. And at every one, poor old Billy Dodds, unaccustomed to the specialist contortions of the hooker's position, was bent out of shape. 'Standpipe, you've sprung a leak, butt,' came from the crowd as he wiped blood from his mouth after one particularly wild retreat in the second half.

The team stayed for a pint or two down the valley after the game, but it was still light when they gathered in sombre mood at the Sherkin for a last drink from the barrel that had somehow managed to work its way into the catering operation at the new clubhouse. Capper was not there. None of the players or supporters stayed long and soon it was only the last few mountain bikers coming down from the ridge at dusk that prevented Our Marnie from pulling down the shutters and locking the door. Just after dark she walked up the moorland path to West Street and entered the old clubhouse. She went upstairs and found Capper curled up in bed – with the light on.

The sun had not risen over the high ridge the next morning when Gonzo pulled up in the Land Rover. He slipped in through a gap in Capper's temporary gable end and went upstairs. Our Marnie was already up and nodded at Gonzo as if she knew that he would be here at this hour on a Sunday morning.

'He still won't turn the light out,' she said. 'It's doing my head in. Though I suppose it's doing his in even more, poor dab.'

Gonzo went into the bedroom and gave Capper a good shake. 'Come on,' he said. 'It's time to confront a few demons.'

Capper knew exactly where they were heading and sat rigid in the passenger seat of the Defender as it bounced across the moor and swung into the bracken.

'We can do this the easy way,' said Gonzo, when they stopped, 'or the hard way.' Capper hung his head. 'You can run. I'll catch you. You can sit there. I'll carry you. Or you can come with me and we'll go down the hole together.' A sheen of sweat covered Capper's blotched dome of tanned and new skin.

Gonzo went round to the passenger side and opened the door. 'Remember the time at school,' he said, 'when I had that thing about rats? And what did you do?'

'I put one in your bag,' mumbled Capper.

'And what happened?'

'You knocked me out.'

'Apart from that.'

'You never minded rats after that.'

'So?'

'So, leave me alone. I don't want to go down that 'ole.'

Gonzo left the door open and went into the back of the Defender. He pulled out the long rope and a rucksack, attached a head-torch and handed a second to Capper. 'Let's go.'

Once the decision was taken and he had willed his muscles to unfreeze and release him from his seat, Capper moved with miserable determination. Gonzo anchored the rope to the boulder, threw the free end into the void and pointed after it.

'You first,' he said.

Muttering about a rat in a bag being a whole lot of different from dropping a man into hell on a Sunday morning, Capper turned his head-torch on, grabbed the rope and lowered himself down. Soon they reached the point where the tunnel narrowed and where Capper's fall had ended. The one single sharp rock shone red when Capper looked at it. He felt sick.

'Right,' he said. 'That's it. I've been here. And feel a lot better. Honest. Let's go.'

But Gonzo was tying a cord to the rucksack he had taken off and was wriggling past him, squeezing head first to the right of the tooth of rock. After a few metres his fingers found a good grip on an edge and he pulled himself forward. He was head and shoulders over a ledge, staring down after the rope that dropped vertically into darkness. There was headroom now and as he looked up, salts in the rock glinted and sparkled in the beam. He reeled in the cord, sat carefully on the ledge, put the rucksack back on and lowered himself down again.

'Aye, that's it,' grunted Capper behind him. 'Well done, Capper. For facing your demons. A rat in the bag. Job done. But oh no, let's give good old Capper another fuckin' rat. Fuckin' black 'ole. Who d'you think I am? Stephen fuckin' Hawking?' He lowered himself after Gonzo.

For a moment Gonzo thought the rope might run out, but then he saw the coil below him and soon he was standing at the bottom. He unzipped the rucksack and pulled out a powerful torch. As Capper landed by his side he clicked on the beam.

'Fuck me,' said Capper. A vast chamber revealed itself

before them. Boulders twice the size of their anchoring point on the surface were strewn across the gently sloping floor, giant balls amid pins of stalagmites. Chandeliers of stalactites hung from a vaulted ceiling.

'What do they call it?' asked Capper as they drove back to the village. 'A makeover. Aye, that's it. A makeover. Come up here and cycle the pathways to the stars.'

'Very poetic,' said Gonzo.

'Spin on the circuit where once the coal trucks turned.'

'Is there no end to this?'

'And descend into the chamber of wonders, nature's gold mine.'

'Thank you, the Welsh Tourist Board. But what about scrummaging?'

'Bring it on. Bring it on, I say. But just think of it: our shit heap, the adventure capital of Wales.'

'OK, Walt Disney, but we might need a bit of planning permission.'

'Planning fuckin' permission. That's the trouble with you, Gonzo Davies. You never see the bigger picture.'

There was a gathering of villagers and cyclists behind the posts on the Thursday evening of training before the first home game of the season. There had been rain at last in the week and the whole area around the mine had been washed. The dust that had swirled in the air over the dry weeks of summer and settled on the roof of the rugby stand and the Sherkin had been returned to earth.

'Perked-up grey,' said Capper as he splashed his way

from the company headquarters to the changing room. 'The ground will take a stud at last. Perfect.'

But he still had to lower himself into the scrummage and the village and the cycle club wanted to check on his recovery. Gonzo asked Daff and Tulip to run the backs' session and came to oversee Capper's confrontation with his claustrophobia. The hooker put his arms up and Daisy and Moss bound on to him. Mystic and Blossom knelt down and put their shoulders and hands into place. Buddleia, Buttercup and Gonzo added the last tier to the formation. They lowered as one and thudded into the scrummaging machine.

'Ready … ready … now,' shouted Capper and the machine rose and shot backwards.

'Oh yes,' shouted the hooker after ten metres of leg-pumping. He raised two arms to the clapping audience behind the posts. 'Capper Harris and the chamber of horrors. He's out. And lives to fight another day.'

The sunshine returned on Saturday. It didn't bring the heavy heat of August but was cooled by a light wind coming up the valley. A rich smell of cooking meat was borne on this breeze across the playing surface and a queue formed at the barbecue sites, manned by the cycle club, all through the day and into the night. When the eating was done, Gonzo kept the fires alight, with coal replacing charcoal, and the many that remained gathered around the braziers and kept the party alive, talking about the game and the inspired performance by Capper. Following his example, the team had won by 20 points against a club from five valleys away, foreigners who were not without serious ambitions in the league. It was rumoured they were paying well and it was one of the talking points of the night and the considered opinion of the Widowers that it was always good to see a club with spirit able to put one over a club with money.

Standpipe had played at full back, filling in for Useless, who had bruised a rib in the first game. It had been a less contorted afternoon and Standpipe had been delighted when Gonzo delivered a short and unnecessary pass to him for his first try of the season.

'You didn't have to do that,' said Standpipe.

'Yes, I did,' said Gonzo. 'You might have to play at hooker again next week. Capper's about to blow a gasket.'

Capper had charged around to the very end, not always in the vicinity of the ball.

'He's like a boxer-dog puppy,' Blossom had said when Capper threw himself into a ruck and gave away a penalty.

'He's senile,' had been Daff's observation.

The one player not to have caught the infectious ebullience of Capper's day was Ragwort on the wing. He had dropped a couple of passes and let his head droop when he missed his opposite number for the opponents' only try of the match. The other players pulled him and his girlfriend, Emma, around the biggest fire and held them tight in their circle but it was clear that Ragwort was waiting to have a word with Gonzo. He kept checking to see where the number 8 was, who he was talking to, and whether there would ever be a gap for him to squeeze into.

Finally he caught Gonzo's eye and approached him at the third fire, whose embers were being stirred for the last time. Ragwort nudged Emma and they made their way over.

Emma was not called Emma. Ragwort had not been at the club very long. He'd been drafted in to replace the Professor, who had been sent off before the Babcock Cup final, but everyone already knew that the new and very speedy wing never went far without his girlfriend, who was his height to the nearest millimetre. They drove to work together from the village – from the room they shared in Gonzo and Capper's house in Straight Row – to Merthyr, where Ragwort stacked shelves in a big printing warehouse and Emma was a trainee seamstress in an embroidery factory unit next door. It hadn't taken Capper long to work out how their relationship worked.

'What's the name of that caterpillar you were telling me about?' he asked Gonzo in the last days of the old clubhouse on West Street. 'The hairy yellow and black thing that turns into a butterfly?'

'The cinnabar?' said Gonzo. 'It's a moth.'

'Same difference,' said Capper. 'Feeds on ragwort, right?'

'That's the one.'

'Well, she's Cinnabar then. 'Cos she's all over our Ragwort.'

'Evening, Ragwort. Evening, Cin … Emma,' said Gonzo now. 'What's up?'

Cinnabar gave Ragwort a little nudge with her elbow. 'Sorry, Gonzo …' said the wing and received another little nudge.

'Don't be sorry,' said Gonzo. 'Not for dropping the odd ball …' Ragwort looked crestfallen; Cinnabar a little annoyed. 'Not for being the bearer of bad news.' Ragwort's look turned to surprise. 'No secrets up here, Ragwort. You've come to tell me about the Welders, right? A hundred and fifty quid a game. Is that what they've offered you?' The Welders, the nickname of a rugby club three valleys away, had a new benefactor – a local hot-tub manufacturer. The Welders, like the opponents the village had just beaten, had been recruiting all summer and were still plugging gaps in their squad, even now that the new season had started. Ragwort nodded. 'And you don't want to go,' said Gonzo looking at him, 'because you like it with us. But,' and he looked at Cinnabar, 'six hundred quid a month would come in very handy.' Ragwort looked down. Cinnabar nodded her head briefly, defiantly. 'Well, we don't pay,' said Gonzo. Cinnabar's lips pursed a little. 'But how about this? You stay where you are – here with us, and here in the house in Straight Row. Rent free, let's say. And when you're ready to move on – for all the right reasons – because you could make it, Ragwort, and one day you'll need better rugby than we can offer here – when you're ready, you'll go with our blessing. How about that?'

'That's … that's …' tried Ragwort.

'That's very kind, Gonzo,' said Cinnabar. 'And you won't regret it for a moment. Will, they … Ragwort?' Emma never called her boyfriend by his nickname. To her he was Ashley.

'That's brilliant,' said Ragwort. 'Thank you.'

Cinnabar turned Ragwort round and led him back to the players' circle. There was a certain wiggle to her walk.

'Somebody looks pleased,' said Capper, stepping out of the darkness and rubbing his hands over the embers. Gonzo explained what he had just done. 'Aye, of course you did,' said Capper, ''cos we're one big fuckin' charity.' But before the night was over, Capper had gone into the Shard and taken a wad of notes out of petty cash and given Ragwort and Cinnabar back the deposit on their room.

6

The next time the players and supporters gathered it was to go south to Cardiff for the reception in the Senedd. The winners of the Babcock Cup were at their smartest, the Children in tight-fitting suits, the older players and the Widowers in club blazers. Grace and Our Marnie were in new dresses, one black, one dark grey, both contrasting with the shimmer coming off Meg and Annie who looked as if they were going ballroom dancing. They all had a quick swig of beer or sparkling wine at the Sherkin before boarding the Owain Owens bus. Only when safely aboard did they give the driver, old Tommy Morgan, the order to fire up the engine. Not even the spangle of Meg and Annie's dresses would have shone through the cloud of black smoke that escorted the bus out of the village.

The reception in Cardiff was on a grand scale, with politicians mingling with as many representatives of the world of business, tourism and entertainment as the Assembly could accommodate in the Neuadd hall and Oriel gallery. The entire workforce from the new film studios in the Bay and the music venue at the Coal Exchange were invited. The village club automatically formed a tight huddle on the edge of the throng, but soon they were opened up by all sorts of partygoers and well-wishers. They even had a mention in the welcome speech. A message had needed to be given in the dark days after the bomb, said the Presiding Officer – that life had to go on. And the Babcock Cup final had marked a small but significant shift back towards normality. 'Good people coming to the city with nothing but goodness in their hearts.'

'That was us, all right,' said Annie, clinking a glass of prosecco with Meg and the retiring Under Secretary of Community Affairs. 'Nothing but goodness in our hearts. And wickedness in our knickers.'

'Thank you again for coming,' the Presiding Officer said once the formalities were over and she was working the room. She had inserted herself into the heart of the rugby circle. She turned to Gonzo. 'I remember you, Gonzo Davies.' The rest of the players groaned. 'I was Carole Williams, barrister,' she said, 'on day one of my first week of sitting as a recorder in Swansea Crown Court when you won your first cap against Argentina.'

'Carole the Wig and Gonzo the Cap,' said Capper.

'And you're Capper Harris,' she said.

'What … how …?' stumbled Capper. The Presiding Officer of Wales tapped the side of the nose and turned back to Gonzo. 'I followed you. I was there in the crowd for the last of the Six Nations after that – the game against England.' Grace had been there too. She gave Gonzo's arm a squeeze. Carole looked at her. 'He was a little young for me, but I did rather fancy him.' The circle groaned again. 'We were starting out on something together … you in rugby, me in the law … and now, well, here I am, doing this. What about you?'

'I'm back in the village …' said Gonzo.

'Looking after us,' said Blossom.

'Aah,' said the chorus.

'Still playing … and doing a little building …' said Gonzo.

'Building is good. It's what tonight is all about. May I ask you … how's the head? Did you ever – how can I put this? – get to the bottom of it?'

Gonzo thought of the beating he had meted out to Danny Mewson. 'Partly,' he said. He thought of Martin Guest, Grace's husband. 'Not entirely.'

'And your head?'

'As empty as ever,' said Capper.

'It's fine,' said Gonzo.

Ten minutes later, Gonzo caught the look of desperation in the eye of Meg and Annie's Under Secretary and went to rescue him.

'Is it OK to go inside the Chamber?' he asked.

'Y Siambr,' said Alun Fry. 'If I were to be pedantic.'

'We do love a man when he's pedantic, don't we, Meg love?' said Annie.

'What is it you do here, Alun love?'

'Not a lot any more. I'm retiring.'

'Is that retiring shy, or retiring from work?' said Meg.

'Pedantically speaking,' said Annie.

'I'm finishing work, after forty-th …'

'Would you like to go out with a bang, Alun bach?'

'I'll sort this, Alun.' said Carole Williams, appearing from nowhere, with Grace on her arm. 'I can see you have your hands full. Do try to behave.' She steered Gonzo away. 'Alun's a shocking bore,' she confided. 'Those two will be very good for him, I'm sure.' She led Gonzo and Grace into the debating chamber of the Welsh parliament.

'May I ask you a question?' said Gonzo.

'Please.'

'Same as yours really. Did you get to the bottom of what happened here?'

Carole Williams the lawyer paused. Then the Carole Williams whose Senedd had been bombed spoke: 'Not really. There are forces at work that do not want this place to succeed. Some we can catch – people within the system who allow themselves to be corrupted. Or are simply corrupt. This is politics. We can root them out – slowly – but we'll find them.' She stopped again. 'But to answer your question – which I'm not supposed to do, politically speaking – who planted the bomb? Who are the corrupters? I don't think we'll ever know.'

'The English?' said Gonzo.

'You are not the first person to raise the suspicion. But as I say, I don't think we'll ever know for sure.'

Walking purposefully down Bute Street, the long straight connection between Cardiff city centre and the Bay, came Kitty Vernon-Evans, wife of one of the corrupt. She had travelled first-class from Swansea to Cardiff by rail and was now on foot, clear of thought, long of stride and devoid of feeling. She carried nothing other than her handbag.

*

Capper and Our Marnie came into the Siambr. They seemed to be giving themselves an unaccompanied tour of the Assembly building.

'Don't let him pinch anything, Your Presidenceliness,' said Capper. 'He's a devil for it.' The Presiding Officer laughed.

'What do they call it?' asked Gonzo. 'Transparency. If everything's out in the open then how can people be so corrupt?'

'Because people always have secrets,' said Carole Williams.

'Not us,' said Capper. 'No secrets up with us.'

'But there will be. Everything in a place like this,' and she indicated the Senedd, 'is magnified, but wherever you are, even up in your ...'

'Shit-heap,' said Capper.

'Language,' said Our Marnie, hitting his arm.

'Even up in your home village, you will have secrets.'

There was a little commotion behind them and a large figure almost ran into the Siambr. It was Brian Griffiths, President of the Welsh Rugby Union, a genial old soul who'd risen to high office largely on account of being permanently available to attend functions.

'Goodness, thought I'd missed you all,' he said. 'Evening, Carole.'

'Good evening, Brian. Look what you've got here, Capper,' she said, 'a pair of presidencelinesses.'

Brian looked slightly bemused, but held out his hand to Gonzo. 'Evening, Gonzo Davies,' he said. 'Didn't want you to think we at the WRU weren't proud. That we couldn't be bothered to acknowledge …' He mopped his brow. 'Sorry, been stuck in a … well, no, been out with the District C boys, really. Catching up … you know how it is … anyway, just wanted to say well done. Congratulations.'

'Thank you,' said Gonzo. 'Congratulations?'

'What, haven't you heard? Well, maybe I'm out of order then. Hope I haven't spoilt the surprise. It's Arthur's fault in the office. I told him …'

'Brian,' said Carole firmly. 'Stop. Or at least pause.'

Brian tried to be quiet. And failed. 'It's just … it'll sound now like I'm breaking a confidence.'

'We were just talking about secrets, funnily enough. I think it's OK, Brian. We'll give you parliamentary privilege.'

'Well, thank you. Much appreciated, I'm sure …'

'Brian.'

'Yes, Carole.'

'Tell Gonzo your secret.'

'Oh, that. Well, yes. You've been selected for the Barbarians squad, Gonzo Davies. Against New Zealand and – let's see if I can get this right – against somebody else, because the last time they played – the Barbarians, that is – they had a right hammering. So the Sheikh – I think he's a sheikh – has invited them – you, that is – to have a warm-up game first. In the Emirates. Dubai, if memory serves.'

'But how …?' said Gonzo and Capper together.

'That's easy,' said Brian, 'because he – not the Sheikh, obviously, but your old coach, Conrad Thomas – was sitting right next to me at the Babcock Cup final, and he said: "There's life in the old dog yet" – about you. They've pulled him – Conrad, not the Sheikh – out of retirement to coach the Barbarians for this special one-off – an extra game on the All Blacks tour. Made life hell for us, I've got to say … you know how hard it is to make plans even five years ahead … and suddenly they want this extra game at the start of their tour in just over a month. Well, so do we, mind, because that Tai McDonald – terrible tragedy; great player – and a number 8, just like yourself Gonzo Davies … and we said yes of course, in his honour. But now it's a two-off, and what with the Welsh camp already muttering … you know what they're like when you start asking them to give a bit – well, sorry, Gonzo, maybe you don't, what with it being a … while, like … since you … anyway, so, yes, you – we, that is … or in this case, Conrad … tried to take the pressure off a bit, because Stuart – that's our Stuart Graves – not that you need reminding, Carole – won't want too many players missing camp in the build-up to the November series. The All Blacks aren't the only tourists here in November – not that they're here, in Cardiff, exactly – except now they are, of course, which is where you come in, Gonzo Davies. If you get my drift. When Conrad suggested you, Stuart said: "Gonzo who?" Only joking, of course. And then he said yes – or was it no? – he didn't mind. I suppose you're entitled to ask what's it got to do with the coach of Wales anyway. But that's how it is. So … I just wanted to say well done.'

Kitty stood at the bottom of the steps leading up to the Senedd, not far from the spot where the white van carrying the explosives had been parked. Security cameras that could not be controlled by any agency other than the command room within the Assembly building swept the area now. There was no visible increase in security – no barriers or wire – and protestors were still allowed to congregate on the steps themselves. At this late hour of the evening, the placards and banners had mostly been taken home, although a small group of demonstrators against the closure of a geriatrics unit in Aberystwyth was still shaking hands with a band of Kurdish refugees seeking justice, and wishing each other good luck when Kitty arrived. She waited for them to leave before she started to climb the steps.

The Presiding Officer had ordered more sparkling wine, much to the concern of the security staff, who recognised that guests were starting to wander and that they were beyond the hour set for carriages to leave on the invitation. There was only so much spirit of reconciliation a security operation could stand. Alun Fry was a long way past his tolerance limit. He still hadn't been able to shake off Meg and Annie and there was a smear of lipstick on his shirtfront. Most of the other guests had already left. The players, unaware that fresh supplies were on their way, were doing the last rounds, swilling down the party leftovers.

Gonzo excused himself. He needed a few gulps of air before recharged glasses were raised to him. He wasn't sure he wanted to be in the public eye again. Grace certainly would want nothing to do with exposure. This wasn't quite as simple as it seemed. They stood at the top of the steps of the Senedd and found themselves staring at their old neighbourhood.

'You used to come and see me,' said Gonzo pointing to

flats not far away to the right, 'over there. In your Mazda. In your brown coat.'

'And later I lived with … him, just over there,' said Grace, pointing to a closer and grander block of flats. She shivered. 'You finished with me. And he nearly finished me. I'm not sure I like this place.'

Gonzo noticed the smart woman with the salt-and-pepper hair only because she stopped in her tracks on the steps and did not move a muscle. Her head was down and she remained rooted to the spot. When eventually she looked up, her eyes were closed.

They were standing in her spot. Not exactly in the very place she had chosen, but they would be near her. The giant and his very attractive partner. Please move, big man and beautiful woman. Kitty wanted a bit of, well, elbow room. It wasn't too much to ask. She needed a little room for her manoeuvre. She needed a little privacy in her very public place. She would will them to leave. Look down, take a long count and then look up – when I open my eyes you will be gone. Ready, ready, now. There, gone. Nobody stood in her way.

She climbed the steps and stopped. She would do it with her eyes shut. She reached into her bag and felt for the grip of the Browning pistol. Ever since declining to commit homicide she had dwelled on the process of termination, and decided that her own was the preferred solution. As if preference came into it. Perhaps not, but Kitty had been sufficiently intrigued to weigh up the options. Intrigued – what an odd thing to be, she thought, and how different from her emptiness now. To have been intrigued suggested an engagement, an interest. Perhaps it was the last flicker of emotion, the force that drove – no, that was too deliberate – the force that bore her from her home in Llanwrtyd Wells to the centrepiece of Horace's polluted life in Cardiff.

And what had those options been which had intrigued her so much? Traduced wives made good assassins, quite adept at slipping poison into a husband's peppered steak, or pressing a pillow down on an adulterer's grey face, but Kitty had decided to leave Horace alive on what she sincerely believed would be his deathbed. She had flirted – and realised what a totally inappropriate word that was – with tracking down Felicity. But the plump child was more victim than temptress, and Kitty was sure that if she was prepared to let Horace drift towards death with his guilt exposed – rather than with his air supply cut off – she would rather Felicity live on, even to a ripe old age, under the curse of what Horace had done to her. Besides, Kitty had to think of this: magistrate and murderer. She was not made for the preposterous. She would be neither – because she would be dead. That would put an end to intrigue and interest in life's twists and turns. Kitty had simply made her decision and would not sway. Suicide it would be. That was the whisper in her ear – not a force that drove her, but a hushed sibilant that bore her to Cardiff. Bore her. How boring it all was. How easy to end.

She would put the Browning in her mouth, not to the side of her head. She was worried that the bullet might exit and hit somebody if she went for the temple, and that simply would not do. Enough harm had been done without adding to it with what Kitty had learned was called collateral damage. She would face the Senedd and fire upwards. But precisely because she shut her eyes, she did not see in the reflection of the glass the return of the giant. As her hand tightened on the grip of the Browning in her handbag, a stranger's held her wrist and an arm was placed around her. On the CCTV screens before the security guards, whose gaze never faltered in the age of reconciliation after the bomb, it was a simple family reunion – a mother in the late evening, embraced by her son.

Gonzo held Kitty and felt her go rigid. Kitty kept her eyes screwed tight shut against the blast of rage that consumed her, flooding the numbness she had felt for weeks, the lack of feeling that had offered no resistance to the acceptance of her death by her own hand. She shook now with outrage that she had been thwarted. Gonzo held her tight.

'I can save you,' he whispered into her ear. 'I can save you.'

Kitty felt the anger die. And she let herself crumple into the arms of the giant and the beautiful woman who ran forward to help him, a daughter joining the family cuddle.

Capper came out to tell Gonzo to get a move on. People were waiting inside. But there was no sign of Gonzo or Grace. They were already on the bus, parked two hundred metres away, reassuring Kitty Vernon-Evans that everything was going to be all right. Capper went back to the remains of the party and joined the final toast to Gonzo in absentia.

7

Nobody came to work early the next day at the Shard. Grace popped in to collect a set of keys for the house in Straight Row, but left almost immediately. She was making her way off the wasteland when the first group of cyclists arrived. She did an about-turn, unlocked the Gherkin and invited them to help themselves. The cycling fraternity were meticulous about leaving the facilities as they found them, in a way that the rugby players were not. Kit was strewn across the floor in the changing rooms under the stand, and Our Marnie and Grace had gone on strike, refusing to sift through the leftovers of match days and training nights. There had been something of a stand-off between these matriarchs of the club – the Children's queens of the washing machines – and the Plant, the worst offenders. In the days when they had gone from the ground to the old clubhouse on West Street, the Children had been relatively organised in their routines: they played, they packed their bags, they drank fast from the free barrel and they left in a rush for the less 'tragically old' watering holes in the cities. But now they were happy to stay at the Sherkin. In fact the cycling club and its full age range of participants had opened up vibrantly youthful social opportunities in the village, and so keen were the Children to engage with the 'lycra brigade' on these fine September evenings that they completely lost their flimsy sense of tidiness. They played, they showered, they made themselves fragrant and in a hurry went out to play again at the Sherkin. Their unspoken understanding in their haste was that Grace and Our Marnie would tidy up after them. Our Marnie had loudly declared that she was a washerwoman to no Child, and that her days of being their skivvy were over.

Reluctantly, the Children had promised to leave the changing rooms tidier, only to find them on their next visit already spotless. The cyclists, like the rugby players, had rather taken to the long evenings after their long days on the mountain and they asked if they could use the changing rooms – Home for men and Away for women – to shower after their exertions and swap their spattered lycra for casual clothes. The Lewises ran a tidy ship and the offending rugby articles of underwear and sweatshirts were gathered up, washed and left the next day in neat piles on the benches for the Children.

Grace went to the house in Straight Row. Ragwort and Cinnabar had left for work. Gonzo, Capper and Our Marnie were in the kitchen and had already introduced a pale and weak Kitty to Dario. Bowls and plates and mugs filled the bowl in the sink. Grace slid the keys across the worktop, avoiding a patch of dried tomato sauce on the way. Kitty did not reach out to take them. Grace left them by her hand.

'You can stay as long as you like,' she said.

Gonzo had been awake most of the night. He had taken the Browning off Kitty and removed the immediate danger, but he was far from feeling in control. He seemed to have taken responsibility for a woman in an extremely vulnerable position. Kitty had told him her first name, but it was the single word she spoke before sitting back in her seat in the middle of the bus, her head hung low, oblivious to the hubbub of a rugby club returning home from a night out. They had been dropped off at the end of the track to the cottage – old Tommy Morgan the driver would not risk his vehicle in the pot-holes – and he had carried Kitty home. Grace had taken charge of the handbag. She had hesitated before opening it, but had then gone through what little there was inside – a purse with a bank card, that revealed that they now had a Mrs Vernon-Evans in the house.

'You realise this is becoming a habit,' she had said quietly to Gonzo later in the night, after Kitty had fallen asleep on the bed.

'What's that?' said Gonzo, putting his arms around her.

'Looking after women in distress. First me, and now Mrs Kitty Vernon-Evans. You're running a refuge for fallen posh totty.'

'It's not as if I'm qualified …'

'You'll think of something.'

'But what if …?'

'Sorry, I said that wrong. We'll think of something.' And Grace had kissed Gonzo and gone into the bedroom. He had carefully lowered himself into the one-armed armchair and tried to sleep, but his mind was racing. Images of Grace falling at the broken garden gate – it was still hanging off one hinge – repeated themselves over and over. He had eventually dropped off but had woken as a rectangle of light around the chipboard windows announced the start of a new day. He'd quietly checked on the bedroom. Grace, still in her new dark grey dress, had lain down on the bed alongside Kitty and they were curled up together.

In Straight Row, Gonzo now signalled to Dario that he needed a word. They went into the garden, a small patch of knee-high grass.

'I'm sorry about the grass,' said Dario. 'Never had a garden. Never had a house that didn't rock in the wind. Never had a dishwasher …'

'It's OK, Dario. Look, I need you to do something.'

'Of course. Anything. What is it?'

'You're our sort of lookout, Dario. Well, instead of keeping an eye on the whole village, I want you to keep an eye on Kitty. If that's OK. She's going to be staying here.'

'Of course. It'll be good to have somebody else in the house. She's got a hell of a tongue on her, Gonzo – that Cinnabar.'

Nobody was speaking when they went back into the kitchen. Grace had taken Kitty's hand, but all was quiet. Capper looked relieved to see Gonzo back.

'Right then, we'd better be making a start,' he said. 'I'm off up to Beaufort Street. Right …' But he did not move.

'Me too,' said Our Marnie. 'I'll be in the office.'

'I'm going shopping,' said Grace, 'for some clothes.' And she inclined her head towards Kitty, who had none, other than what she was wearing.

There was a pause. And then Kitty looked up.

'May I come with you, my dear?' she said.

'Of course,' said Grace. 'Whenever suits you.'

'Shall we say an hour, then? It'll give me time to sort this kitchen out.'

On the pavement outside, Capper handed Gonzo an envelope. 'There's no end to the fuckin' wonders that drop through our letter box,' he said. 'It's your invitation to the Barbarians. Looks 'ell of a trip.'

'You didn't open it?' said Our Marnie.

Capper shrugged. 'A man in the public eye needs a sniffer dog,' he said.

'Please,' said Our Marnie. 'The very thought ...'

'Tell you what, though,' said Capper. 'It's 'ell of a fuckin' trip.'

'Language.'

'And you know that tradition they have, them Barbarians? You know, the famous black and white shirt ... well, you wear their shirt, Our Marnie, and your own club socks. 'Kin' 'ell, Gonzo. Our club socks.' He headed for the van, but turned around. 'And another thing, Mother Teresa,' he said to Gonzo. 'That's three rooms now. The orphanage is filling up.'

Gonzo was in the Shard on his own going through the Barbarians' itinerary. It would be a twelve-day adventure, starting at the Willows Spa on the banks of the Thames in Berkshire, where the invitation side would assemble before flying to Dubai from Heathrow for the warm-up game against the United Arab Emirates. The following week would be set in Cardiff, where the main event, the memorial match in honour of Tai McDonald, would be played, at the Millennium Stadium. There would have been no difficulty in raising a team for the fixture against the New Zealand All Blacks – who had immediately agreed to this add-on, this prologue to their tour of Scotland, England and France – but to persuade players from around the world to commit fully to twelve days was more challenging. There was no fee on offer for the two games. All proceeds were to go to a new Tai McDonald Trust. The only thing the Barbarians could offer, thanks to the Sheikh's sponsorship, television rights and huge public support for the game, was luxury all the way. And not just for the players. Gonzo Davies plus Partner, it said on the invitation. The adventure would begin in five weeks' time. Would Grace go with him? Could Gonzo go, now that he seemed to have taken responsibility for Kitty? He tapped the card against the tabletop and stared out of one of the Shard's windows.

A large head in a hard hat suddenly filled the frame. Gonzo gave a start. There was a loud rap at the door and three men and a woman came in without waiting for a reply. They were all in white hard hats and two were carrying clipboards on which they were making notes even as they marched up to Gonzo's table. The face in the window had vanished and as light returned Gonzo glanced out to see not the usual swirl of cyclists on their circuit or dotted around the site of the old mine, but more people in hard hats and high-visibility coats, walking up and down, pacing out distances and taking pictures on their mobile phones of the Sherkin and everything around it.

Gonzo turned back to face the four people in front of him. One after the other they produced their official ID and gave spoken confirmation:

'Blaenau Gwent Planning Department.'

'Blaenau Gwent Licensing Authority.'

'South Wales Electricity in conjunction with Western Power.'

'Dŵr Cymru Welsh Water in association with Making Wales Grow.'

Gonzo thought they looked like the Four Horsemen …

'Any wisecrack,' said the man from the Planning Department, 'about us looking like the Four Horsemen of the Apocalypse, and there'll be a fifth person in here right now, showing you his warrant card and saying "South Wales Police". Got it?'

Gonzo nodded, seized by an old feeling of helplessness. When the scouts from the world of professional rugby had first come to see him, his brain had seized up. Give him time and he could formulate a response, but put him on the spot and his head turned to mush. Fortunately, it did not appear he was yet required to talk. The quartet looked as if they subscribed to the diktat: Speak only when we say 'Speak'.

The woman from the electricity company leaned forward. 'We should very much like to know what is going on here.' Gonzo stared at her. 'You may speak,' she said. But Gonzo couldn't.

The silence was broken by the sound of a motorbike pulling up outside. When the engine was cut, the hush resumed, followed by the crunch of boots on the gritty, grey waste outside. There was a light knock on the door, a pause and the sound of it opening. A man in leathers and a crash helmet walked in. He took off his headgear and shook free a mane of shoulder-length hair.

'Good morning, Brian … Tony. Gill, isn't it?' he said. 'Hello. It's been a while. And … I'm sorry?'

'Jim Griffiths. Licensing.'

'Good to meet you, Jim. Now, perhaps I can be of service?' said the Professor.

Twenty minutes later, Capper ran into the office, with Our Marnie not far behind.

'Where are they?' he said. 'The cyclists said there's been an invasion of the shit-heap.'

'There was,' said Gonzo. 'The electric, the water, the licence, the planning. They've all been.'

'But they never come here.'

'Well, they've been here now.'

'And?'

'And what?'

'Well, where the fuckin' 'ell are they now?' shouted Capper.

'Don't know. They went off with the Professor.'

'The Professor?' cried Capper and Our Marnie.

'Yep,' said Gonzo. 'It's been quite a morning.'

Our Marnie held out a hand of restraint. 'Whoa,' she said. 'I'll put the kettle on – while we've still got power – and you can start from the beginning.'

Two hours later, the Professor drew up in his motorbike again. This time when he walked into the Shard, he was greeted by Gonzo with a big embrace, followed by hugs from Capper and Our Marnie. The last time they had seen him was after the Babcock Cup semi-final. He had cut a forlorn figure, in trouble in his own eyes for having been sent off, and in chronic disgrace for having allowed Martin Guest to be his puppet-master for far too long. Gonzo had told him to stay, to stick with the team – that together they would find a way through. The Professor had nodded his head, but when Gonzo came to walk with him to the celebrations in the old clubhouse, the Professor was gone – into thin air. And now from out of it he had reappeared. The Professor sensed a bombardment of questions was coming his way, but managed to speak first.

'I want to introduce you to someone,' he said and quickly went to the door and let in another biker in leathers. The newcomer was in his early forties, slightly older than the Professor, slightly taller than Capper but just as bald, and much more Scottish than anyone in the room.

'I remember you, Gonzo Davies,' he said. 'I was at Murrayfield for that drawn game. Jammy Welsh …'

'This is John,' said the Professor, 'my partner.'

'Since when … where have you been … what have you been …?' said Our Marnie, Capper and Gonzo together, and all five laughed.

'Like the hair, Professor,' said Our Marnie.

'Professor?' said John. 'I've been calling him George.'

'His real name is the Professor,' said Capper.

The Professor nodded. 'I suppose it is,' he said.

'Anything else I should know?' said John. 'You've not got a wife and three children up here …? Where are we, by the way?'

'Welcome to the village, John. Scotland is three hundred miles that way,' said Gonzo, pointing over the Blorenge. 'Welcome back, Professor.' They all paused. 'Are you back?'

The Professor looked around the office. 'I see there have

been some changes,' he said. 'No,' he said to John. 'No wife. No three children. Just a fresh start. Back here. Not that I've ever lived here before. But, yes, I'm back.'

'Are you available for Saturday, then?' asked Capper. ''Cos you might have to go to full back. Useless is still out and Standpipe …'

'I'm not going to play,' said the Professor. 'My nerves couldn't stand it …'

'Nor mine …' said John.

'But if you need a hand on the coaching front …'

'It's a deal,' said Gonzo.

'Right,' said Capper, 'I don't want to be hurrying you, Professor – what with you being just back and all that. But that's the odd thing, ain't it? You've only just got here and yet you may be the only person in this room who's got a fuckin' clue what's going on.'

'Language,' said Our Marnie.

'OK,' said the Professor. 'You've broken about twenty laws already, setting up this place and starting a cycle club and running a café-cum-clubhouse without permission. But I've had a word.'

'How do you know all those people?' asked Gonzo.

'Look,' said the Professor, 'it's not something I'm proud of, or want to talk about again … but this is what I did when I worked for …'

'For him,' said Grace, coming into the office. The Professor stood up and the two people who knew Martin Guest best in the world looked at each other – Martin's wife and Martin's fixer. Neither of them had really known him so well after all. 'Hello, Professor,' said Grace and hugged him.

97

John introduced himself to her and Grace went outside and gently pulled Kitty into the office. 'This is Kitty,' she said.

'The stray cat,' said Kitty. Grace found her a chair and she joined the group.

'Right,' said Gonzo and then looked around the table. 'Look at us. It's like a proper board meeting. Anyway, this is to kick off: I arrived here and the clipboards descended. An army of them, swarming everywhere. And then the Professor arrived. I managed to tell him about the clubhouse up in West Street and the subsidence before he ... well, I reckon you'd better take it from there, Professor.'

'Well,' said the Professor, 'I have to say that was a bit of a game-changer, seeing the old clubhouse. I hadn't seen the damage for myself and it came as a shock. And I think the ... er, the interested parties understood that. The whole of West Street on the mountainside, cracking up, abandoned ... although there was a moment when Job-Shy Joe started shouting about the revolution coming. But I think they got it – not Job-Shy, but the clipboards – I think that's when they started to come around ... when they saw our ... predicament. All you're – all we're – trying to do is rebuild an essential hub of village life. So, we made a deal.' The Professor paused to take a last sip of the tea Our Marnie had made. Kitty stood up and started collecting the empty mugs around the table.

'I like to be busy,' she said, feeling everyone's eyes on her.

'Come on, Professor,' said Capper.

'Oh, he's a right old drama queen,' said John. 'He'll milk this for all it's worth. Won't you – Professor?'

'I'm merely collecting my thoughts. Thank you, by the way, Our Marnie.'

'You're welcome. Don't expect this every day, mind. This is an exception. Grace and I are still on strike – which makes you a strike-breaker, Kitty.'

Kitty stopped. The table watched her carefully. She slowly raised a fist. 'Sister power,' she said in a deadpan voice.

'So,' continued the Professor, 'this is how we stand. The utility companies will come and put in a metered supply of electricity and water to the caravan and the shed ...'

'We can stay in the fuckin' Sherkin?' said Capper. 'Pardon my French, Kitty.'

'I've been saying far worse inside my head lately,' she said.

'We can stay,' said the Professor, 'but as they pointed out, these are temporary structures. If this ... project – the cycle club and the rugby club ... I couldn't tell them you were running a building business from here, Gonzo ... if this is going to work, then this whole site has to be cleared for proper redevelopment. A mountain cycling centre is just the sort of thing, weirdly enough, they are looking to promote and they're already talking about building a back-to-back stand. One side looks over the cycling facility, the other on to the rugby field. New changing rooms, to be shared by both sports.'

'Well, that's all very grand ...' said Gonzo.

'There's more,' said the Professor.

'That's some meeting you had with them, Professor,' said Our Marnie.

'It was most constructive,' he said. 'First extra thing – what's the one thing we have in abundance up here?'

'Rain,' they all said.

'Right. Water. There's a rugby pitch here because a long time ago there was a project to build an entire sports complex alongside the mine, including a lido. Volunteers came from France and Germany to work on it. They got so far, but then the Second World War came. Years later, it was your father, Gonzo, that resurrected the plan for the rugby pitch. We can go further now, go back to the original plan.'

'Bloody hell, Professor,' said Capper. 'All this in five minutes ...'

'Just think, Capper, a water park. Slides coming down off the mountain into the lido. Cyclists and swimmers in the summer; rugby in the winter.'

'What's the second thing?' asked Our Marnie.

'Something to do with ... what did you call it, Professor?' said Gonzo. 'Clearing the site?'

'It's true. Soon, this will have to go.'

'Knock down the Sherkin? You just said ...' said Capper.

'And build something bigger, better.'

'And where would that be?' asked Gonzo.

'The Miners' Institute. Your father kept it going. You two have kept it going. The council will sell it to us and we can make it into something that's not just to be kept going, but made into something really special. A headquarters for ... everything. Clubhouse. Company office ...'

'It's huge,' said Our Marnie. 'We could have a flat at the top. Without a wall you can walk through.'

'Hang on, hang on,' said Capper. 'All this buying and redeveloping – that costs money. Where's that coming from?'

'There are grants for leisure and tourism projects that create jobs ...'

'That's about five per cent of the outlay ...'

'And there's European funding ...'

'That'll have to be matched …'

'And Lottery grants …'

'That'll have to be matched.'

'Bloody hell, Capper,' said Our Marnie.

'Language,' he said.

'Just for a minute, we dared … I don't know, dream a little …'

'We live in a shit-heap.'

'It's just … you don't have to keep reminding us …'

'It's real life.'

John suddenly clapped his hands. 'You Welsh,' he said. 'You're as bad as the Scots – permanently on the lookout for misery.' He looked around the table. Everybody did look downcast. 'Look,' he continued. 'Finding the money to match what's on offer is not a problem.' They all turned to him, suddenly interested again. 'And don't you all go looking at me like that. I'm no sugar daddy. Am I, Professor?'

The Professor laughed. 'No, you're not. You're church-mouse poor.'

'So?' said Grace.

'So,' said John. 'Shall I tell Grace?' The Professor nodded. 'His nibs has got the money.' Grace wasn't the only one to look surprised. 'And the Professor has the money because he stole it from your husband.'

There was a knock on the door and three Lewis heads appeared. They went no further. They were in their road bike gear and never clomped across the floor in their stiff shoes.

'Everything all right?' asked Mike.

'Only we heard, you know …' said Dai.

'There were … strangers in the village,' said Tom. 'Anything we can do to help?'

'Everything,' said Capper, 'is … well, lads, either we're discussing … what is it, Gonzo?'

'An investment opportunity.'

'Aye, an investment opportunity, or we're asking for another offence to be taken into consideration.'

'Er, right,' said Dai. 'Have we got time to do the Flying Five before we're sent down?' The Flying Five was the five-mile road between Blaenavon and Brynmawr, a new time-trial semi-sprint addition to the Graig's portfolio of informal events.

'Half an hour,' said Gonzo, 'and we'll be able to give you an update.'

'Just remember your Highway Code,' said Capper as the Lewises stepped back from the door, fastening as one their lightweight helmets. Capper turned to the Professor. 'Where were we? Ah yes, the international man of mystery. Come on then, let's be having it. Can't be any worse than what you've told us before.' Our Marnie kicked him under the table. 'No offence like, John,' added Capper.

The Professor looked a little uneasy in his chair. He looked up at Grace. 'It's true,' he said. 'And it's the reason we're here. I didn't steal the money … I liberated it. After what he put us through, I couldn't help it. I knew where it was and I transferred funds into an account he doesn't know exists – one that I can access. Don't worry about him. He's got more than he can ever spend, wherever he is. But here's the thing, Grace. John, what you said isn't strictly true. We've discussed this, remember?'

'Aye,' said John. 'Sorry, I just wanted to ramp up the drama a bit myself.'

'It's yours, Grace. I don't want it. And by rights, it's simply yours, anyway. We're going to make a fresh start, John and me, and I don't want anything to do with … him.'

'Is there … much?' asked Grace.

The Professor shrugged.

'Enough to do what John said?'

He shook his head. 'I've only been back, as Capper says, five minutes, but there's a rule of thumb about these projects – and that is: however much you've got, you always need a little bit more. It used to drive … him … mad. But that's the way it is. We wouldn't need much more, but …'

'OK,' said Grace. 'Now, I'm going to sort of blurt this out, so, if I do it wrong, Gonzo, you can tell me … but I'm just going to say it. And it's this. I don't want the money. I'm making a fresh start, too. So, let's use the money – his money – for something good. That would stick in his throat.' Grace stood up, with more colour in her cheeks than Gonzo had seen. 'There, I've said it.'

Kitty stood up. 'I want to say something, too. I've known you for all of one night and one morning. But I've been talking with Grace and I just want to tell you all this: first, I'm not going to do anything … silly, because, second, I too want to make a fresh start. What is more, for someone who has never worked a day in her life, I bring – and I think this is the vernacular – something to the party. I have been on a little spree – not the shopping trip with Grace just now, but a somewhat longer spend. I won't bore you with the details … but to my surprise, I have scarcely made a dent in the

103

money I should not wish my husband to have, even if, strictly speaking it is his. Too bad, I say, Horace, too bad. And that's the last time I shall mention you by name. You are Him Two. And what was his is mine now. And that means I can make it yours. As I suspect they no longer say in the movies, count me in.'

'Sister power,' said Our Marnie and led the table in a round of applause.

'In that case,' said Gonzo, 'I declare the first board meeting of the Fresh Start Co-operative closed – unless there's any other business.'

Capper stuck up his hand. 'All this generosity,' he said, 'is all very well, but tell me, you two ...'

'Oh no,' said Our Marnie. 'Don't throw a bucket of cold sick on them.'

Capper was looking at John and the Professor. 'I'm just saying,' he continued, 'or I'm just asking these two, who've just given away all their money, if they've now got two pennies to rub together.'

John and the Professor looked at each other and shook their heads.

'Right,' said Capper with a sigh and opened the key drawer. He took out the last set for the house that was no longer their show home. 'That's the last bedroom gone in Straight Row. I declare the Orphanage full.'

'Where did you say it was?' asked John.

'Straight Row.'

'From the word go in our new life, we're living a lie,' said John.

8

As Dario reported to Gonzo, there was no need most of the
time to monitor Kitty. She spent more time at the Shard than
in the Orphanage, helping Our Marnie run the office, now
that Capper and Gonzo were back at work on their various
sites. Or she helped the Professor there, as he went through
the infinitely detailed interaction between several public
bodies and their speck of enterprise. Kitty kept her new home
shipshape and she provided an electronic valet service to
the Professor, processing his many contractual negotiations
with a sense of order that saved him swathes of time. Having
worked all his life with an arm, as it were, twisted behind
his back, he found it quite difficult to adjust to freedom of
movement. He almost went too quickly and started to confuse
his lines of communication. He was asking people to do a
second thing that was dependent on a first that could not yet
have been started. Kitty gently applied a brake. One evening
she emailed him a review of his day's work, based entirely on
listening to him and observing him, and suggested an agenda
for the following morning. The Professor frowned when he
first read this intrusion into his working ways – processes
whose confidentiality he had for good reasons until now
guarded jealously – but he followed the advice to the letter.
Now he found he consulted Kitty more and more frequently.

John came and went. One moment he could be seen
spinning around the circuit in bright yellow – his *maillot
jaune* – fluorescently and uproariously coming in last behind
the Graig cyclists; the next he was serving lunch in the
Gherkin. His cooking – Mediterranean Scottish, he claimed

– drew more and more people to the cycle track. One day Capper arrived in a grizzly mood, complaining about their plasterer who had let them down in Beaufort Street for the third time. Later that day Capper went back to the site, still fuming, and found John applying the finishing touches to a beautifully skimmed wall.

'Fuck me,' said Capper.

'I can't,' said John. 'The Professor would go crazy.'

'I mean, fuck me, you're hired.'

'Let's call it in lieu of rent.'

Where once Capper had rolled his tongue around 'ingress of water' as a favourite phrase, now he found himself repeating 'in lieu of' to himself.

Dario was not totally redundant. Once a day, Kitty would walk from the village out on to the moors, and Dario would follow from afar, swinging himself up to one of his many vantage points and tracking her progress. She did not go far and she walked not out of loneliness or to let any residual inner despair rise to the surface of her being. When she said she would put Horace out of her mind, she meant it. She did not turn her face to the sky to sob or cry in anguish at the evil her husband had done. She looked upward to breathe in clean air and to offer thanks that she had been given an opportunity to begin again.

She took these walks at first at lunchtime, but then she was tempted, as they all were, by John's midday fare and she couldn't resist. Besides, there was a problem to resolve and to do so she needed to tinker with her timetable. If there was a problem at the Orphanage it was Emma. Somehow, Kitty could not quite bring herself to call her Cinnabar. Emma was finding it difficult to adjust to having 'two of those', as she referred to John and the Professor, in the same house. It wasn't homophobia per se; more jealousy. The Professor was making it his personal mission as a coach to improve the player who had replaced him on the wing – to transform him into the village's special one. Ragwort, slightly under the thumb of his Cinnabar away from the rugby field, was anything but cowed on it. He was fast and well-balanced and elusive. And he had that streak peculiar to small participants in a sport dominated by overgrown physical specimens – scarcely concealed belligerence. For eighty minutes a week, Ragwort was a nasty piece of work, and was all the better for it as a rugby player. It was the Professor's job to channel all that aggression in a positive direction. He worked on his student's physique and his gait and the timing of his runs. He reworked the wing's positioning in attack and rebuilt the way he approached the ball coming at him out of the air. Ragwort was not the tallest but he was fast becoming the safest pair of hands under the high ball. And every time he talked of how the new coach was doing wonders for his game, Cinnabar felt herself pushed a little further away.

Kitty invited Emma to walk with her early one evening. Emma was not keen. She had barely set foot through the door after coming home from work when Ragwort was changed into his kit and heading down to the rugby pitch.

'That bloody rugby club,' she spat. 'I hate it.'

'I'd like you to see something,' said Kitty.

'Where?'

'Out on the moor. Not far.'

'I don't know. I hate the bloody moor.'

'It won't take long – just a short walk.'

'I hate walk … oh, listen to me. I hate myself.'

And with that, Cinnabar let herself be taken out in the fading light to the wilderness. 'I'm losing him,' she said after a minute of walking in silence. 'I could kill that Professor.'

'No, you're not, and no, you couldn't,' said Kitty. 'He loves you, your …'

'Ragwort. Even I call him it now.'

'Well, he loves you. It's obvious to everyone in the Orphanage.'

'Is that what it's called? The house …'

'So it seems.'

'I like it.'

'Well, that's a start.'

They walked on and soon the path narrowed into a thin straight line of cropped, springy grass, aiming at the top of the Blorenge in the distance.

'You're right,' said Cinnabar. 'This is good.'

Something large lumbered out of a hollow in the moor and stood on the track thirty paces in front of them.

'Oh my God,' cried Cinnabar. 'It's a bloody horse. I hate horses.'

'No, you don't.'

'Well, I'm scared of them then.'

'That's different. We can work on that. Come on.' Kitty took her hand from her pocket and held out an apple. The horse walked slowly towards them. Cinnabar stepped behind Kitty and held on to her waistband.

'Oh, I don't know about this, Kitty.'

But Kitty was already stroking the horse, who was nuzzling the other palm, that held the titbit.

'This is Arkle. Arkle, this is Emma. He's what I wanted you to see.'

With extreme caution, Cinnabar reached out a hand and the horse pulled away before coming forward again to see if it held any more food.

'If you reach in my pocket, I've got some Polos in there,' said Kitty quietly. 'He loves a mint, does Arkle.'

'Where did you find him?'

'We met one day up here. I used to come out at lunchtime, but I prefer coming for a walk at the end of the day now. He's always here.'

Cinnabar held out a flat palm and Arkle took the mint. Cinnabar giggled.

'He tickles.'

Gonzo had not replied immediately to the invitation to play for the Barbarians. A polite email was sent to him from the secretary of the invitation side, wondering whether he had received the card in the post. Gonzo replied that he had and that he would be honoured to play. He apologised for the delay and explained that he was just waiting to see whether he would be accompanied or not by his partner. The secretary thanked him and asked him to provide confirmation one way or the other as soon as he could. An early response would be much appreciated – the secretary was sure Gonzo would understand – given the logistics of the two-game operation and the schedules to be prepared for players coming in from all over the world. Gonzo lived thirty miles from Cardiff.

He did not want to be the boy from the backyard who held everybody up – Gonzo Davies, too old and slow and not strong enough to say yes or no on behalf of his partner. But he waited.

Grace wanted to go. And she didn't want to go. She knew Gonzo needed an answer and she knew that her reasons for not going were dissolving. The characters in her bubble, the people who to varying degrees might depend on her – who might anchor her to the village - seemed to be thriving. The Professor was busy at work and positively glowing as a coach at the club and personal mentor to Ragwort. John, far from being envious, was the life and soul of the Sherkin social scene and the Graig club, and was fast becoming something of a guru in Capper's eyes. Our Marnie was anything but unhappy at seeing her man besotted by someone other than her.

'I love him more now I see him less,' she said.

Dario reported that Kitty had gone from being fragile to steady as a rock almost overnight. 'She's like a mam to Cinnabar,' he said. 'Talks a lot of sense does our Kitty. She's so patient … and tidy. I've never been so … looked after.' There was a little choke in Dario's voice. Kitty wasn't being a mother only to Cinnabar, it seemed. Dario coughed. 'Cinnabar's her work in progress, of course. She's taken the sting out of that young madam's tongue. Listen to this, Grace – one night Cinnabar and Kitty come back to the Orphanage and the next morning there's a horse in the garden. Arkle, they call him. She'd been nagging me for weeks to cut the grass, that Cinnabar. "Look, Dario," she said, "a lawnmower." I'd never heard her laugh before.'

There was no reason now why Grace could not go to Dubai for a few days. The supplementary week in Cardiff – so close to home – could be forsaken if it didn't work out. But what was this 'it' that couldn't work out? Why did she not say she would love to go wherever her Gonzo went, let herself be swept along on his last adventure? There was no pressure playing for the Barbarians. It was a game without stress and he was its romantic oddity, the little sentimental inclusion in a match designed to be without a trace of malice. And yet she still hesitated. She knew it was not other people that might stop her from leaving the bubble. There was only one person who feared exiting the village, and that was Grace.

The trip to Cardiff had affected her. The sight of the places in the Bay, where her affair with Gonzo had ended, where she had lived unhappily as a wife, had filled her with trepidation even before the upheaval of the incident with Kitty. There was only one place Grace wanted to be and that was back in the village, back on the mountain, the place where Gonzo had once said could never be a home for her. Well, it was. To such an extent that even the trip down to Abergavenny the next day had filled her with unease. Taking the part of the listener, the soother, and offering a hand of friendship to a woman in such distress had allowed her to conceal her own anxiety. Only when they were back on the road up the Blorenge, the back of the van filled with bags of clothes for Kitty – the shoppers' statement of belief in a brighter tomorrow – did she feel the pressure in her head ease. Only when they were heading a little too fast – as she had driven all those years ago – through the dark tunnel of beech trees and over the cattle grid into the daylight and across the open mountainside towards the Keeper's Pond, where she had first clapped her eyes, through the steam of her overheated Mazda, on Gonzo Davies, did she feel reassured. Only when she was beyond Garn-yr-Erw and deep in the heart of the wilderness did she feel safe. She did not want to go.

'I think you should let them know,' she said to Gonzo one night when he came home from training, a few days after he had promised to inform the Barbarians, 'that I'd be honoured to come with you.'

They were picked up in a Mercedes, a luxury coupé that was taken with extreme reluctance by its driver, Tony from Grangetown in Cardiff, down the track to the cottage. 'No offence, Mr Davies, but this track is well out of order,' he said as they were bouncing their way out.

'Please, call me Gonzo.'

'Fair enough, Gonzo, but your track's still a nightmare. A man of your standing, like, you should have a flat drive.'

'A man of my standing?'

'Of course. I remember you playing.' The car swung out off the track and on to the open road. Tony took his hands off the wheel and pretended to give a little pass. 'D'you still do it?' He moved his head in order to see Grace in his mirror. 'Doing a Gonzo, Mrs Davies. That's what your old fellah did. Every time he did one, we kids would bang the hoardings and yell: "He's done a Gonzo."'

'Call me Grace, Tony. And yes, I suppose, he's still doing it. Doing a Gonzo.'

Gonzo was, but he was worried that what he could still do down in the lower reaches of Welsh club rugby would be exposed on the grand stage. He was a grass-roots player about to play alongside the best players in the world against the best team in the world, the New Zealand All Blacks. Doing a Gonzo. Looking a right Charlie, more like.

'I'll shut up when we reach the Severn Bridge,' said Tony. 'I promise. But can I ask you something? That game against England – your last one. Gonzo's finest hour. Was it all planned – you taking a battering like that?'

For the next three-quarters of an hour Gonzo was pulled back in time to his last international match for Wales, the last of his six caps. Grace had been there – in his thoughts as he sought inner peace before kick-off – in the flesh. She had been there with Martin and Konstantin Mordashov, who had just bought her husband's steelworks. Gonzo had played the game of his life. And that would be that. He'd never play for Wales again, and he wouldn't see Grace for many years, until the day she turned up in a state of collapse at the cottage.

Tony wanted more and more details about every aspect of that final game of the Six Nations, and the 45 minutes passed quickly. The driver had one more question – whatever happened to your head, Gonzo Davies? – but the Mercedes was sweeping towards the Second Severn Crossing, and true to his word, he stopped talking and allowed Gonzo and Grace to doze their way up the M4 to their exclusive Willows Spa hotel.

'It'll be all right,' said Grace in Gonzo's ear as they swept through the pillared gates. She could feel the heat coming off him. Gonzo felt ridiculous. Nobody could push back the years, especially not in a sport where each new generation was faster and stronger than the one before.

'Here we are,' announced Tony, pulling up in front of the mansion on the banks of the Thames. 'We're all behind you, Gonzo. Just look after that old head of yours, and it'll look after you.'

They had been told to pack nothing larger than an overnight bag. On the vast bed in their suite were laid out clothes for Gonzo and clothes for Grace – more designer dresses than she had worn in a year; more shirts than he had worn in a lifetime. A card on the pillow informed them that pre-dinner drinks would be served in the Windsor-Lewis Room at 7 o'clock. Before then, if Grace cared to phone reception a treatment could be booked for her – or them – in the spa.

'A hammam …' she said. 'Come on, let's give it a go. In for a penny …' And Gonzo found himself being led to a world of steam and gentle massage, far removed from the ice baths and the probing fingers that used to assault the contusions deep within his muscles. A large, cheerful woman called Rachida, from Marrakech, introduced herself and asked them to strip. He was lying next to Grace and found it disconcerting to see her stretched out, being oiled and massaged. Grace had put on a few healthy pounds and looked … well, she looked perfect to Gonzo. At some stage he would have to start thinking about rugby and not making an idiot of himself in Dubai and Cardiff, but for the moment he was well and truly distracted.

It was as if Conrad Thomas, Gonzo's coach when he had briefly played for Wales, had been waiting for nobody else. He was charming with everybody, welcoming the players and their partners as they arrived in pairs and groups for the drinks reception – but in his reserved Kiwi way. When he saw Gonzo, however, he limped as fast as his arthritic knees would permit him and slapped his old charge on the shoulders and threw his arms around him.

'Good to see you, Gonzo Davies,' he said. 'How's the head? You must be Grace. Nice to meet you. Are you still up there on your mountain? Have you become a cave dweller, too, Grace? Hell, I must stop talking …'

'The head's fine, coach. Yes, we're still on the mountain, and yes, she's a cave dweller now. And how are you?'

'Hobbling, mate, on these old knees. I'm in retirement on the Coromandel Peninsula, but I wouldn't have missed this for the world. Did you ever meet him? Tai? No? You'd have liked him. You were a lot alike. Hell, it would have been a good scrap.' Conrad leant towards Gonzo. 'You know you're the only Welshman here. That Stuart Graves – would you believe it? – said he couldn't afford to release anyone. Look around. Every other country willingly gave us a player or two – even if they're going to be just as busy as Wales in November. The others – England, Ireland, Scotland, France and Italy – said we could have more. We took two from each. Then two from Argentina and Fiji – for a bit of grunt and a bit of running. And one each from, let's see, Romania, Tonga, Samoa, the USA, Canada and Japan. Plus one South African … and an Aussie to lower the tone. Do you know any of them? I don't. I'm old enough to be their grandfather.'

'And I'm old enough to be their father.'

'Did you ever see the old boy play, Grace?'

'I did – I still do.'

'He was bloody good back then. How's he going now?'

'Oh, they tell me he's still getting stuck in.'

'Well, we'll need a bit of that.'

The French players were the last arrive. Until Maxime Ferry and Noa Diawara came into the room the atmosphere was cordial but unrevealing. Gonzo, thinking he looked puny and wrinkled alongside all these muscled athletes in their mid to late twenties, was the most reserved of them all. He didn't even have a fellow countryman in the room. He watched the other players, all accustomed to attending receptions and being gawped at for their size and their chiselled, stubbled and often bruised appearance. They were going through their ritual reluctance of not being seen to be the first to drop their guard. They sipped their soft drinks and talked quietly in small groups. Maxime Ferry changed all that. He swept in and worked half the room in five minutes flat. It was impossible but he seemed to know everybody in the Barbarians' squad. He suddenly seemed to notice what everybody was drinking and he jumped up on a chair and clinked the glass of champagne he had just finished.

'Everybody, s'il vous plaît,' he shouted. He reached down and took the glass of orange juice out of the huge hand of Radu Murariu, the Romanian second row. He held it up for everybody to see. 'This, my friends, is an insult,' he shouted. 'An insult to the traditions of the Barbarians and an insult to my good friend, Tai McDonald. It is an insult to the cellar of the Willows, to the *vignerons* of Champagne … and, Radu, to the wine-growers of Romania. You should be ashamed. I know that you, Matt … where are you, Matt Miles?'

The American prop put up his hand and shouted: 'Over here, buddy.'

'I know that you are from California where they grow oranges. So, please do not be offended. This is not an insult to you. But no more of this ... waiters, champagne all round.'

Immediately, the mood of the party changed. As Maxime worked the second half of the room, the pairs split up and groups intermingled. Grace was absorbed into an Irish-Argentine quartet and Gonzo found himself clinking glasses with the South African scrum half, Jacques du Plessis and his wife, Hentie.

'Take care, Gonzo Davies,' said Maxime, finishing his tour of the room. 'I have been saving you till last – to save you from these Huguenots.' Jacques and Hentie laughed and gave Maxime a kiss on both cheeks before the Frenchman reached for Gonzo and planted two big kisses on his. 'You know,' he said to the South African couple, 'why I really saved grand-père Gonzo to last?' He still held Gonzo's face in his hands. 'Because you, monsieur, are the reason why I am playing rugby and not winning gold medals in the Super G at the Winter Olympics. The day Wales came to Paris – do you remember? We called it the Game of the Century. And I was a child in the stands and I said to myself that I wanted to be like them – like you – one day. A god, out there, playing like that. It was incredible, that match.'

Having gone round the room, Maxime – 'Just Max,' he later said to Grace as he introduced her to his wife, Perrine – stuck with his Welshman. He pointed to himself, Gonzo and Jacques and said, 'Six ... eight, nine. We are missing the seven ...' But Noa Diawara was already there, behind him. It was said he had never lifted a weight in his life, but had the strength of three men. He was on this tour on his own – 'He has fifteen fiancées in the Côte d'Ivoire and couldn't choose …' said Max – and said almost nothing. He and Max were inseparable, both on the field and off it, playing partners in the back row and friends. They played for the club that was an amalgamation of Stade Français and Racing Métro '92, a resurrection outfit formally titled Paris Maximum, but known universally as Paris Max. 'After me, of course,' said Max, who was born and bred Parisian and had been at Stade Français until it went into financial meltdown, with an international arrest warrant issued for the apprehension of their owner and former player, Thibaud Fernandez, who was wanted for questioning in connection with a series of money-laundering scams.

Racing Métro's slide out of business began with a bit more grace than their rivals' across town, but a vote by the players to carry on playing for nothing in the light of an internal audit that revealed the cupboard was bare, quickly became a rancorous split in the camp. The Racing schism became a strike supported by half the squad and the whole club soon ceased trading. The simultaneous liquidation of the two famous names was the second notable French double that year – after Montpellier became both the champions of France's Top 14 domestic championship and the winners of the European Champions Cup. Montpellier were the southern pride of the nation; Paris Max were the offspring of what *Midi Olympique*, France's rugby newspaper, called 'an inevitable collapse through hubris'.

Noa came to Paris Max as a non-striker from Racing and

his partnership in the back row with Maxime Ferry was the pillar on which a faltering rugby revival in the capital was built. The amalgamated club was unveiled one Tuesday in May and relegated on Wednesday for any number of sins of their illegitimate parent clubs. As the lawyers waded through the old regimes' financial irregularities and breaches of French employment law, the players battled their way out of the Pro D2 second division and back into the Top 14. They were still often fair game on the road, and in the strongholds of French rugby in the South and South-West they won vary rarely, but they had succeeded in making their own home a difficult away destination for those that treated them with disdain elsewhere. In one recent and particularly combative round of the Top 14, Noa had knocked out a player from Clermont Auvergne, who had just opened up a gash in Max's head, causing blood to cover his mop of blond hair. 'Joe Louis takes care of Marilyn Monroe,' had run the caption beneath a photo of the incident in *L'Equipe* magazine.

Now, in the Willows Spa, the putative back-row and scrum-half combination for the Barbarians – the numbers 6, 7, 8 and 9 – led the bonding session. They drank and talked and others came and drank and talked with them until 4 o'clock in the morning. The entire squad followed them off to bed and they all slept for five hours. They went out for a gentle – very gentle – training session before returning to their rooms, where all their new clothes, bar their travel kit, had been packed into all their new bags. They showered and changed, had a restorative lunch, and boarded the coach that took them to Heathrow.

On the plane that would land in Dubai early in the morning of the eve of their warm-up game against the United Arab Emirates, they all slept again. Bleary-eyed, they checked into Raffles Hotel. Conrad had organised a team meeting for the players, and their partners were invited to take full advantage of all the hotel's leisure facilities. Briefly the tourists had a moment to admire their accommodation. Before they went down to the lobby, Gonzo and Grace stood in their room, whose luxury made the Willows Spa seem like the Miners' Institute, and looked out over the Gulf.

'I was really nervous about coming,' said Grace. 'I'd been locked safe inside the village and I didn't want to leave.'

'I'm still a bit nervous about playing. And I was worried about you too. But I feel better. They're a good bunch, aren't they?'

'They're great. I feel fine. And you're going to shine, Gonzo Davies.'

They walked to the lift, pressed the button and waited. Gonzo slipped an arm around Grace and kissed the top of her head. Inside the lift she leaned slightly against him. He did not notice her weight and lightly ran a finger down her back. Three floors down, the lift stopped. 'Doors opening,' said a disembodied voice. Almost silently they parted and there in front of Gonzo and Grace stood her husband, Martin Guest.

9

After leaving Penarth Marina aboard the boat skippered by Frank, usually his driver but now his skipper, it had taken Martin three weeks to reach Dubai. They touched land in Ceuta, the Spanish enclave on the coast of Morocco, where Martin immediately ordered Frank home. Frank was reluctant to leave Mr Dennis Coates, as Martin's new passport revealed him to be, alone in North Africa. Trustworthy Frank – through loyalty, unlike the suborned, coerced and blackmailed Professor – wanted to stay. Martin's obedient delivery driver – his true deliverer – felt it was premature to abandon the man who paid him to do his occasionally unsavoury bidding. Frank was not given to much outward expression of pleasure or even satisfaction, but Martin knew the former commando enjoyed the execution of duties that would have horrified his rather shrewish wife, Marlene. Martin and Frank shared much in common. Frank was almost his friend. But he was not. Martin thanked him and ordered him back to his house near the edge of a cliff in Cardiganshire. There would be money in his bank account. Frank could live well in his retirement.

Martin was on his own and felt neither fear nor any sense of anticipation. He flew out of Casablanca and into Cairo as Dennis Coates and from there he arrived in Dubai as Clive Parfitt. And in Dubai he was nobody. Or he was another wealthy somebody, and could therefore be anybody. He rented an apartment that overlooked the desert, not the sea. It was billed as unfurnished but luxurious. Martin deliberately kept it minimalist. Spartan. Empty – all bar a single bed.

He slept at night, but did no more there. He needed no office space by day, not because he wasn't interested in this crossroads of commerce, but because so much business was conducted in the hotels of the city that these became his waiting grounds, where he sat for three weeks, listening and watching.

Ravi Kala was larger than life. He moved his bulky frame between the Burj Al Arab and Jumeirah Beach, between the Ritz-Carlton and Raffles and appeared in the foyer of each hotel slightly sweaty, until the air conditioning cooled him back down, and always a little loud. He lived with a mobile phone clasped to his ear. It didn't take Martin long to hear about his consignment of scrap metal on a container ship stuck somewhere in the Red Sea on its way to China via Mombasa.

'Where?' said Ravi one morning within earshot of Martin at the Ritz-Carlton. 'How the hell should I know where? Bloody somewhere, that's all I know.'

It took Martin three days to work out that an agent to an intermediary, who tended to work out of the Jumeirah Beach, was the cause of the problem, playing Ravi, the vendor, off against the Chinese purchasers. The ship was already docked in port in Mombasa, racking up fees from which the agent would take a cut. The old organiser in Martin – the proud re-jigger of a bakery's timetable, the maker of space in a cluttered furniture warehouse, the master of a brief in the production of steel – couldn't help but make his play. He wrote a note, put it into an envelope and slipped it into the free hand of Ravi as he walked past. The Indian on the phone was too agitated to notice.

The next morning, Ravi presented himself, without a phone to his ear, at the corner table of the coffee shop in Raffles. 'So, here I am, Sherlock bloody Holmes,' he said, not sitting down, but taking a handkerchief from his pocket and wiping his brow. 'Eleven o'clock in the coffee shop. Who the hell are you and how the hell do you know where my ship is?'

'It's Krishnan. He's screwing you.'

'He wouldn't. We are like brothers.'

'Ask him how much Chilemba Onyango is paying him.'

'Who the hell is he? And who the hell, I say again, are you?'

'He's like another of Krishnan's brothers. Your ship is in Mombasa. My name is Martin.' And with that, Martin stood up and began to walk away.

'Is that it, Mr Martin?'

'I'll be here next week,' said Martin and left.

Ravi sat down at the table at 11 o'clock on the dot the following week. He snapped his fingers and ordered tea.

'Any particular blend, sir?' asked the waiter.

'English bloody breakfast,' said Ravi. He wiped his brow. 'So, Mr Martin, it seems you were right.'

And Martin was no longer on his own in Dubai. Once a week they met, not in the same hotels but always at 11 o'clock in the morning. And then they met twice a week. Ravi sought advice on how to shift these goods here and those products there, and Martin gave the objective view of an inexperienced businessman a step back from the calculatingly devious haggling and bartering that went with every deal. He watched and he listened and he told Ravi who to avoid. He introduced him to a Korean, the utterly humourless Mr Park, whom Martin had heard in faltering English on his way through reception trying to explain to a company in New Jersey that he had twice narrowly avoided being robbed of every last cent of his commission. Mr Park and Ravi sealed a contract with nothing more than a handshake and honoured it, much to their mutual benefit and somewhat to Ravi's surprise.

'They can be bloody difficult, I can tell you, Mr Martin. The Koreans.' Martin said nothing. 'I say that, Mr Martin, in the expectation that you might ask me a bloody question. "Is that so, my good friend Ravi? How come, Ravi?" But no, you never ask. Not even, "How much are you going to pay me, Ravi?"'

'I don't want any money.'

'What do you want then, Mr Martin?'

Ravi one morning suggested lunch the following day. 'I feel we have gone beyond the-tea-and-coffee stage, Mr Martin,' he said. 'How about some bloody champagne and a toast to Mr Park, eh?'

He was expecting a cold no, but Martin gave him a chilled yes. Ravi plied him with the best Krug Clos du Mesnil in an attempt to loosen his tongue. All that happened was that Ravi ended up in tears, talking about his wife and five children back in Mumbai. In the bar there was a large gathering of expats. They were holding what looked like a working lunch. Beer bottles and folders filled the table. Ravi wiped his eyes and his forehead.

'I am a very wet man, Mr Martin,' he said. He glanced across at the expats. 'Look at them. How the Empire was run. Beer and written orders.'

'Orders, carried out by people like you. They do all the ruling and you do all the running. It's why you end up … so damp.'

Ravi shook his head. 'I am a free agent. I answer to no British master.'

'Except me.'

'You are a cruel man, Mr Martin. A bloody cruel man. And Ravi is not making a bloody joke.'

There was a smattering of laughter from the expats' table and an order was placed for more beer.

'So, tell me … cold Mr Martin in your watchtower, what do you see there?'

'They are the organising committee of the rugby game to be played here in Dubai between the United Arab Emirates and the Barbarians.'

'How …?'

'Powers of observation. They're on the big board in the foyer. They've been meeting here all morning.'

'Ah. And this rugby, does it mean anything to you?'

'Not now.'

'But?'

Martin shrugged.

'Come on, Mr Martin. Tell me what you know.'

'I know it can be painful.'

'In India, we might say you were an enigma, Mr Martin. You might even be honoured as a mystic. But I see only your dead British eyes. Were you ever alive?' Martin looked at him and felt nothing. 'But I owe you,' said Ravi. 'So, I make one more bloody effort. I'll show you something, Mr Martin, no bloody joke. Saturday night. Eleven o'clock, we meet here.'

Ravi turned up at the appointed hour not in the sleek limousine in which he went from hotel to hotel, but a battered taxi. They drove out of the sparkling city towards Sonapur. It was called a camp but contained row after row of permanent housing – dilapidated and filthy, but built to last. The township was occupied by the labourers who toiled on the building sites in the city, now in the distance. The taxi bounced and turned through the streets, until it came to a halt outside a square box on scrubland.

Ravi knocked on the heavy front door and held up a small red plastic square to a peephole. The door opened. The single room of the building was a dimly lit club, with a bar to the left and chairs and table spread out across the floor as far as a dais against the wall on the right-hand side. On the raised platform was placed a small table. The music was loud, the smell of booze and sweat almost overpowering. Vodka was the spirit of choice, served in bottles made of frozen water. Blonde waitresses wearing very little pulled them out in clouds of vapour from a deep-freezer behind the bar. The serving girls walked fast through the hands that reached out for them, shimmying out of contact, never spilling a drop or dislodging a glass from the trays they delivered one-handed. They took only cash.

'Welcome to the Red Square Club,' shouted Ravi.

Every table was full and was defined by nationality, it seemed. There were Russians around seven or eight, Chinese at three, Koreans at the two closest to the dais. Japanese, Germans, British and French had a table each.

Martin and Ravi stood at the bar and Ravi ordered vodka. He paid a $100 and received no change. For half an hour they watched. Then a Russian held up a red square and swayed to his feet. A roar went up and a waitress placed without great ceremony a wooden box on the table on the dais. Another escorted the Russian out of the crowd and up to the table. The music faded and there was silence as, without ado, he opened the box, threw his square inside, pulled out a revolver, gave the chamber a spin, put the gun against his head and pulled the trigger. There was a click, followed immediately by both a roar and a groan that quickly turned to applause when the Russian retrieved his red square. Before he was back in his seat, having swayed through the throng with his hands held above his head like a victorious boxer, the music was pumping again and the tables resumed their shouting as if nothing had happened.

'You can become a member when a red square becomes available,' shouted Ravi. 'Twenty thousand dollars. Cash, of course.'

Three weeks later, Ravi took him to the club again. There was a different crowd – fewer Russians, but more Americans. The air was still rank and the music loud. The Koreans filled only one table, but they were drinking furiously, consuming frozen bottle after frozen bottle of vodka. One of them lunged too aggressively at one of the Russian waitresses. A pair of bouncers – not hulking goons in suits, but lithe athletes in black T-shirts – appeared from nowhere and in no more than three seconds they had the aggressor tied in a knot of his own limbs. They knocked him senseless with a sharp blow from a cosh made of bamboo and left him slumped in his chair. Nobody was ejected by Red Square security on to the streets of Sonapur. It was familiar justice at the club and the incident caused hardly a stir at the other tables.

Only a 'play' held their interest. That night, three players, accompanied by the same ritual of the red square and the wooden box, took to the rostrum; three times the revolver clicked.

In the early hours of the morning, when the club was at its fullest, two waitresses took to the rostrum without a player and the music stopped. They held the box and opened it for all to see. Inside was a red square.

'There is a vacancy,' said Ravi.

The waitresses went from table to table, lifting their chins as an order to those present to show their squares. If there was a guest without a membership token they held out the box to them. An American declined, then a Frenchman. An Italian reached out for the box, but the second waitress held out her hand for payment. The Italian gave a rueful shrug and the waitresses continued their tour of the room. When they came to the bar, Ravi held up his token. One of the waitresses looked at Martin. He stared back and without blinking held out his hand to Ravi who reached into his damp jacket pockets and pulled out two envelopes, each containing one hundred $100 bills and handed them to the second waitress.

10

'Doors closing.' Nobody had moved and soon the lift was going down again. Martin had come and gone. When the doors opened again on the ground floor, Grace flinched, but on the other side stood nothing more menacing than a group of tourists. Even so, Gonzo did feel the weight of her now as she almost fell against him, and he had to support her and half carry her out.

Punctuality when it came to the 'business end' of rugby had always been one of Conrad's watchwords and it was no different even for a festive game. Max was always running a little behind time, but now he was late even by his standards. When he came down with Perrine and Noa, he immediately saw something was wrong and ushered Gonzo and Grace to the coffee shop in Raffles. He told Noa to go ahead and warn Conrad that there would be a delay, and now Perrine and he listened as the tale was told.

'So, the lift doors open … and there he is … le mari,' he said. 'In French we call that the bedroom farce.'

'No, Max,' chided Perrie. 'No jokes … not now.'

'But it is true, my angel. We know about these things. You and I … we began on the run.' He looked at Grace. 'Perrine in the wardrobe; me through the window … she had a first husband …'

'It's true,' said Perrine. 'But Max …'

'Yes, yes … but it means we have experience. We know what to do. And it is this. Gonzo, we are not in the business to lose. We will not be beaten by this. So, come, my grand-père, we have to stay together. And Perrine …'

His wife nodded. 'Grace, you will come with me. We are *une vingtaine* of women, too strong for one man.'

Grace looked up, her pallor gone. 'You're right,' she said. 'I'm done with this. With him. Go on, you two. I'll be fine.' She reached out for Perrine's hand and they left together.

Conrad had it in his mind to put Gonzo on the replacements' bench for the first game and more than likely the second. He was mindful of the player's age and he was slightly irked that the Welshman, who knew Conrad's ways better than anyone in the Barbarians squad had broken the cardinal rule of timekeeping. But then he started to watch Gonzo, Max and Noa in training together. It was obvious from the moment they began to warm up at the stadium where the game would be played the next day that their back-row relationship on the field would be special. Even as they casually kicked and passed the ball among themselves they began discussing who should go where and what might happen if one of them went over here and another ran a line from over there. To see them as a unit stripped back the years for Conrad and he quickly changed his mind and knew that they would be in the starting team – that they would form the central plank of his team. He left them to their own devices and concentrated on putting together combinations elsewhere.

Grace worried – as if she wasn't in an agitated state already – that she would stand out now, and therefore disrupt the partners' easy-going togetherness. The other wives and girlfriends interacted fluidly around the pool, sifting themselves naturally into smaller groups that weren't quite as daunting as a single party, twenty-odd strong. But they remained bonded by their own team spirit. Perrine went from pocket to pocket and seemed to organise some sort of rota, whereby somebody was always by Grace's side on her giant mattress of a sunbed. From here, they could scan all the comings and goings at the hotel. Max's wife slid alongside her and did not move – the constant in the slowly moving turning of the guard.

'Look,' she said. 'You have the Amazonians to protect you.'

'This is mad ...'

'Please do not take this the wrong way. But you do not live in our rugby world, Grace,' said Perrine. 'Every one of these girls has to send her man off to foreign places, on long tours. The players are young; it is the nature of their work that they can be a little ... over-excited. We love them because they are a bit wild, but we do not trust them. Or if we trust them we do not trust the world they live in. It is full of temptation. The girls have all done this before. It is part of our life of self-preservation.' Four waiters appeared carrying ice buckets and trays. 'Besides, they can be bribed. It is a little early in the day, but we are on tour, *non*?'

Later that night there was an inversion of rugby tradition. It was not in the ways of the Barbarians to enforce any curfew, but the players had taken an unspoken vow, that if this was to be a true adventure, the rugby side of things had to go well. They would be sensible on the nights before the two games. They were generally abstemious anyway during the season and it was no sacrifice to go without, especially since they were still feeling the effects of the first session at

131

the Willows Spa. They had a glass of wine with their evening meal in the sumptuous Pearl Fisher restaurant, overlooking Dubai Creek, but they remained sober, in contrast to their partners who to a woman by the end of the evening had to be scooped up in strong arms and carried back to their rooms.

The next day the combination of Gonzo, Max and Noa lasted only twenty minutes before Noa had to go off with blood streaming from a cut to his eyebrow. The French wing forward was replaced by the Canadian, Dan Hollister, whom Max soon called The Mountie – 'Because he always gets his man, no?' Dan played horizontally, as a missile that flew through the air and cut opponents down, whether they had the ball or not. Back home in Victoria on Vancouver Island, he was known as Solar, for being a star of the Canadian game and for all the damage he inflicted on others' solar plexus, but he took Max's sobriquet in his stride, and such was the getting of his man that The Mountie became an instant favourite of the 50,000-strong crowd at the Dubai Stadium. This audience was roughly the same assembly of expats and rugby tourists who came to watch the annual seven-a-side tournament, the difference being that the spectacle before them was a concentrated game of 80 minutes on a single night, rather than the two-day, all-day action of the Sevens. The crowd respected the protocol that it was not acceptable to be drunk in public and provided willing but relatively restrained support for the game, and Gonzo was almost relieved that he did not have to force his way through a barrier of noise – unlike the first time he had run out for Wales at the Millennium Stadium in Cardiff, when his ears had been assaulted by the din, another unnerving element to the experience of winning his first cap.

Dave the Mountie lacked the finesse that went with Noa's marginally less physical approach. Not that there was much evidence of subtlety in the Frenchman's play – or in anybody else's – in the opening quarter of the game. While Noa was on the field, there was a lot of indecisive, clumsy misfiring as the entire invitation side struggled to co-ordinate their efforts against the UAE team that had had two preparatory matches. It was the nature of these games, that it took time for players to grow accustomed to the ways of strangers who were suddenly their team-mates. On top of this exercise in calibration, there was the heat. Even though the game kicked off after dark, it was still hotter than the finest day of the summer in the village. Gonzo was not made for this and within seconds he was gasping for air and was slippery of fingers as the sweat poured from him. He missed scrum half Jacques with his first pass and dropped the first one that came his way from Max.

One thing in this chapter of mishaps, however, made Conrad, sitting up in the stands, purr. Noa, Max and Gonzo came away from the back of a line-out in a tight trio, the ball going from first to second at the first touch of contact on the man in the vanguard. This player who had just released the ball twirled himself out of the tackle and reattached himself as the third to the back of the threesome and helped push and slide and spin the mini-maul forward until he became the ball-carrier again. The swirling, pirouetting dance troupe went across the field and at the same time forged ahead, starting at the line-out twenty metres from the goal line, and touching down – with Max in control of the ball at the end – between the posts. Faced with a lot of arm raising and protest from UAE players who simply could not lay a finger on the ball or bring down any of the opposing back row, the referee, who was – in his own words – an inexperienced local expat from Abu Dhabi, declared, without knowing precisely where, that there must have been some sort of obstruction inside the spinning top and disallowed the try. The Barbarians took the decision in their stride, Conrad expressed his frustrated admiration, and at the next breakdown, Noa accidentally clashed heads with an opposing prop and trotted off, dripping blood.

In the third quarter – after Gonzo had gulped in as much air and water as he could at half-time – the Barbarians scored four tries and the result was secured. Gonzo put Jacques over for a try and Max gave the scrum half his second. Gonzo thought that Conrad might do his life expectancy a favour and pull him off after an hour, but the coach kept the number 8 on the field to the end. Dave the Mountie rampaged to the last and stopped the UAE team from scoring more than a pair of consolation tries. Gonzo could not remember anything of the last ten minutes.

He sat in the changing room at the end, shaking and downing one bottle of water after another until Max restrained him. 'Beware, grand-père, of overhydration. This water can be dangerous.' He opened the changing-room door and a line of stadium catering staff brought in crates of lager and champagne.

The post-match reception was held in the desert, far enough inland for the city to be visible only as an orange crescent low in the sky. This night of the game was as uproarious as its eve had been subdued. There were short speeches of welcome from the representatives of the Sheikh, and then, with a clap of the hands, a spread of food was unveiled and musicians began to play, soulfully at first but with a gathering intensity. Gonzo, Max and Noa – with a bandage around his head – were pushed into the middle and ordered to reproduce their dance of the dervishes. They ate and they sang and they laughed within their ring of tents under the stars, and Grace felt comforted by being surrounded by the wilderness. Much later, they stood around a brazier and listened to the silence of the sands. As the sky over the eastern edge of the desert began to lighten, Grace steered a gently wobbling Gonzo towards a fleet of all-terrain vehicles and they joined the convoy that aimed itself at the fading orange glow of Dubai and took the Barbarians to their beds.

Just after midnight at the Red Square Club on its patch of scrubland in Sonapur, Martin showed his token to the peephole in the door. He was alone. He stepped inside and breathed in the sweat and the fumes, felt the throb of the music and sensed above it the Koreans at their loudest and most leering. He saw Ravi at a table, in the middle of a group of Indians and nodded in his direction. Ravi waved him over and introduced him to his 'treacherous brother, Krishnan'. He then kissed this brother firmly on the cheek and told him to move over and make way for the man who had laid bare the devil's work. Krishnan did not seem to resent in any way having his scam exposed by Martin and rose to shake him vigorously by the hand. Martin shook the proffered hand and then his own head. He did not join Ravi's table, but moved to the bar, where he took up his usual position. He was offered vodka, but ordered water. He held out a $100 bill and received no change.

Two players came to the dais; a Russian, who casually tossed his red square into the box, gave the chamber a spin and then aimed the gun at the ceiling. There was a click, followed by uproar at the tables. The Russian looked contemptuously around him as fingers were pointed at him and jeers rang out. He spat at the crowd, just before the bouncers arrived. They did not bother with any martial-art niceties. They simply clubbed him mercilessly with their bamboo truncheons, picked up his inert body and threw him out of the door. Ravi had told Martin that scavengers lurked in the darkness of Sonapur and anybody ejected from the club was theirs. The Russian would be lucky to make it back to the city.

The incident changed the mood of the club. There was a restlessness in the fetid air and the vapour billowed from the deep freezers behind the bar with increasing frequency. The waitresses kicked out at the ever-more daring hands of the punters and on this one night, glasses and frozen bottles toppled off their trays and smashed on the floor. Table flared up against table as insults were traded. The bouncers circled the perimeter of the club, not invisible now but issuing warnings to those on their feet: sit down or be expelled.

A terrified Englishman was thrust towards the rostrum from his table. His drinking companions all wore rugby shirts and they seemed to have picked on the single white shirt in their midst. A proxy red square was held up as he stumbled forward, but before the player was halfway to the table, his knees gave way and he was hauled back to safety by the other rugby shirts. The bouncers wagged their fingers and pointed their batons at those that would disrespect the club's protocols.

The return of the deadweight white shirt to his place among his now crazed friends distracted the audience, and Martin was halfway across the room from the bar, with his red square held up, before anyone noticed. The music did not end with a fade but stopped suddenly, giving a clumsy urgency to proceedings. The audience turned their attention from the table of failure to the man on the move, but instead of providing an accompaniment of silence they began to beat out a rhythm, thumping their table tops. A waitress had to run after Martin and place the wooden box on the table before he had to wait more than a second or two. But it was in that second or two that the Korean table sensed something. They had seen many players in action, but never anybody as icy as this. For a moment they let the image sink in, of this model of calm about to take a gamble with his own life – and then they began to join the thumping, pumping rhythm, letting their drunken wildness take them over.

Martin dropped the red square into the box and pulled out the revolver. He looked at it, but only briefly, and then ran his palm hard down the side, spinning the chamber. He looked straight ahead and began to raise his arm. At that moment, one of the Koreans leapt forward, his mouth a round, screaming O, veins protruding from his forehead. He knocked the waitress flying and before the bouncers could leap forward, he snatched the gun from Martin's hand. The rhythm stopped.

'You a lucky man,' screamed the Korean. 'You a lucky fucking man.' And he put the gun against his head and blew his brains out.

Martin was left with the faintest trace of finely splattered blood on his shirt. He looked down at the corpse at his feet. Already the bouncers were moving in, extricating it from the circle of onlookers, removing the red-square token from a trouser pocket and carrying the dead man at a practised trot towards the bar. A hatch opened, a curtain parted and the Korean was gone. The club's entry fee covered discreet disposal. There was room now for a new member and the token would be put on sale the next night – to allow for a period of mourning, according to the cemetery humour of the club. To tout it on the very evening of a player's exit might be considered ghoulish. Certainly a little tacky.

A lucky man, thought Martin, allowing the waitress who had run after him with the box – and who was left untouched by any of the Korean's vital fluids – to escort him back to his place at the bar. For a half-dressed whore, thought Martin incidentally, it was strange that she now held his arm as if he were an elderly person being helped across a busy road. His mind returned to the Korean. Did he think I was a bringer of good luck – that he was safe usurping me at the dais; that he would not die? Or that I was the lucky one, because he was going to take the shot for me – that he knew that whoever pulled the trigger was going to die? What a strange thing, thought Martin, thinking only that. How strange it all was: that O-mouthed Korean, this whore-carer Russian.

He stood at the bar almost in an exclusion zone. If he was a lucky man, nobody wanted to go near him. And then the remoteness of Martin's mind gave way to a rush of sensation. At first, he felt suddenly cheated, that something had been snatched from him. Obviously not his life – but perhaps it was the loss of control, however momentary, that stung. Even to feel piqued was something. And that made him want to laugh. Piqued. He liked the word. Because a stranger had snatched him from the jaws of death? Had sacrificed himself. Who had he been? Was it the unsmiling Mr Park? He was sure it wasn't. Mr Park didn't have veins that could pulse on the side of his head.

Martin was aware that somebody had breached his isolation. Ravi stood before him. Martin lingered a little on being cheated, feeling piqued, wanting to laugh.

'Are you OK, Mr Martin?'

'Would you like a drink, Ravi?'

Ravi was about to insist on spending several of the many $100 bills Mr Martin had made for him, when a thought struck him. 'A bloody question, Mr Martin,' he exclaimed. 'You have asked me a bloody question.' Martin looked up and Ravi gave a start. 'You are alive, Mr bloody Martin. I can see it in your eyes. You have come to life.'

11

Nothing advanced quickly with the redevelopment plans for the old mine site and the Miners' Institute. The process, as the Professor explained on innumerable occasions to Capper and Our Marnie, took time and above all – when they interrupted him or pressed him for news – patience. One of the spin-offs of the Professor's return and involvement in the project, however, was that through his experience and knowledge of the systems, smaller matters could be attended to without delay. He could not influence the undoing of the Sherkin's illegal connections to the rugby stand's power and water – the metered reconnection was dealt with as a priority and performed with a reproachful sternness by the utility companies – but it wasn't long before he was putting it to the engineers on site that since they were in the locality, might they not be persuaded to undertake some other jobs that had been on the to-do list for some time? Namely, the supply of power and water to Gonzo's cottage.

Gonzo had a folder that he kept in what he thought was a secret place in the Shard. It may have been hidden well enough to prevent Grace from discovering what plans he had for their home, but the Professor and Capper found it in seconds flat, steered by Our Marnie, who had watched Gonzo tenderly compile his measurements and brochures and sketches. Spurred into action by the question – 'So, what's this other job, then?' – from the teams sent to legalise the Sherkin's power and water, the Professor and Capper launched a slightly improvised project to complete as much of the work on the cottage as possible in the time Gonzo and

Grace would be away. Almost before they were out of sight down the mountain in Tony's Mercedes, the diggers moved in. The Professor, co-ordinating with Our Marnie in the office, concentrated on materials and delivery. He expedited the arrival of the eight small sash-windows Gonzo thought would never be finished, and within two days, Capper, head of labour, had them installed. Within four, they were painted. The bio-mass boiler that Gonzo had almost forgotten was on order was taken to its destination in the cottage's scullery, and the plumbers and electricians moved in with it. Copper piping and plastic-coated cabling snaked their way around the house. With only five rooms in total – two bedrooms, a bathroom and the two big rooms downstairs – the workers sped along, fuelled by John's food from the Gherkin and cash in hand.

'What can I do?' asked Kitty one day.

'You, Kitty, can be in charge of the kitty,' said Capper. 'I've been dying to say that.'

'What can I do?' asked Dario.

'You can direct the traffic,' said Capper. And Dario became the banksman on site, monitoring the flow of delivery vans up and down the track, directing them safely in and out, even as the diggers worked on the trenches that criss-crossed the land.

'The banker and the banksman,' said Kitty as she and Dario walked from the cottage one evening to meet Emma on the moor, where they would feed Arkle.

Capper poured and levelled the screed floor in the kitchen and then, deep into the night, laid oak boards over the cellar in the living room. His pride and joy was the oak door he made from the off-cuts, following a sketch Gonzo had placed in his folder, a few scribblings that allowed for a certain rustic charm above the precision of a master joiner. Capper kicked the chipboard front door down the next morning, lovingly hung his creation and mended the garden gate, which was soon swinging on two new hinges. He'd stopped on the first Saturday to play – the village lost a dreary game in the suburbs of Newport – and then, because the electricity supply to the Gherkin would not be switched on until the next day, treated Our Marnie to chicken and chips in the Colliers' Arms in the village where there was a large gathering to watch the Barbarians game on the television. It turned into the most prolonged drinking session of the season and a close-up of the exhausted Gonzo trooping off the field in Dubai was greeted with wild cheering.

'Done all right, mind,' said Capper, and they all raised a full pint to Gonzo and downed it in one.

They had rested on the Sunday, which was just as well because the rain began to fall. Not the light rain of the past few weeks, but a drumming, slanting downpour that seemed set on making up for the summer drought. The Blorenge and the moor, parched for weeks, readily absorbed all the weekend's water, but by the time Gonzo and Grace returned unexpectedly on the Monday, pools were starting to form in the dips and hollows of the wilderness, the Keeper's Pond was full again and a stream of water was rushing down the road to Govilon.

Capper was starting to lay the slate floor in the kitchen when Gonzo came through the new front door. The hooker was not best pleased to have his surprise ruined. 'What the fuck d'you think you're doing here?' he shouted. 'Pardon my fuckin' French, Grace,' he added when she followed Gonzo into their house. 'But shouldn't you two be in Cardiff?'

Grace was having a wobble, a sort of delayed reaction to seeing … him. She could not call him anything, and certainly not her husband. He was her rapist.

'Did we really see him?' she asked Gonzo on the flight to Amsterdam, from where the Barbarians would fly to Cardiff. 'Perhaps, it wasn't …'

'It was him,' said Gonzo. 'I always knew we would. One day. Somewhere. I thought I was braced for it. But when those doors opened, I couldn't move.'

'Nor me,' said Grace. 'Mind you, neither could he.'

'As a showdown, I suppose it lacked …'

'Movement.'

'Doors closing …' They managed a chuckle and Grace snuggled up to him as close as their first-class seats would allow.

'D'you mind if I don't come to Cardiff?' she asked. 'We're booked in down the Bay and there's something about the whole place … and after seeing him, I feel a little sick the whole time.'

During the night in the desert, Gonzo had sought out his old coach and they had wandered away from the tents into the desert. Gonzo told Conrad all about Grace and Martin and what Danny Mewson had done to his head.

'You Welsh,' said Conrad. 'I always thought you were the sensible one.' He shook his head. 'Seems you're a cave dweller

143

after all. What's surprising is you've made one of the lovely Grace too.'

'D'you think?'

'She's surrendered her heart to you. You take care of her, Gonzo Davies.' Gonzo nodded his head. Music drifted towards them on the faintest gust of wind as they walked slowly back towards the party. Conrad stopped. 'I had great plans for you ... for us. Once. You silly bugger.'

'We've been given a last chance, coach. So, let's give it a go, eh?'

Now, while they waited in their executive lounge between flights at Schipol Airport in Amsterdam, Gonzo asked Conrad if he could take Grace home, rather than head for the Sir Tasker Hotel in the Bay. Conrad was at work, going through the game on his tablet. He was in a no-nonsense mood – his old Welsh players would have said he 'had his sensible head on' and would have hesitated before breaking his concentration. When Gonzo interrupted him, he frowned, before growling, 'We're having Tuesday off, anyway. As long as you're back first thing Wednesday morning. That's when we start again. There's a lot to do. You and Jacques need time together. Don't be late.'

At Cardiff Airport there was no Tony in a Mercedes to greet Gonzo and Grace. They caught a taxi that took them home via a hole in the wall in Brynmawr. The cash dispenser they normally used had been ram-raided in the night and there was crowd around the scene of the crime.

'Oi, Gonzo, what you doing 'ere?' shouted an old man. 'Didn't them Baabaas pay you enough?'

'You should be getting ready for them All Blacks,' said another. 'You looked knackered in the desert, butt.'

It wasn't quite the homecoming Gonzo would have wished for and Grace felt responsible for the deflation. When Capper shouted at them as they stepped into the cottage, she could have cried.

'Whoa,' said Capper, suddenly seeing the look on her face. 'It's just I haven't finished … oh shit, it's good to see you. Welcome 'ome.'

At the same time as the taxi was driving down the newly gravelled track to the cottage, now illuminated and heated, the All Blacks crossed the Second Severn Crossing into Wales. They had landed at Heathrow four days earlier and had been recovering from their jet-lag and making their plans for their matches in the 'hub hotel' of their tour, in Richmond-upon-Thames. There was no relaxation in their ranks, no nights when lager and champagne arrived by the crate. Their evolution as the latest embodiment of rugby at its most advanced had been jolted by the death of Tai McDonald. The All Blacks had insisted on putting their grief to one side and completing their programme of matches in the Rugby Championship, but they were obviously affected. They had lost at home to Australia in the immediate aftermath of the captain's demise and had been lucky to escape with a two-point win over Argentina in Wellington. Tai haunted them. George Pai Taihonga did not berate them for their lack of customary efficiency, their listlessness. He shared their grief. But as soon as they all arrived in London, he gathered the squad and said it would soon be time to move on. The game

145

against the Barbarians would be the team's own farewell to Tai, and after that they would start afresh. There was a World Cup approaching and New Zealand owed it to their Tai to win it unprecedentedly for a third time in a row. Nothing would be achieved if a natural period of mourning became a despairing slide that could not be stopped. Their bespoke bus, with its giant silver ferns emblazoned on both sides against the black livery, picked up a police escort at the toll booths on the Welsh side of the bridge and swept down the M4 towards their 'satellite' hotel in the Vale of Glamorgan to the west of Cardiff.

Ravi went to the coffee shop in Raffles at 11 o'clock the next day. And to all the usual meeting places in the days that followed. Of Martin he could find not a trace. Nothing moved in the empty apartment that overlooked the desert – not that Ravi knew where Martin laid his head at night.

At the same time as the All Blacks began to lever their lean, honed, big-boned limbs out of their coach and make themselves at home for their brief stay in Wales, a scheduled flight from Paris landed at East Midlands Airport. Sitting inconspicuously in Arrivals was Frank. He did not greet Clive Parfitt when the passenger came through the doors, but rose from his seat and walked ahead of him to the short-term car park. Two hours later they crossed into Wales. Martin was home, too.

Grace forgave Capper his bad language. She loved what he had done – what they all had done. She couldn't stop crying. She said she loved the cottage the way she had just found it.

That there was no need for Capper to keep working now that they had spoilt his surprise. Grace didn't need a kitchen or a bathroom or a bedroom. She and Gonzo had … them. The people who had done all this for them. Capper was about to point out that there was a whole lot more to do and that he didn't mind doing it all because, well, he'd only been joking about being angry – although he had felt a little cheated out of the moment of wonder that would have come with the unveiling of the whole job in all its finished glory – but not to worry, that it was all fine and there was stuff on order, that was about to be delivered in fact …

'Who's been paying?' said Gonzo.

'The Bank of Kitty,' said Capper.

Gonzo scolded him for doing what might well be construed as taking advantage. Grace was afraid Gonzo was going a little far and felt more tears welling, but at that moment Our Marnie arrived with Kitty, Dario, John and the Professor and they all sat on the new floor in the living room and exchanged tales of Dubai for stories of the project. John, who had never met Martin, gasped in horror when Gonzo recounted the opening of the doors.

'Had to be …' said the Professor. 'Had to be.'

They all went to the Shard that afternoon and were still there when darkness came, finishing off the meal John cooked in the Gherkin, in celebration of legal power. Capper reluctantly washed up in celebration of legal water, but his spirits were lifted when John produced a bottle of whisky and suggested they have a little nightcap as a house-warmer.

'In the house that Kitty built,' said Gonzo, wagging a finger at her. 'This is no way to run a co-operative.'

Kitty linked arms with Grace and Our Marnie. 'We'll see about that,' she said and climbed into the back of the Land Rover. All eight squeezed in and soon they were on the new track. The approach to the cottage wasn't so smooth that the headlights didn't move up and down, and it took a couple of rearing and falling beams for Gonzo to realise there was a car he did not recognise outside the property. 'Anybody know that car?' he spoke into the back. Faces no longer laughing turned to the cottage. Nobody said anything. Capper and Gonzo ran down the track, long shadows going ahead of them, cast by the headlights. They disappeared from view around the side of the cottage, leaving the unknown car in view. Suddenly there was a roar and Grace gave a little whimper. He was here.

Four figures came back into view, Capper first, followed by Gonzo between Max and Noa. John jumped into the driver's seat and the Land Rover completed its journey. The introductions were made and John was just about to suggest they go inside, out of the rain that was about to fall, when there was a loud snort behind them. They all jumped. It was Arkle, standing at the garden gate.

'And so, Grace, you leave us. Perrine is not here because she is not speaking to you.' Max swirled the whisky in his glass and raised it appreciatively to John. 'Bravo.' He winked at Gonzo. 'Or, it could be said that she is going shopping. She says she will see you at the game, Grace. But she says to tell you – like a referee always says to Noa – this is a final warning.'

'I won't snub her, I promise,' said Grace.

'Snub ... I like it. I shall tell Perrine she will not be ... snubbed.'

'But what on earth brings you up here?' asked Grace.

'Well, I said to Perrine that once you have been chased naked through the old port of Marseille – it is true, Perrine's first husband found us – after such a thing, this Cardiff Bay is not so special. But in Dubai you tell me about your wilderness, Gonzo, and about Capper the famous caveman, and I say to Noa that it is our duty to see such a place – and meet such a man. Also, I say to Conrad that you are not to be trusted, Gonzo. Everybody in France knows about you Welsh – always crying, always singing sad songs about going home. So, he says to me that I am responsible for you. His last words: "Bring him back."'

Capper had often wondered about the other men in Gonzo's life. He'd thought that just as Gonzo had the village – the Plant and the Twins, Mystic, Useless and the Professor – so he had once had team-mates at a professional level. He must have made new friends in Cardiff and in the Welsh team. He never spoke of anyone. And here, now, was this new bloke – these blokes, Frenchmen, real living current French international players – who obviously liked Gonzo. Should Capper be jealous?

'Who're you calling a caveman?'

'He said it not in a bad way, Capper,' said Max. 'He said there is a ... perception of you in the outside world, that you are, yes, cavemen and that you live in your wilderness. But it is not the truth, he says. There is more to you and to here than that. Is that not how it was, Gonzo?'

Gonzo shrugged. 'Sometimes take a bit of finding,' he muttered.

'But that's what you said, is it?' said Capper. Gonzo shrugged again. 'Well,' continued Capper, 'it's not every day I agree with him, but I'd say he got that about right. Just as well, really, 'cos otherwise I'd have to fuckin' snub 'im.'

'Language,' said Our Marnie.

'So, tell me, Capper,' said Max. 'What is there that is more? I arrive here with Noa and we see … wilderness. Beautiful, but a wilderness. And you Capper, if I am making the Flintstone movie, you are my number one star … beautiful, but a caveman.' They all laughed.

'Well, for starters,' said Capper, 'there's the mountain cycle club.'

'Oh no,' groaned Gonzo, 'he's off on the tourism trail. More whisky, John, quick.'

'Exactly,' said Capper, 'the tourism trail.' And he talked about the new cycling centre and the plans for the lido. 'And now you mention it,' he said to Max, 'we do have a cave.' And he told him all about his chamber of horrors.

'But I must see this,' exclaimed Max. 'Seriously, it is my passion. Every summer, I go to the Ardèche and do precisely this.'

'Well, if you and Noa want to see it …' But Noa was shaking his head vigorously. Max laughed. 'Noa has a fear of such places. He will die for France, but only above ground and with a light on.'

Noa nodded furiously and broke into a huge grin. 'It is the truth,' he said.

'I was like that,' said Capper. 'I know a cure.'

Noa shook his head again until it seemed the stitches over his eye would come apart. 'Impossible,' he said. 'But the mountain bike – that is different. For me this is a passion.'

Well, in that case,' said John. 'I'd be honoured to show you what we've got.'

'So,' said Max, 'I see. After all these years, you are to snub me, Noa.' And he held out his glass for more whisky. Next day – the last before the Barbarians started to prepare for their game at the Millennium Stadium – it was all organised. Capper and Max would go caving; John and Noa would take to the high mountain trails by bike. Gonzo would continue to work in the cottage, which was his way of saying he wanted to stay with Grace. Kitty, Our Marnie, Dario and the Professor would run the Co-operative from the Sherkin.

Max, the experienced caver, seemed quite happy with the improvised gear – ropes and torches and even a pair of hard hats – that Capper brought to the cottage the next day. Capper showed him a spool of nylon thread that they used to mark out plots, and Max nodded for it to be included. He looked tired. Noa and he had shared Grace and Gonzo's old mattress in the spare room, and Noa, turned flat on his back by an instinct to protect his stitches and because of the whisky, had snored all night. The former occupiers of the mattress were still asleep in their giant new bed in the main bedroom when Capper and Max set out across the neck of the Blorenge towards the boulder and rock in the bracken. Along the way, Capper told Max the story of the old mine, the rugby ground and the old clubhouse on West Street.

'I am from Paris,' said Max as they stopped to look back at the village. 'But I know of the traditions of the village club down in the south-west of France. It is tough rugby in the Basque Country, in the Pyrenees and over on the other side of France in the Auvergne. It is a little crazy in Béziers and Narbonne. I have played in Oyonnax and Castres, where they defend their home like madmen. But I have never seen anything like this. But what do I know? As I say, I am from Paris, which makes me a little out of the ordinary in French rugby. I am a rich kid from Paris – that makes me maybe very unusual.'

'I'm a poor bloke from Wales,' said Capper. 'That makes me totally run-of-the-fuckin'-mill.'

'Run-of-the-fuckeen'-mill. I don't understand it, but I like it. It makes you special, Capper.'

'We're here,' said Capper, levering the rock off the boulder and exposing the entrance to the tunnel.

'This? This is your cave? It is a peep hole.'

John and Noa spent all morning on the mountain dram roads. Noa tried not to be reckless, to spare his bones and his eye. But he was not one to throw himself into sport half-heartedly and before long he was tearing down the slopes at breakneck velocity. He pedalled back up much more sedately, looking a large rugby player aboard a machine too small for him rather than a king of the mountain. On these upward pulls John could keep up with his guest and stayed close to Noa's massive backside and thighs.

They sped down to the Gherkin and Noa became the lunchtime sensation of the Graig. He blasted around the circuit with them. As he tired he became more unsteady out of his saddle and at one point he took a wrong racing line and it was obvious to all that he was going to have a spill. John who, without the Professor knowing, had spent the early hours of the morning researching Noa online, could see a terrible headline: 'Joe Louis falls off his bike and misses the All Blacks'. All that happened was that the seventeen-stone Noa sprang from his machine and executed a perfect forward-roll, ran on and completed his floor exercise with a full somersault. His bike, now with a buckled front wheel, was reverentially handed back to him and he wobbled it towards the Gherkin, where the awning was being pulled out. Dark clouds were gathering overhead.

Gonzo worked all morning on the slate floor in the kitchen. Grace stayed with him. She liked watching him at work, his attention to detail combining with the sheer brute force required to lift and lower the square and rectangular slabs. She knew he had a pattern torn from a brochure in the living room, but he never consulted it. He constantly checked his levels and tip-tapped at edges and corners to make sure his jigsaw came together without a tripping line. Occasionally a drop of sweat would fall from his brow and create a little splash of brightness on the matt surface of their kitchen floor. He quickly wiped it away, along with any smudges of grey adhesive, with a damp cloth he kept in a rinsing bucket by his side. They spoke little.

'Would you like the radio on?' she asked.

'No thanks,' he replied. 'I like listening to you.'

153

'I'm not saying anything.'

'I know,' he said. 'And you don't have to. Sometimes I hold my breath so I can listen to you doing nothing.'

Capper did not want to go down the tunnel. The peephole stared up at him and told him not to enter. But he knew he was in some sort of contest with Max. He liked him; he wasn't jealous. But this was a contest, all right, or a trial – a test. And Capper anchored the long rope to the boulder, turned on his head-torch and led the way down into the innards of the Blorenge. Soon they stood in the chamber that Capper and Gonzo had discovered. Max, to Capper's relief was impressed: 'Mon dieu, it is true. You have a cave, Capper.'

Capper felt relief but he knew that this wasn't the end of the trial. The chamber was different. The floor that had been damp on his first descent was now knee-deep in water. Water fell in drops or streams from the vaulted ceiling – or even in a pressurised spurt here and there. There was noise now, whereas Capper could once have heard the echo of a whisper. In the foreground was this plopping, streaming, hissing sound of water entering the chamber. And in the background was a deeper rumble.

'Can you hear it?' asked Max. Capper nodded and Max's face came and went. 'We go, yes?' said the Frenchman. And Capper's beam bobbed again, before both torches were turned towards the far side of the chamber and they went in search of the source of the distant roar.

*

Our Marnie arrived at lunchtime with soup and bread. She shook an umbrella and her coat outside, but still left a trail of drops from Capper's front door to the boiler room.

'Noa and John are down off the mountain,' she said. 'Looks as if this rain's going to last all day. You don't think ...'

For the first time Gonzo became aware of sounds beyond his and Grace's space. He could now hear the rain drumming on the roof, the swish as a blast of wind threw a curtain of water against the new windows.

'They'll be fine,' he said. But ten minutes later he went and peered outside. The clouds were so low and thick it was as if night had arrived four hours early. Twenty minutes after that he took the first slab to be cut – to fit into the floor's perimeter, up against the walls – and saw that it was raining harder than ever. 'Shit,' he said under his breath. He leant the heavy slate against the outside wall, where it instantly turned bright and shiny. He went back inside and asked Our Marnie for the keys to the van.

'You're not to worry,' he said. 'I'm just going to check, that's all.' Our Marnie, of course, started to worry. Grace took her into the living room and anxiety spread over Capper's oak floor.

Now that he had taken his decision, Gonzo moved at speed. Capper had taken the two head-torches, and Gonzo was left with the heavy hand torch. At least it was waterproof. It was all he took. He trotted towards the van. As soon as he knew he could not be seen by the two faces pressed tight against the living room windows he went as fast as the van allowed down the track and deep into the wilderness.

*

Just before they started to climb down the steep tunnel out of which the roar came, Max stopped Capper and felt for the spool of nylon thread. He tied the end to the base of a stalagmite, tapped the structure for good luck and attached the spool to Capper's belt. He then took the second, thinner, coil of rope – the first still hung from the boulder on the surface into the chamber – from around Capper's shoulder, cut a five-metre length and attached himself to Capper. He thought about taking the coil with them, but shouted at Capper that if they found anything so vertical that it required a rope, they would save it for the next time. He threw the coil over the stalagmite, tapped an inwardly relieved Capper on the shoulder and led the way down.

The climb was steep but not difficult. They came to a second chamber, fed by a wider tunnel to the right. This feeder tunnel seemed to have its own sound, a distant gurgling, but Max and Capper followed the greater roar below them. A few more difficult metres further on, they came to a third expansion. Each chamber was a quarter the size of the one before; each access tunnel to it tighter and lower. Water rushed past and they were up to their waists in the third chamber. Max surveyed the next drop and held up a finger. One more. They squeezed into the next tunnel.

Kitty and Cinnabar battled through the elements to feed Arkle. He appeared on the path before them and led the way to the cottage, where he waited at the gate. They opened it and he led them to the empty old log-store lean-to on the sheltered side of the cottage. He manoeuvred as much of himself as would fit inside, patiently munched on the Polos and prepared to ride out the storm. Kitty and Cinnabar found themselves knocking on the door at the same time as the Professor, Noa and John arrived in the Frenchmen's hire car. Our Marnie opened the door and let them in. Like the horse half-in and half-out of the storm, the gathering in the cottage could do nothing but wait.

It was as if the mountain had soaked up as much rain as it could and had then been squeezed by hands cupped over it, forcing water down. The contents released by this vast sponge of rock fell with gravity and the gurgle of the feeder tunnel into the second chamber became a cold cascading spew. The roar below Capper and Max was overwhelmed by the approaching avalanche from above. They had time to link their arms before the water hit them and tore them apart, ripping the spool from Capper's belt and the hard hats and the torches from their heads. They were tumbled into a fourth chamber, where their connecting rope snagged on a rock and they were jerked to a halt. They clawed their way together, sucking in air. Their feet found rock. But in pitch darkness the chamber was filling fast with water.

Gonzo found the second coil of rope just before the rising water in the first chamber lifted it off the stalagmite. As fast as the water surged down the tunnels and cracks towards the bottom of the mountain, more was coming in from above. He shone the torch into the water and saw the nylon thread. He ducked under and took the thread and pulled it up. He could sense a vibration through his fingers but when he pulled, he could reel the thread in without much resistance.

He slackened his grip and the nylon line slipped through his fingers until it was taut. He took the coil of rope and fastened one end securely to a pillar of rock. He thought about trying to unwind the coil as he went, but he had the torch in one hand and he needed to follow the nylon. He threw the rope down the tunnel. He then reached again for the thread that he still hoped was a slender lifeline and set out to find what had become disconnected from it.

He reached the second chamber where the water from the other tunnel was flooding in. He waded up to his chest through the chamber and then climbed down the tunnel towards the third, water crashing all over him. There was a sort of ebb and flow to the surge and he managed to catch his breath between waves, but by the time he reached the next place where he could breathe without fear of taking in water, he was frozen and exhausted. His feet were tangled in the rope which snaked in the current and he had to duck under the surface to free himself and see where the nylon thread went next. The tunnel ahead was full of water. Gonzo resurfaced and refused to think of anything but the symmetrical marvel of nature. There would be a chamber ahead. There would be air. He was not about to drown. He took a deep breath and dived into the tunnel, following the rope that twirled and danced around the nylon thread.

Capper and Max could no longer touch the floor of the fourth chamber. They had six inches of air between their mouths and the roof of the cave. The rope had slipped off the rock as they had to rise with the water and they clung to the roof with fingertips fast losing their strength. Why bother?

Capper was thinking of letting go, but held on because he wanted to see Max go first. He knew he was still there because they were chest to chest in the blackness. Neither said a word. Max would go first. That way, Capper would win the contest. And then he could let go and be taken away by the torrent, never to be found, the perfect burial ground for a caveman.

The six inches shrank and they now had to press their faces to the roof of the chamber to breathe. They did not see the light of Gonzo's torch in the tunnel until he entered the chamber. He broke the surface and all Capper could do was plant a kiss on his head. Nobody said a word as they grabbed the rope and prepared to go underwater and fight uphill against the torrent to the relative sanctuary of the third chamber. Max went first, with Capper not far behind, taking care to avoid the flailing feet that sought a grip on rock or beat against the water in the struggle to make progress. Gonzo shone the light after them to show them the way as far as he could, but he needed both hands on the rope. He turned the torch off, stuffed it inside his shirt and started the return journey.

Once Max was in the third chamber he began to haul on the rope. He held it in one hand and pulled Capper out with the other, and then they both pulled Gonzo the last few feet. Gonzo turned the torch on and they had time to give a roar as loud as the emptying sponge of rock before the light suddenly cut out. They had to follow the rope blindly now, which meant there was much banging and bumping against rock. They felt their way around the walls of the first chamber until they came to the first rope, their route to the surface.

An hour later they fell through the front door of the cottage. They lay on the floor staring up at a circle of seven faces: Grace, Our Marnie, Noa, Kitty, Cinnabar, John and the Professor.

'You know, Gonzo,' said Max, 'you know, I think we have already played the All Blacks.'

'Any of that whisky left, John?' said Gonzo.

12

Suddenly Noa was the Barbarian back-row forward with the fewest blemishes. His split eye was nothing compared with the bruises and lesions all over Gonzo and Max's bodies. When they reported for duty at the Sir Tasker Hotel in Cardiff Bay, the other players fell about laughing at the sight of them. Their mirth continued until Max told them every detail of their 'little adventure', as he called it, as they travelled by coach to their training ground in Penarth, the spiritual home of the Barbarians.

'We took on this mountain, and the mountain won,' was the beginning of his tale. Conrad found himself listening rather than telling the players that the time had come to focus on the four days ahead, culminating in the game. Max finally brought the story to an end: 'We are bruised but not beaten, coach. We are here. And if you think that after our adventure we cannot be stimulated by this game, then you make a mistake. For us this contact with the All Blacks is anything but run-of-the-fuckin'-mill.' Gonzo raised an eyebrow. 'It is strange what stays in your mind when you are so close to death.'

'OK,' said Conrad. 'It is time now to concentrate. We have the next mountain to take on.'

At the media briefing after the training session, questions were asked about the state of Gonzo Davies and Maxime Ferry. Conrad, entirely serious, said that training had been so intense since Dubai and the competition for places so fierce that things had 'got a little out of hand'. Pressed for details, he would say no more, but in the *Western Mail* the next day a photo of Noa, Max and Gonzo appeared. 'Ready for the All Blacks?' the caption ran. 'The Three Mauled Musketeers.'

A Canadian journalist with Agence France Presse managed to track down Dave Hollister. 'Is it true, Solar, what they're saying about the fight for places?' he asked.

'Sure,' said a poker-faced Dave. 'I told those guys that if they wanted my spot they'd have to take it from me. They call me the Mountie. I showed them I'm the Lumberjack.' His words were faithfully reproduced in three national newspapers, and each cutting was pinned up in the team room of the Sir Tasker. Every time The Mountie walked in, the squad shouted, 'Timber'.

Grace told herself that she would go down to Cardiff on the Tuesday night, but Our Marnie and Capper appeared early that morning. Capper set about finishing the slate floor.

'For goodness' sake, Capper,' Grace told him. 'You can't be doing this. Look at your hands.' Capper stared down at his swollen, bruised knuckles. 'Didn't touch them in the mountain, Grace love. They're always like that.'

'Well, your head then.'

'Just a few nicks. A few more nicks. That mountain, I tell you. You're right, mind. It's done my head in … if I don't do anything I keep seeing … well, I keep seeing nothing. Pitch-black nothing.'

Our Marnie said: 'Come on now. We saw you last night. Sopping, freezing and shaking … but tight-lipped, saying nothing. The three clams. You haven't slept a wink. So, come on. How close was it?'

Capper nodded. And now that Gonzo wasn't there to play down his role in the rescue, he told them the full story.

Gonzo phoned Grace that evening on the cottage's new landline – there was no mobile reception in the wilderness – and told her that Max and he were going to have an early night. Why didn't Grace stay another night in the cottage? She wanted to see him. She wanted to wrap herself around him and make sure he was all right. 'Capper's told us,' she said. 'Are you all right? Really all right? Your head. Think of your head. You can't …'

'Grace,' said Gonzo quietly. 'I love you. But … be quiet. My head needs a good kip, that's all.'

The next day the kitchen units and work surfaces were delivered and Grace, for all her promises to herself that she would be on her way to Cardiff any moment, spent the whole day labouring for Capper who seemed equally keen to install it.

'It can never be a full surprise any more, can it?' he said. 'But we can still give him a bit of a homecoming, can't we?'

Gonzo phoned again on the Wednesday and told Grace it was getting a little serious in the Sir Tasker. What had started as a fiction about the ferocity of training was turning into reality. Testosterone was the new flood. Why didn't she stay at home? He sounded brighter. Grace was pleased on both counts. She wanted to finish the surprise, take another step towards making it their home, where they would settle into unexciting bliss, into a mundane paradise where nobody drowned or had their head stamped. She longed to curl up in arms that didn't have to wrestle and rip and pull on ropes in underground death traps. And she didn't want to feel trapped in the Bay. She told him she missed him. She said she'd be down on the Thursday. And she was in fact packing her bags, ready to drive down in the Land Rover to the capital on that day when there was a knock on the door. She opened it and there stood Perrine.

'Those men,' said Max's wife. 'They have gone into "the zone". What a place. I have never seen Max like it. Normally he is Mr Cool. But he is like a … how can I say it …?'

'A man possessed.'

'Exactly. Mon dieu, your kitchen, Grace. I adore it. Yes, a man possessed. Only your Gonzo is normal. Well, Noa of course … but the rest, they are like Max. I cannot stay with them. I cannot shop any more. I cannot go to one more restaurant. Grace, can I stay here?'

'Of course.'

'Can you show me the place … you know, where it happened?'

'Of course.'

*

Word reached the All Blacks about the seriousness of the Barbarians in training and they believed it. It suited them to have a formidable foe. It showed there was respect, which they valued and which brought out the best in themselves. They approached the farewell game to their great captain with a renewed intensity. In typical New Zealander style, they piled the pressure on themselves, firmly believing that the tighter the strain, the more ferocious would be the response of the All Black rugby player. And nobody felt the pressure – or put more of it on himself – than Cutter Bartholomew, the young player, the next big thing, who was to step into Tai McDonald's boots. Cutter was indeed very big – and fast and strong – but he was not a modest young man. He was an Aucklander who had excelled at every level of the game. The only interruption to his record-breaking rise through the ranks was George Pai Taihonga's insistence on sticking with Tai McDonald, the superannuated South Islander. Cutter had consummate belief in his own ability. He had felt for a year that he should have been in the starting line-up of the All Blacks, ahead of old man McDonald.

In truth, George knew too that Cutter was already better than Tai. But it pleased him to see the 'arrogant young prick', as he called him, restless in the wings. It pleased him that the kid, when he was finally given a chance against Australia and Argentina, had not found rugby at the highest level quite as easy as he had imagined. Cutter had done some wonderfully athletic things in the air and with his tackling, but he had been selfish on a couple of occasions and chances had been missed. George had watched Cutter's reaction to the exposure of his egotism in the team room and knew the critique had been badly received, but the lesson had been absorbed. Cutter was ready.

He was nearly half the age of Gonzo, of whom he had never heard. He did not care who this Welsh nobody was or what he did well or badly. Cutter only cared about what Cutter did, and that mostly involved making coach George choke on the words of criticisms he, George, had dared make of him in front of the squad. Cutter was going to show George a thing or two. He was going to make a statement in the farewell game. Farewell and good riddance. Tai was dead; Cutter was the future.

Grace took Perrine to see the peephole into the mountain on Friday morning. She also took a camera and spent half an hour trying various exposures – the sun came and went between scudding clouds – until she knew she had the shot of the boulder and the rock and the mountain and the sky that she liked. She suggested to Perrine that they go down to Abergavenny, where they settled into the Angel for a coffee, which became lunch. Grace asked Perrine if she would excuse her for half an hour. She wanted to have the shot of 'the place' blown up and framed – one picture to present to Max, one to keep for Gonzo. She also had another errand to run, but it wasn't long before they were heading back up the Blorenge. Grace told Perrine this was the very road on which she had driven in her overheating Mazda and first seen a very naked Gonzo at the Keeper's Pond. Perrine laughed and they both checked the temperature gauge in the old Land Rover. They swept on past the pond and didn't stop until they reached the Sherkin which Perrine said she simply had to see.

The club had postponed their home game the next day – with the blessing of the Welsh Rugby Union – in honour of Gonzo's participation, and the team seemed to have assembled at the Gherkin for an early toast to Gonzo's Last Stand, as Capper called it. John had lit the barbecues and Our Marnie pulled up the shutters and started pouring the pints. The storm was done and the evening was clear and cool. The cyclists were still in action and Annie and Meg wandered down to meet the glamorous French player's wife. The Professor appeared to announce that the bus had been ordered and that Owain Owens would be leaving at 11 o'clock in the morning.

'Why don't you come with us, Grace, darling?' said Meg.

'And Perrine, love, you too,' said Anne.

'Do you know,' said Perrine, 'why not? The night before the game is no time to be with the players. And I am having such a good time here.'

'Know what I think, Perrine my darling?' said Meg. 'You're a Welsh girl like us – who just happens to speak French.'

It was agreed that Grace and Perrine would go to Cardiff on the club outing. Perrine was a bit giggly on the way back to the cottage and fell on the new bed. Halfway through saying how worried she was about Max, how he seemed to take this surfeit of excitement in his stride and yet how perhaps she alone knew that there would be a swing the other way – 'There is a Max noir to go with the blonde,' she said – and how she almost dreaded thinking about what he would do when his playing days were over, she fell asleep. Early the next morning, Grace eased out of the cottage and made her way down to Abergavenny to pick up the framed pictures.

Cutter Bartholomew finally found out what Gonzo looked like, but only because he wanted to eyeball him during the haka. It took him a while to marry the photo in the programme with the ravaged old man that stood twenty metres away. Cutter was to play against a beaten-up geriatric. Even better. Putting old men away was what this day was all about. As he went through the haka's rituals, the collective expression of naked aggression, he did not blink or take his eyes off this Gonzo Davies, who had once played no more than six times for his country.

Gonzo was a little emotional. Conrad had named Jacques du Plessis as captain, but they had both then approached Gonzo and asked the one Welshman playing at the home of the Welsh game if he would like to lead out the team. Gonzo hit the wall of noise from a full house of 73,000 and it stirred all sorts of memories. In fact, these flashes of times past hit him as a physical force – not a torrent that could bowl him over like a surge of water inside a mountain, but a shock to the mind that made him stop in his tracks, causing Jacques, behind him, to have to make his first side-step of the game. Gonzo remained so affected by this assault on his emotions that he forgot to look up into the stands – as once had been his ritual – and seek Grace in the crowd. The crowd sang the Welsh anthem, unaccompanied, and he listened to every note, every word behind his closed eyes, reliving times past, feeling this moment, forgetting what he had to do next to survive. He needed to clear his mind and he needed to concentrate on his opposite number, a young giant who was looking at him with pure hatred.

Grace liked the throb of the Land Rover and she knew full well that the word came with connotations. Throb. But she liked it anyway. She liked it because of that suggestiveness. The old Defender was strong and it had a beat that reassured, a vibration that made her quiver in the upright seat with its cracked plastic and leaking foam padding. Gonzo could not drive for more than half an hour without seizing up. The Defender, strangely for a vehicle built to go off-road to places where only real men went, was built for people her size. Grace had plenty of room for her legs and she often volunteered to drive. Whenever she turned the key in the ignition she looked for the spider, but had never seen it or even the threads of a web in the bottom corner of the windscreen.

Early in the morning of the game, she carefully put the framed photographs on the passenger seat. She had plenty of time to make it back up the mountain before the bus left for Cardiff. She had lingered in Stan's shop, thanking the Polish framer for delivering on the rush job. She had given him several bits of work and now trusted his judgement – 'It's my sad Polish soul,' he'd told her. For the pair of photos he had chosen a thicker pair of dark grey, almost black, frames than she had suggested, but she loved how Stan's gave more weight to the brooding sky and more menace to the rocks, and depth to the moor that stretched towards the mountain in the distance. She had handwritten a caption on the photo that she thought would look good on the softly lit landing in the cottage: 'Gonzo's Finest Hour II'.

Cutter Bartholomew caught the kick-off one-handed over his head. It caused a ripple of appreciation around the stadium. 'It's a day to say goodbye to Tai; it could be a day to say hello to Kid Cutter,' said the New Zealand television commentator. Cutter caught the first line-out throw that came his way with his other hand and flicked the ball with a snap of his wrist to little Waka Sturridge, his scrum half. The All Blacks were back to maximum efficiency, masters of their skills and not shy about putting them on display. This was, after all, a celebration game. Cutter stayed outside Joey Panafu'uano, the fastest player on the New Zealand team, and took the winger's pass in his own ground-eating stride to score the All Blacks' second try in the opening ten minutes.

He also blocked Gonzo off the ball. He pulled his opposite number's shirt to prevent him being in position to stop the first try and he tripped him as Gonzo set off into midfield where the Barbarians were putting together their first promising move. 'You shouldn't be out here, old man,' he said in Gonzo's ear. 'You're an embarrassment.' And Cutter loped into midfield, looking for action, looking for trouble, looking for the next move to join – a set-piece move; a career move.

Grace put a third photo between the pictures on the passenger seat and started the engine again. There was no need to rush. Abergavenny was scarcely starting to stir on this Saturday morning. Out of superstition, she glanced at the place where the mysterious spider didn't live, smiled and then froze as she glanced in the side mirror. For a second she thought she saw … him. But when she craned her neck, there was nobody there, except the early-bird queue outside the mobility-buggy cabin in the car park. Grace saw him everywhere – on every street corner in Dubai, at the airport, on the mountain looking down on her. She once served him a coffee at the Gherkin, but the cyclist had taken off his visor and turned out to be Wiggins Jones, a Graig regular, a cheeky student from Llantilio Crossenny.

'You OK, Mrs Gonzo?' Wiggins had asked. Grace had nodded and cursed … him. Cursed Him viciously for creeping ever closer to her refuge. Only in the cottage could she slam the door. Her home was her place of safety. Whatever happened, Gonzo would save her, just as he saved others and brought them home. But she would certainly see him in Cardiff – and even more dispiritingly, she would feel him, sucking her enjoyment out of the occasion. No, he wouldn't. She had Perrine in her home. She had Our Marnie and she had Annie and Meg. She had Kitty. She had an entire body of support. She had Capper and the Children and the Professor and John and Mystic and Useless. She had a guard that would take her to her Gonzo. She started the Land Rover and let the engine's throbbing beat settle her, before she pointed its green bonnet toward Llanfoist, crossed the Monmouthshire and Brecon canal at Govilon and headed for home.

At the start of the second quarter, the All Blacks had an attacking scrum, with a gap on the right-hand side that invited Cutter to combine with Waka and Joey and Gordie

Bates from full back. The 8-9-14-15 move had been a speciality of the Tai McDonald age and now it was Cutter's opportunity to pay homage to it. All he had to do was pick up at the back of the scrum, head right, draw the first tackler – usually the blind-side wing forward, and on this day Noa Diawara – set this defender on his heels and put his scrum half into the gap. If he was lucky – and it had certainly worked more than a dozen times for Tai – the number 8, by staying in support, could well pick up the prize of a try. Tai had made the sequence of shirts so well-known that the crowd used to count them off as each shirt-number received the ball: '8 ... 9 ... 14 ... 15 ... 8.' The trick was not to be greedy.

Gonzo spoke to Noa before the scrum went down: 'Take the dummy.' Noa nodded. Cutter picked up and sensed that the first tackler, Noa, was willing to give him a yard. Cutter couldn't help himself. Instead of fixing the big black slow African and taking him out of the defensive equation by straightening and passing to Waka, Cutter elegantly feigned the pass and had a moment of delicious satisfaction when Noa followed its imagined flight. Cutter hadn't expected a dummy to be so easily bought at this level, but perhaps he was just very good at the art of deception. Cutter had made space for himself and prepared to accelerate to top speed, every sinew straining to put him on a solo run to glory.

And then Gonzo hit him. Cutter was picked up and turned horizontal. Noa rushed in to keep the young New Zealander suspended safely but helplessly above the ground. However hard his huge biceps and strong hands tried to keep the ball under his control, it was eased out of his grasp. He shouted in frustration as Noa completed the extraction and slipped the ball to Gonzo, who with one hand flipped it to Jacques who was already running at full speed. The scrum half scored between the posts. Noa gently put Cutter on the ground and patted his cheek.

At the next line-out, Gonzo gave Cutter a little push – an illicit little nudge – as the ball was launched and Cutter lost his balance for a moment between the two players who were about to propel him into the air. By a fraction a second he mistimed his jump and the throw missed his fingertips by a centimetre. It flew on, into the hands of Max at the back of the line-out. As Cutter took a wild swipe at Gonzo, who swayed out of the way of the blow, Max set off, a blonde streak into a midfield of black shirts. He took out three defenders and set up the ruck from which the Barbarians scored again.

The Television Match Official asked to see the start of the move again. Gonzo's push was invisible; Cutter's punch was there on the big screen for all to see. Cutter spent the next ten minutes in the sin-bin. When he came back, he tried to barge his way through Max who flipped him over. Noa stripped him of the ball again and, as he screamed in anger again, Gonzo gave him a short sharp punch that left the stunned Cutter with a swelling over his eye the size of a pigeon egg. Coach George replaced him on the hour and Cutter left the field, head down and heavy of tread. It hadn't quite been the new kid's day after all, was the informed opinion at the microphone. It just went to show how good Tai McDonald had been. Cutter sat disconsolately on the sideline with an ice-pack pressed to his egg. He had to watch as Gonzo, Max and Noa performed a dance of the dervishes, with Gonzo spinning away to score under the posts.

The match swayed back and forth, try following try in the third quarter. Just when it seemed that the impossible might happen, the Barbarians became a little too extravagant in the three-quarters and a little too far out for safety and the All Blacks scored two tries that made the result safe. This brace of typically clinical scores – punishment tries, they were called – would normally have heralded an extravagant finishing flourish, but to their slight consternation the All Blacks spent the rest of the game on the defensive, protecting their six-point lead. Gonzo felt good. The Mountie was on for Max who had run himself into the ground, but the balance of the back row still felt good. Gonzo had never felt stronger in the closing stages of a game. He was slightly surprised then to see Radu Murariu, the Romanian second row, trotting on and himself being called off. He was even more surprised to see Conrad walking on to the field towards him. Hands were already applauding Gonzo as he walked off, but at the sight of the number 8 being given this personal escort by his old coach, limping on his arthritic knees and with an arm around Gonzo's waist, the entire Millennium Stadium crowd rose as one and gave them a standing ovation. A few All Blacks came over to shake Conrad and Gonzo by the hand.

'Now that would have been a contest,' said the commentator. 'Tai McDonald against this Gonzo Davies.' Gonzo was quite happy to linger, to milk the moment but Conrad pulled him down the tunnel towards the changing room. 'Well played, old fellahs,' was the commentary line that carried them to the doors at the end of the corridor.

*

As she approached the Keeper's Pond, Grace began to relax. There was always a risk, going up the Blorenge and overtaking the bunches of cyclists on the long pull through the beech trees, that one of them might wobble out of line. But it was still a bit early for the Graig to be so high and Grace rumbled over the cattle grid into daylight with the road to herself. It stretched out ahead of her, rising as a black diagonal line against the green and purple of the mountainside. She could see she did have company after all. A rambler was coming, head down, towards her on the mountain side of the road. She eased into the middle to give him plenty of space.

Three seconds from the Land Rover, Martin walked into the middle of the road. Two paces from it he looked up. One second away, he threw back the hood of his jacket and walked even further into the path of the oncoming vehicle. Grace saw the first movement and swerved. She saw the second motion and swerved again. She saw it was Him and couldn't make the adjustment that would have brought her back in line with him. She couldn't mow him down. Instead, she went off the side of the road. The Land Rover was built to survive the first part of its sudden off-road journey. It bounced hard against rocks, slewed on the wet ground and remained upright. But there was nothing it could do about a plunge through thin air off the edge of a vertical wall of rock. When the Defender landed, it began to tumble end over end and then side over side, quickly and then slowly until it settled in a crumpled, disfigured heap – but, remarkably, the right way up – in a hollow, out of sight of the road. There was nobody on the open road to witness the end of the fall. Martin was already in Frank's car and they were already over the cattle grid and speeding away downhill, into the darkness of the beech trees.

'Sit down, Gonzo. Please.' said Conrad. 'I'm afraid I've got some bloody grim news, mate. It's Grace …'

Perrine had waited at the cottage for Grace. And the bus had waited at the Sherkin for the two of them. Our Marnie and Kitty had gone to the cottage when the bus could wait no longer, and found Perrine prowling the track. They drove down to Abergavenny and back again. Eventually, with a terrible feeling, Our Marnie, Kitty and Perrine, who refused to go to the game, sat in the cottage and waited.

A lone fell-runner, working her way up the tracks of the Blorenge came across the Land Rover late in the morning. Grace was still behind the wheel in the seat too uncomfortable for Gonzo. The panting runner checked for a pulse and put her ear close to the mouth of the slumped driver. She felt no beat, sensed no breath. A small spider was climbing across the seat-belt that held Grace in place. The athlete tried to call 999, but had to run for half a mile before she could find a signal. She ran back to the Land Rover – not that there was any need for haste now – and began to climb up towards the road, where the emergency services would arrive. Along the way, and before she had to take a diversion around the low cliff, off the top of which the Land Rover had flown, she found evidence of the subsequent tumble. And among all the pieces of plastic and metal she came across two photographs, one without a frame, the other remarkably intact, with just a single crack across the glass. And a third photograph –

the picture Grace had picked up the day before, the image of what the ultrasound scan revealed to be the cause of her recent nausea. She had been feeling sick not because of Him, but because of the him that Gonzo and Grace had made, and that had died with his mother.

13

Three of the four regional rugby teams in Wales expressed an interest, as much in the light of the publicity generated as by the power of his performance against New Zealand, in signing Gonzo. The season was two months old and there were holes to plug in their ranks. As well as being a potential short-term answer, however, he was also very much a question. How could it be, it was asked in several media outlets in the days that followed the game at the Millennium Stadium, that a home-grown talent had been allowed to languish in the near-total obscurity of village rugby while the professional game of Wales was apparently prepared to bankrupt itself on the purchase of imports from overseas – players who were not that much younger than the forgotten man and certainly not as effective? Gonzo was briefly a *cause célèbre*, but when there came no response from the player himself, the regions shrugged and said there was only so much they could do when it came to recruiting on the home front. A few freelance representatives of the regions – and even a couple of agents – followed up this lukewarm interest by knocking on the door of the cottage, but there was never any reply. Business cards and notes to contact so-and-so collected on the floor.

There was a spin-off from the interest in Gonzo. A scout from Newport stayed a little longer than all the other envoys and came to the village's first home game after the death of Grace. Gonzo was not playing and it was a dismal occasion. The players did their best to lift themselves by saying that they owed it to the memory of Grace to put on a performance, but their hearts were not in it and they lost for the first time on their own patch. The scout, followed with grave suspicion and visible hostility by Dario, reported that Gonzo Davies had not only been absent on the day, but also had not been seen for a fortnight. On the other hand, he wrote by way of justifying his claim for expenses, there was a winger in the village team who, despite receiving few opportunities, showed real potential. Still slightly embarrassed by all the unflattering publicity surrounding their employment of players from outside Wales, the region invited Ragwort for a trial. With no Gonzo to apply a brake to his ambitions and prodded by Cinnabar, Ragwort headed south and the trial period soon became a short-term contract. One of the bedrooms at the Orphanage now stood empty.

Kitty missed Emma. She missed walking across the moor to feed Arkle and talking to Ragwort's girlfriend about nothing in particular, lightweight chats that had helped soften the young woman's outer shell – Cinnabar's carapace. It hurt Kitty to hear her companion revert to type in the Orphanage, urging Ragwort to take the offer and take her south. 'Just don't take leave of your senses,' Cinnabar warned her man.

It hurt Kitty to hear Dario – worried, twisted Dario – flare up at the Professor and for the discord to hang around the Orphanage like the smell from Ragwort's trainers until Kitty had put them in the washing machine. No trainers, no Ragwort. Kitty walked one day to the cottage to see if there was anything she could do. She found Our Marnie cleaning up a pile of post and paper on the floor behind the front door and she helped her tidy up in the half-finished kitchen and the empty living room.

'I need some advice,' said Our Marnie, when their housework was done.

Gonzo spent most of his days at the old clubhouse on West Street. Occasionally he would go and sit in the Miners' Institute, in the reading room where he had begun his recovery from the injury to his eye and head, the malfunctions that had ended his professional career. He didn't believe in any healing power of the room; he didn't read there; he simply went there.

The Professor gently knocked on its door twelve days after Grace's funeral. The village was returning to full volume. The Professor had been berated by Dario for allowing the scout to infiltrate the village, for allowing a process of team deconstruction to begin. 'Think what Gonzo would say,' shouted Dario.

The Professor had seen Gonzo in the dark days and knew that there was no repeat going on here, no shrinkage of the will to go with an expansion of the waistline. Our Marnie was keeping him fed and watered, and the village would sometimes see Capper and Gonzo on the mountain. He was not in physical decline, but he was withdrawn. Sometimes he didn't say a word for hours on the dram roads. He did, though, in his unspeaking way seem to invite updates about the club and the Co-operative and the village. As yet, he had not proffered any opinion on life after Grace.

Capper had already told Gonzo about Ragwort, but the Professor wanted to know if he, the mentor, should do something about his protégé, as demanded by Dario. What, the Professor wanted to know, did Gonzo think? Gonzo said nothing. He barely seemed to hear. When he looked up, the Professor braced himself for a shock, to recoil before lifeless eyes. But there was something there, even if nothing came from Gonzo's mouth. The Professor waited in silence and then muttered an apology and prepared to leave.

'Let him go,' said Gonzo almost as a whisper.

The Professor nodded, waited and, when there seemed to be no more, stood again to leave.

'Was it Him?' said Gonzo.

Nothing from the investigation into the crash suggested anything other than an unfortunate accident. A swerve, a skid at just the wrong place. No scorched rubber marks, no tyre-shredding jacks, no lingering trace of malevolence. But they knew. The Professor did not want Martin to re-enter his life. He did not want to sense the hand of Grace's husband in her death. He never wanted to spare a single thought on his former employer. He nodded. 'It had to be.'

Gonzo looked at the pile of untouched folders on the table, full of original plans of the Institute. 'I'll come through this, Professor,' he said. 'In fact, it's the thing that's keeping me going. We're going to have a ...'

'A reckoning.'

'A reckoning. That's it. But to have it …'

'You need me to find him.'

Gonzo nodded. 'You know him.'

'He knows me, too, Gonzo.'

'Can you … find him? Is he still in Dubai?'

The Professor swallowed hard. 'There's one possible … one line of inquiry … I can't promise anything …'

'Will you try?'

The Professor nodded. There was one thing he would need. He didn't have to say what it was. Gonzo placed a credit card on the table. The Professor glanced at it. Grace Courtney was the name on the bottom. The money the Professor had liberated from Martin and given to Grace was going to be returned, co-operative funds used to find Martin.

'What about the Fresh Start?' the Professor asked.

'There can be no fresh start until this is done.'

The Professor nodded. Gonzo picked up the card. 'How did you score all your tries, Professor? What was the old routine?'

'You, Daff, me.'

'That's it. Me, Daff, you. Gonzo, Daff, Professor.'

'8, 9, 14.'

'That's the PIN. 8914.'

Kitty walked one lunchtime to feed Arkle. She approached the hollow from which he normally emerged, but there was no sign of him. She was beginning to think that perhaps he had sensed a storm and had headed for the cottage. She checked the sky but it was no more laden than usual. When she looked back down, Gonzo and the horse were standing on the track.

'Dear Lord,' she said. 'You gave me a start.'

Grace had told Kitty the story of Gonzo and herself. And Him, of course. She had recounted it with the slight dread of a protagonist conscious that there was still unfinished business, but also with the hope that love would conquer all. Kitty now sat down on the moor, with Arkle occasionally nudging her in the back for another mint, and told Gonzo for the first time about the life – her dull, safe provincial life – that had been shattered by Horace. An existence destroyed by him; a life saved by Gonzo.

Kitty wasn't sure what she expected her saviour to say. Gonzo said nothing and she started to feel a little awkward. He was looking at his feet. She was about to stand and leave when he spoke: 'I need some advice, Kitty.'

In the time he had been spending in the old clubhouse, it had struck Gonzo that, even in his grief, he might be upsetting the balance of a relationship. Maybe because of his grief and the vulnerability it imparted. At least he asked himself the question: was he an intrusion into the shared life of his oldest friends, Capper and Our Marnie? They all knew that Gonzo and Our Marnie had once upon a time seemed destined for each other. A long time ago they were meant to be, and they knew it was Grace who, if she had not snatched Gonzo from her, had certainly dashed Our Marnie's hopes of making a go of it with him. They all knew that years later Grace had returned to the village on the run from Martin, back into the life of Gonzo. Grace came back – just before Our Marnie lured Capper into her bed, and he all too willingly let himself be led there, and from the bed into love with her. Had Our Marnie been on the rebound? But on the rebound from what – a go of it with Gonzo that had never been? A go that had never gone past Go. Not a rebound, but a sort of bounce – off Grace. And Grace was gone. Four were down to three and three did not make an easy ménage. Or was it all in the head of a grieving Gonzo? How could a man in mourning even entertain such a thought?

It was a shared thought. Kitty had already seen Our Marnie at the cottage. Why was Our Marnie there? To have a moment on her own. In Gonzo's house. Our Marnie sensed that her Capper sensed Gonzo in their space, the clubhouse. Senses were on full alert. This was her Capper, who had gone into a place he feared and gone two chambers beyond common sense, way out of bounds of reason. He had gone there out of obstinacy, not to be beaten in friendship to Gonzo. But now Capper sensed Gonzo in the same living space as Our Marnie. And there would never be an overheating sports car, a cashmere coat, a figure at the garden gate to divert Gonzo, to give him, Capper, just for once, a chance.

And Kitty had seen Capper. He had knocked one late afternoon at the Orphanage, dusty and subdued. He knew he was going to lose His Marnie to Gonzo. 'I need some advice,' he said.

Kitty invited Our Marnie to the Orphanage. Ten minutes later, Capper appeared. He went into the kitchen and looked surprised to see Our Marnie there.

'Tell him,' said Kitty.

Our Marnie stepped forward without hesitation. 'I love you with all my heart and nothing will come between us.'

'Tell her,' said Kitty.

Capper looked a little coy. 'The same …' he mumbled.

'Say it,' said Kitty.

'I love you so much it fuckin' hurts,' he said, and a big tear ran down his cheek.

The front door opened and in came Gonzo.

'Tell them,' said Kitty.

'You are the best couple in the world,' he said. 'And I vow to do everything I can to keep you that way. I love you both – but only as a both.'

That afternoon Kitty found herself packing one of her small bags and ordering a taxi to Abergavenny station. She waited in the shadow of the one Sugar Loaf mountain before travelling all the way north to Shrewsbury, then down the Heart of the Wales line to her more familiar – and yet already fading – Sugar Loaf Halt, not far from Llanwrtyd Wells. She put up the handle on the case and pulled it behind her. The case wobbled home on its small wheels with a rumbling of plastic on tarmac, louder than the soft swoosh of the pair of cyclists who passed her, heading in the other direction to the station.

The front door to her house was locked. She looked under the loose flagstone outside the porch, where a key for the carers was usually kept, but there was only a beetle in the hiding place. She went to the back of the house and wiggled the handle of the back door until there was a clunk. One of the little jobs Horace had never quite got round to doing.

She gave the bottom of the slightly warped door a kick and it opened. All was quiet. Kitty went upstairs and found on the cover of their made matrimonial bed a terse note from Dilys, dated eighteen days earlier, saying that Horace had been taken to hospital. The letters Kitty had left on the bedspread were in a neat pile in Horace's bedside drawer. Kitty left them there and went downstairs to the kitchen, where she boiled the kettle. She listened to its rising pitch, watched the vapour billow from its spout and heard it click itself off. Instead of reaching for her favourite mug, however, she turned to the drinks cupboard and poured herself a large glass of sherry. She then phoned the hospital and went through the various holding patterns until she was finally directed to the right ward, seeking news of Horace Vernon-Evans.

'Are you a relation?' asked a nurse.

Kitty hesitated. Reluctantly, she said that he had once been a close friend. Reluctantly? A close friend? She hadn't thought about what questions might be asked of Mrs Vernon-Evans, but she didn't want to admit she'd ever had anything to do with her husband.

'It's just that, well, there was quite a stir, I have to say,' said the hospital voice. 'Quite a bit of interest, you know, what with all the reporters. It was really quite inconvenient for a couple of days.'

'Inconvenient?'

'Well, it's always stressful for the other patients when somebody dies, but when reporters and television cameras appear, it throws the whole hospital into a spin. He was quite a character, as I'm sure you know. By all the interest, it would appear he was rather well respected. A lot of people went to his funeral, they say.'

Kitty put the phone down. She went to Horace's desk and noticed that the fragments of the drawers had been removed from the carpet. She sifted through the innocent files of his life – his lies – and found a copy of his last will and testament. She wanted to make sure he hadn't played one last terrible trick on her and left his money to Felicity or some child he might have sired on another philandering mission. Horace the missionary, in the prime of his life, slavering over a plump child. Horace the spokesman of tolerant decency in the Chamber, pumping his polluted seed in the bed chamber. Horace the stroker; Horace the stroke victim. Kitty wanted to double-check that the inert degenerate – burst of brain but sound of mind – hadn't managed to dribble out a codicil that bequeathed something to Dilys and Pat. She could see canny Pat, nursing him to within days of his end, but at the same time holding his numb hand and penning a bequest to herself. Here you go, Horace, you vile old man. One more document to sign. For Pat. There, that's better.

It seemed Kitty remained the sole beneficiary of his estate. She downed her sherry. A toast to you, Horace. And she found herself wondering at the nature of life's confusions. As quickly as she had been turned upside down and spun through a vortex, she was back where she had always been. Home in Llanwrtyd Wells. She wondered what would become of silly old Kitty. She also wondered what had become of the Browning pistol.

*

185

The next day, John, who refused to allow the Professor to go unaccompanied into what he called – and not without a thrilling little shiver – 'the great unknown', packed their bags and they left on their motorbike. Dario found himself the sole occupier of the Orphanage, and he rattled his way around its rooms on his crutches, blaming himself for the collapse of its micro-society, and yet determined to remain the house-sitter who would watch over it.

Nothing at the Shard moved on the redevelopment front. There was nothing to do in the office and Our Marnie simply locked the door. Mildew began to grow around the sink and the bits of paper on the tables began to curl. She opened the Gherkin only if the Lewises asked her or if she spotted cyclists on the circuit. But the weather closed in and the short days of November seemed to keep the Graig off their machines. Equally unused was the rugby ground. Without a coach and the best player, the club went into an unofficial winter break, an extension of the postponement for Gonzo's last adventure. Home games that would never normally have been deemed unplayable beneath even the most violent of storms were now called off at the first sign of rain, ostensibly because of a waterlogged pitch. Then real frosts hardened the playing surface. The village shut down and cold winter closed its grip around the wilderness.

At 11 o'clock one morning, an espresso was served at the corner table of the coffee shop of Raffles Hotel in Dubai. Ravi was sitting at a table on the other side of the room, cooling his damp brow in a gentle current of conditioned air, a phone to his ear and the treacherous friend who was like a brother to him, Krishnan, by his side. Ravi thrust the mobile at Krishnan and said, 'Speak to the Turk.' He went quickly to the corner table and sat down.

'You look good, Mr Martin. You look bloody good. Where have you been?'

'Business, Ravi. You know how it is.'

Ravi nodded and told him that Krishnan had expressed a strong wish to go to the Red Square. They would be honoured if Mr Martin joined them.

'I won't be going, Ravi. I've no need for that now.'

14

Ten days before Christmas, Gonzo dragged a gas heater into the Shard and re-opened the office for business – personal business, but at least a sign that he was re-emerging. He had received a call from the Professor and had asked everyone to convene here. And now he waited. Our Marnie came down an hour later and opened the Gherkin and began to cook a fry-up for the boardroom next door. Capper soon pulled up in the van, shaking cement dust from his jeans. He picked up the hose that ran to the outside tap at the back of the Gherkin and with a gasp rinsed his head and mouth. His dome glistened in the cold air and he ducked inside the Shard and wiped it with a tea towel, spotted with mould. He sat down around the table and waited with Gonzo for the bacon to fry and for the sound of the Professor and John's motorbike.

As a light rain began to fall there was the sound of an engine, but not theirs. In through the door instead came Kitty, somehow putting a set of car keys into her handbag, shaking an umbrella, holding down the button on the handle of her suitcase and retracting the telescopic pulling frame all in one go.

''Kin 'ell, Kitty,' said Capper. 'You're like Mary Poppins there.'

'Take no notice,' said Our Marnie, giving her a big hug. 'Are you ...?'

'Am I back?' said Kitty. 'No. I'm home.' And she told them that she'd had an offer on the house in Llanwrtyd Wells, sold all the furniture and anything else that had a trace – 'an odour' – of Horace on it. She'd made a bit more money, trading in his BMW for a second-hand pick-up truck, a vehicle she thought might serve a better purpose up here. Capper put his smeared head to the dirty window.

'The Kittymobile,' he said. 'I bet you were queen of the highway in that.'

'If I'd brought Horace's arsenal of weapons with me, I think I might have been given right of way,' said Kitty. 'But I didn't, tempted though I was. I am the head of an orphanage, not an arms smuggler.' Even Gonzo smiled. 'I sold them. Goodness, they were worth a small fortune.'

Capper peered out of the window again. 'Right,' he said. 'Here they are, the biker boys.'

John had found Frank through Marlene's ponies. While the Professor tried to locate the house on the cliff in Cardiganshire through the world he knew best – computers and libraries and local authorities – John cruised the coast road between Cardigan and Aberystwyth. A man in leather looking for a dangerous homeowner on a cliff – he couldn't help but view this through a prism that contorted the undeniably serious into a stifled titter. He thought he could post something in the Personals of the *Tivyside Advertiser*: Scotsman, seeking the shrewish wife of the dangerous man.

And then one morning, on his way back from Aberaeron to their Bed and Breakfast in New Quay, he was filling up the bike at a service station on the A487 – the sort of garage that had diversified and expanded to become a local-food shop, ice-cream parlour in the tourist season and purveyor of farm supplies – and saw a woman who could only ever be described as shrewish, buying pony nuts. Thinking that this whole caper was still a little absurd, John pretended to check his tyres as Marlene set off with her cargo of feed. He ran in to pay, put on his crash helmet and roared south until he saw the van and maintained a discreet distance. She led him to a paddock on the inland side of the main road, and after unloading the bags – going back and forth between the van and a spotless stable block on bandy legs, and easily picking up her loads in wiry arms – he followed her to her home on the cliff-top just outside Aberporth.

The next day, the Professor and John walked the cliff-top path that ran along the bottom of Frank and Marlene's property. They were just another pair of seal watchers on this stretch of Cardigan Bay. And they did the same thing the next day. They saw Frank only as a shadow behind a veil of lace over the windows, but it seemed Marlene had a regular outdoor routine with her ponies. On the third day, John went ahead of her and when she arrived he stepped out from the stable block. If she was startled in any way by this bald biker, she did not show it, but looked him up and down.

'Marlene, isn't it?' said John, who was caught between still seeing the funny side of the encounter and extreme nervousness. Marlene did not move a muscle. 'Can you give Frank a message, please?'

'Why don't you tell him yourself? Presumably you're going to tell me at some stage you know where we live?'

'That obvious, eh? But seriously, Marlene, I'm about as menacing as a hay bale is to your wee ponies, unlike your Frank who …'

'My Francis is a retired chauffeur,' said Marlene. 'A driver, who's never taken kindly to people on two wheels.' She glanced at the motorbike and sidecar. 'Beg your pardon, three. How sweet. You know what he'd say?'

'Aye, I've a fair idea,' said John. 'On my bike?'

'On your bike. Exactly.'

'And I'll soon be on my way. But can you give him a message, please?' Marlene pursed her thin lips and gave a brisk nod. 'Just tell him we're looking for Martin Guest.'

Well, of course they were. Would there never be any release from that man? Her Francis was no more in retirement than a … Marlene didn't know what. No freer than a Roman bloody galley slave. I've done my stint, master … think I'll just pop up on deck for a smoke. As if that would ever happen. Francis was in shackles.

'Does Gonzo Davies want to do him harm?' she asked. 'Well, give him a message from me. Tell him to join the bloody queue.'

That evening, the Professor and John stood on the footpath at the edge of the cliff. Frank stood six feet away, listening on his mobile, with a finger of his free hand stuck in his other ear. The sea wasn't crashing on the rocks far below, but it was a constant bass rumbling in the background, mixing with the louder but more intermittent onshore wind. The Professor couldn't take his eyes off the phone. It was an old model, dating back to the time when both the Professor and Frank had been in the employ of Martin Guest. It had rung only once since Frank delivered his fugitive by sea to Ceuta, and that had been to tell the boat skipper to revert to the road, pick him up at East Midlands Airport and drive him to the Keeper's Pond. And there, to shut his eyes and see nothing; hear nothing. And then carry Martin to Bristol Airport. And remember nothing. It was the phone that the Professor had been trying in vain to hack into for the past few days. Frank took it from his ear and ended the call.

'Tell him to meet me here,' he said loudly into the wind. He turned to go and then checked. He looked at John. 'And if you ever come near her again – you or your boyfriend – you'll both go the way of this.' With a casual flick of his wrist he tossed the phone over the cliff, and John felt his overactive sense of the absurd impaled on a spike of fear. 'Try hacking into that,' said Frank and went to sit down for his tea, with his Marlene.

Gonzo listened and called the meeting to order. 'Capper and the Professor,' he said, 'you have a rugby club to resuscitate. John and Our Marnie, you have the Shard to dry out and the Gherkin to reopen. Kitty, you have what's left of an

Orphanage to run. I'm saying this not because I'm ordering you to do any of it … it's just I don't want any of you saying you've got nothing on, and you want to come with me. Right. So, I'll be going.'

Nobody moved or said anything. Not even Capper. Kitty reached into her bag and threw the keys to the Kittymobile on the table. The Professor reached into his wallet and put the credit card alongside the keys.

'Are you going by the cottage?' asked Capper. Gonzo nodded. 'Take the gun,' said Capper. Our Marnie took a little intake of breath. Kitty could not bear to listen. It was she who had mentioned guns. Making light of them so soon after what she had put everyone, including herself, through. She willed Gonzo to make the right decision.

'I'll take these and this,' said Gonzo, picking up the keys and credit card, 'but not the other.'

Frank rarely wondered about what he did. It didn't bear thinking about, he thought. But he was not uninterested in the lives of others and sometimes sat in his house and watched the watchers – the seal watchers who stood for hours on the edge of his cliff, looking down at the coves and rocks, on the innocent lookout for new life. Frank sometimes imagined putting on a show for them. He remembered the days of Canadian seal-clubbing, helicopter shots of men on ice floes, arms raised and then falling, splashing red on white. He wondered how a person became a seal-clubber. Was there a course? Was it taught at school? What did you do today, Francis, in class? In History we did the mutiny that left Henry Hudson stranded in Hudson Bay. In Geography we did the melting of the polar ice pack and in Seal Clubbing we did seal-clubbing. Frank reckoned he had done the same sort of course anyway. He had come to Wales as a marksman in the foot-and-mouth outbreak. He was coming out of the Commandos and somehow seemed qualified. Not that he needed to be a marksman. He simply needed to be a shot not bad enough to miss a target the size of a cow. He remembered the farmers more than the piles of carcasses. The animals had all looked the same: legs up, burning on the pyres. Some of the farmers couldn't watch any of it. Not the rounding-up, not the massacre of the innocents, not the bulldozing of the bodies across their yards and into the paddock. The one thing they couldn't miss was the stench, from the fuel chucked on the fires, from the flesh not burning at a temperature high enough to sterilise the crematorium, from the oily black smoke that crept into every crevice of their farms. Some farmers had wept for their prize herds and pedigree flocks. All had held out their hands for the cheque that came with being selected for slaughter. Frank had packed up his gun and gone to work for Mr Guest. And now the doorbell of his house in Cardiganshire was ringing. Frank opened the door and showed Gonzo into the kitchen.

'Bricks and mortar,' said Frank, slapping the wall. 'What we all want to own.' Neither seemed to want to sit down. They were too wary, looking for the first move, the first twitch. 'Marlene's pride and joy,' said Frank. 'When we first came down here, this was a railway carriage, you know,' and he indicated the house. 'Holiday homes converted from old railway stock. Think I'd have preferred it if they'd left it as it was.'

Marlene came in. She looked tired, her hair lank and her face drawn. She looked less mean of spirit, thought her Francis. Older. Kinder.

'I'll leave you to it,' she said. She squirted moisturiser from a plastic dispenser and gave her face and hands a good rub. 'But before I do, I want to say this to you. You did a bad thing, Gonzo Davies. You're going through something terrible right now; heaven knows you are. But you started this. You and Grace … You're not a good person. And you should think of that when it comes to … well, whatever comes next.' She put her hands together again, not so much rubbing them as wringing them. 'I'll be going now.'

'You can stay,' said Frank. 'What I've got to say won't take long.'

'No. I'm done in, Francis.' said Marlene and left. 'I'll leave you to it.'

They sat there in silence. All the way down, Gonzo had seen this Frank only as a face below him, held at the end of a strong arm. The ex-commando was strong and tough but Gonzo knew, and he knew Frank knew, that any contest between them would be short-lived. No, not a contest. That suggested rules. Any fight between them. Any hand-to-hand struggle to the death. Gonzo would smash him and have him wrapped up in seconds and have him suspended over the cliff and have him begging for his life. Except Gonzo knew Frank wouldn't beg. He wondered if Frank had a gun; if their fight without rules of engagement would be unarmed.

'He says,' said Frank eventually, 'that he'll be where you last saw him. Eleven o'clock in the coffee shop. Corner table.'

Gonzo nodded. Neither of them moved.

'Are we good?' said Frank.

'We can never be good,' said Gonzo.

'Are we … done?'

Gonzo looked up. 'Did you know?' he asked. 'Did you know what he was going to do?'

Frank sighed. 'Look,' he said. 'I knew it wasn't going to be good. But …'

Gonzo stood up. 'If I don't find him I'll be back.' He made for the door.

'I know,' said Frank. He stood and followed Gonzo. 'She wasn't right, you know. Marlene.' Frank opened the door. 'Yes, you did a bad thing. But you're not a bad person. That's why you couldn't do what you thought you were coming all the way down here to do. You thought about it, didn't you? Hanging me over the edge, maybe even in front of my wife. Letting go, watching me drop. That's what you thought you were going to do, isn't it? Tell me I'm wrong.' Gonzo went out into the night. 'No, you're not a bad man, Gonzo Davies. And that's why you can't win in this.' And he closed the door gently after his guest.

Gonzo drove through the early hours of the morning from the west coast of Wales to the car park of Newport station. He slept behind the wheel of Kitty's pick-up, texted her where it was and caught the first train to Heathrow, sleeping all the way in the train and the bus link from Reading to the airport. He had to wait for several hours, but managed to catch a flight to Dubai that day. On arrival – on his return – he had nowhere to stay, but Raffles did not seem surprised in the slightest to see a guest back so soon, even one with no luggage.

'Good morning, Mr Davies,' said Reinhard at the reception desk. 'With us again. We are delighted to see you.'

'I haven't booked,' said Gonzo.

'That is no problem whatsoever, sir.'

'But you know who I am.' Gonzo had been thinking about predictability. Ever since the door had closed behind him in Aberporth, he'd been thinking about lots of things, but especially about this whole process of thinking. So many thinking thoughts. Was he being out-thought? Even Frank seemed to read him. And if Gonzo was so easily interpreted then it could be that he was simply blundering into a trap laid by Martin. But by thinking he was being manipulated, was he learning, or was this alertness to danger already anticipated? Was it worth … thinking at all?

'Mr Davies? Sir?' Gonzo blinked and came to. 'Mr Davies, of course we know who you are. I am Reinhard from Stuttgart. That is to say: this is Raffles and I am German. Remembering our guests is what we do. Now, sir, how long will you be staying with us?'

Gonzo didn't know. He had an 11 o'clock appointment. Would he be finished here by quarter past? 11 o'clock of which day? Would he still be here in a month's time?

'Shall we say four days?' said Reinhard. Gonzo nodded. 'Excellent. Will you be paying by credit card? May I take an imprint?' Reinhard of course noted that the card was in the name of Grace Courtney. He remembered Grace. He said nothing and the card was accepted.

'I have an appointment in the coffee shop at 11 o'clock,' said Gonzo.

'It is just through there,' said Reinhard, pointing.

'With a man called Guest. Do you know him?'

Reinhard looked serious as he considered the name. And then he laughed, before making a visible effort to bring himself under control. 'I am sorry, Mr Davies. It's just ... well, it is my job to know the guests. But it seems I do not know the Guest that matters.' Reinhard coughed. 'I am sorry, sir. I'm afraid I do not know him.' He shuffled a piece of paper in front of him and looked up again. 'May I say what ... fun we had when you stayed last time,' he said. 'Yes, fun. When you were here with the Barbarians. You know, we were the Barbarians to ... the Germans. It's what the Romans called us. We are brother Barbarians.' When Reinhard held out his hand, Gonzo thought that if this was a trap it was too well laid for him, and he reached out with his and shook it.

'Welcome back, Mr Davies.'

For three days Gonzo went to the corner table in the coffee shop at 11 o'clock. 11 in the morning, 11 at night, 11 UK time, 11 Dubai. And nobody came. When he wasn't on his own at the table, Gonzo lay in his room on his bed. Thinking. Caught in a trap. Thinking the next knock on the door wouldn't be housekeeping or room service, but the assassin. A knock, a phut, a neat hole that would complete the revenge of Martin Guest. The mortal wound of Gonzo Davies. He lay there, thinking. Not thinking. Not remembering Grace. Not seeing lift doors opening.

*

In his almost empty apartment overlooking the desert, Martin sat and thought about being the last person to see Grace alive. He thought about being the person keeping Gonzo Davies alive. For three days at 11.15 in the morning, Dubai time, he picked up the phone on the first ring and listened to Ravi describe the man sitting at the corner table. Ravi's portrait of misery.

On the fourth day, Reinhard was on duty again. He went from behind the reception desk, having seen Mr Davies walk past at 10.55 in the morning. The guest went by with his head up, scanning the foyer, devouring faces, but not seeing Reinhard. The duty manager followed him to the coffee shop, took in the scene and went back to his workstation. At quarter to twelve Gonzo came back out and headed to the lifts. Reinhard joined him there.

'Good morning, Mr Davies.'

'Morning, Reinhard.' Reinhard wore his name on the breast of his suit jacket, but he knew Mr Gonzo Davies had remembered it. He felt pleased.

'May I ask how your meeting went? Well, I hope.'

'No meeting, Reinhard. No meeting.'

'Ah.' The lift arrived and the doors opened. Nobody emerged and Gonzo and Reinhard did not enter. 'May I be permitted to make an observation?' asked Reinhard. Gonzo nodded. 'I could not help but notice where you sat, Mr Davies. At eleven o'clock. It's just that … perhaps it is a coincidence … but there is a man who sometimes sits at that table. But his name is not Mr Guest.'

Gonzo felt a surge of adrenaline, a changing-room flush of excitement, a first upward shift above flatline nothingness since Conrad told him in the Millennium Stadium of Grace's death. 'What is his name?' he said.

'He is called Mr Martin. That is what I hear him called … and this may be an indiscretion … and I should ask you not to turn around, Mr Davies … but there is an Indian gentleman in the coffee shop … and it is he who calls him Mr Martin.' Reinhard withdrew with the very slightest of bows and went back behind the desk.

Ravi was on the phone to Martin when Gonzo came striding towards him. He immediately overheated and sweat coated his brow. 'Dear bloody God, he is coming towards me.' Ravi tried to end the call but the phone was taken from his slippery grasp.

Martin sensed the change at the other end. He did not move a finger; his thumb did not seek to press any button. The faint static of an open line without voices filled the ears at both ends.

'We need to meet,' said Gonzo eventually. He thought he could hear breathing at the other end, but he couldn't be sure – couldn't trust anything he might think. There was no reply, but still he waited.

Martin concentrated hard on keeping his voice steady. He swallowed and took a breath. 'Ravi has something for you,' he said and ended the call.

Ravi had already reached into his jacket and pulled out a slightly damp envelope. Gonzo tore it open. Inside was a plastic red square.

'Mr Gonzo,' said Ravi. 'I am only the bloody messenger. I ask you to respect my right to leave without …'

'Do you know his wife?' asked Gonzo.

Ravi's eyes opened in surprise. 'He has a wife? No, no, I ...'

Gonzo held up the red square. 'What comes next?'

'A taxi,' said Ravi. 'Here, tomorrow night.'

'Don't tell me ...'

'Tell you what?'

'Eleven o'clock, right?' Ravi nodded. 'Go,' said Gonzo.

Ravi did not go to the Red Square Club. Part of him wanted to, to see what Mr Gonzo made of it. Mr Gonzo, the man who made Mr Martin do ... do what? There was no 'do' about it. This Mr Gonzo, he made Mr Martin, full stop. And Ravi was interested in seeing the making of Mr Martin. But another part of Ravi – a bigger part – feared Mr Gonzo. Never mind the making of a man, Ravi sensed that there was a lot of unmaking in this desert drama and that nobody would unmake anything – or anybody, like poor bloody Ravi – quite as well as Mr Gonzo. Not even Mr Martin, or at least not Mr Martin on his own. He would need help, which brought Ravi back into the equation and Ravi had sweated quite enough on this deal already. No bloody commission on this deal. So poor bloody Ravi kept his distance from the Red Square Club.

And Martin stayed away too. He had been right. He did not need it any more. Killing Grace had brought him back to life and keeping Gonzo Davies alive was feeding him. Or Gonzo's suffering was his sustenance. Martin had recovered from the slight shock of losing absolute control of his puppet theatre – of having to speak to Gonzo and present the red square before Martin had extracted every last drop of pleasure from his loneliness – and now it was time to bring the chapter to its end. He phoned Ravi, to tell him that he expected regular live updates from the club, but Ravi did not answer.

Gonzo reached the club at midnight and knocked on the door. The peephole opened. Gonzo stared back and the peephole closed. He knocked again and held up the plastic square. The door opened and he went inside. He stood at the bar and drank vodka and watched the floorshow. Three players took to the dais, and three clicks kept them alive. Gonzo felt nothing. He sensed the humour of Martin Guest in all this and knew he had been played. He returned to the hotel and asked to check out. Reinhard was just coming on duty. He took the credit card and prepared the bill, noting that Gonzo had put nothing on his room in any of the bars or restaurants, except cups of tea in the coffee shop. He had bought two shirts and some underwear from the hotel shop. Otherwise he had slept on his bed and eaten room service on it. Gonzo didn't even glance at the bill before putting in the PIN, 8914.

'It has been an honour to see you again, Mr Davies. Please come again soon,' he said. With great deliberation he handed back the card. 'If I may be so bold, how is Mrs Grace? I remember her so well.'

'She died, Reinhard,' said Gonzo.

He returned to the village via a 250-mile detour to Aberporth. Frank's house on the cliff was empty. Gonzo went to the stables and was told breathlessly by Elspeth, a 16-year-old from the Cardiganshire village that it was the chance of a lifetime – what she'd always dreamed of – to be put in charge of her own yard. Where was Marlene? Gone. Didn't know when she'd be back. The girl was sorry she couldn't be of more help – or even to stop to chat more.

'Although,' said Elspeth, 'it was kind of weird. Not Marlene, mind you – because I never saw her. But her husband, Frank. Never had much to do with him really. I saw him here a couple of times when I was mucking out, but it wasn't like he was a horsey kind of bloke. But it was Frank who came and made the offer. Did I want to look after the horses? As in, for keeps.' Elspeth paused and scratched at the ground with her shovel. 'Of course, I said yes there and then. And he said – and this is the strange bit: "That's the right answer, Elspeth." I can see him standing here now. Let's see if I can get it right now, what he said. "Because otherwise, they'd all be legs up in the field, cooking. Burgers-to-go." Kind of odd, right? And then he was gone. Haven't seen them since.' Anyway, if Elspeth could be excused, there was so much to do. She had to get on.

15

The turn of the year in the village came not with a meteorological miracle – a burst of January warmth that would have allowed construction work to begin – but it did bring planning news. The redevelopment of the land around the mine for the cycling centre and lido seemed to chime with a fresh push for leisure and sport improvements. The Welsh Assembly, as if in the full flush of a New Year's resolution to embrace fitness, made money available, especially in 'areas of multi-generational economic stagnation', a phrase underlined by the Professor and used in all his correspondence. Furthermore, a new European stream of grant money came on line, as long as a suitable partner could be found, at which point a Franco-Spanish consortium, that had built aqua parks and 'waterworlds of wonder' along the Mediterranean coast and had recently collaborated with the Irish government on a successful joint-venture in Kildare, suddenly appeared in the uplands of South Wales. These pioneers from their company headquarters in Barcelona did not seem put off by the lack of a sea and they even joked before the Tourism Committee at the Senedd that they were amazed to find that Britain and Ireland were not actually in the Arctic Circle. In truth, the seed money on offer had melted the chill of their resistance, and it would be all systems go in the village as soon as – and here was the little irony, they admitted – the weather permitted. The finished product would be weatherproof, but to begin work the developers needed a little help from the skies above. Still, it was good news and the Professor was kept almost too busy in the Shard to give his full attention to matters on the rugby pitch next door.

There was more good news. So generous were the pledges of start-up money from Brussels, allied to the long-term investment from the consortium in Barcelona, that the Assembly money could be devoted to the restoration and development of the Miners' Institute. There was no need for anything more than a token contribution from the locals – from the Professor, that is. Or, strictly speaking, from Martin Guest. Once commissioned, the project was too grandiose for Capper and Gonzo's building company – the company that comprised the two of them and Our Marnie – but there was so much sub-contracted work that Capper was soon being paid to carry out work on a building he had maintained for free most of his life. It felt strange to be stripping out the furnace in the basement and knocking out the sash windows that they had lovingly kept going, but work was work and the end product, the centrepiece of inner-village regeneration, was all that counted.

The Professor was busy by day, but the rugby club too was on the move and he was excited by what was happening there. Ragwort came back in January, declaring that full-time professional rugby was not for him. In fact, he'd been playing very well in Newport, but only in small portions of games off the replacements' bench and for the development team. This apprenticeship in the professional game fitted ill with the rather swifter career path Cinnabar had planned for her man. She declared she was finding it hard to settle in Newport, responding to the counter-argument that they were only twenty miles from home by declaring: 'Exactly. That's exactly how it is in Wales.' She persuaded Ragwort that they needed to bargain collectively – that it would sound more persuasive if they both missed home. They moved back into the Orphanage, Ragwort agreed that it was good to see everyone and Kitty had a full house to run.

She soon had to find room for an extra occupant. Ragwort brought with him from the region a cast-off by the name of

Bendigeidfran Jones – at least, that was what it said on his birth certificate. Nobody had ever called him Bendigeidfran. He had been known, ever since he emerged as an 11-pound baby from his poor mother's loins, as Whopper Jones. He was from Bethesda in North Wales and had been sent south to seek his fortune in rugby. He was twenty years old, spoke less English than the four non-English speaking imports at the region put together and longed for Llyn Ogwen and the mountains of home.

Somehow, little Ragwort and Whopper had hit it off in Newport, perhaps through all the time they spent together on the replacements' bench. Even though it was a friendship no more than a few weeks old, it was clear that if Ragwort went, Whopper might go too. As in, go in the head. And then somebody on the coaching staff suggested that if Ragwort was going back to the village, it might not be a bad idea to send Whopper with him, to give him some game-time and put him under the tutelage of Gonzo Davies. The region hadn't been able to prise Gonzo back into serious rugby; perhaps they could go to the mountain, or at least send Whopper there, to be mentored. And so it was that the village had a new recruit, and he in turn had a mountain and – even if the Keeper's Pond wasn't exactly Llyn Ogwen – a lake to remind him of home. Kitty laid out a mattress in the living room, built an extension of cushions for the overhang of the newcomer's feet and ankles, and stocked up with food, trebling the provisions now that rugby was back in the Orphanage.

Whopper had all the game-time he needed in his first couple of weeks. He played instead of Gonzo. It wasn't that

Gonzo had shrunk into semi-darkness, the half-light that he had once made his home. He used to lie in that penumbra, oppressed by it but grateful to it for not triggering one of his blinding headaches, safe in the invisibility where it didn't matter if he saw two of everything. Twice nothing was still nothing. Gonzo wasn't hidden away now. He came out into the light of the village's reawakening, to work by day with Capper at the Institute. Head down, he got on with it. But he couldn't be stirred out of the emptiness that had come home with him from Dubai, a desolation that hadn't been eased by violence in Aberporth. There had been no frank exchange with Frank. No bloodletting. No relief. Emptiness in Dubai; emptiness in Aberporth. Two times empty was nothing. He worked by day and he worked by night at the cottage. Double shifts. Two times work was something. Something was not thinking of Grace. He couldn't think of Grace. Nothing could stop him thinking of Grace. A thousand times nothing. Still nothing. He worked on.

It was Whopper who finally lured him one training night to the rugby ground. It was Capper who literally pulled Gonzo there. Capper stood up on the top floor of the Miners' Institute at the end of work and stopped Gonzo leaving for the cottage.

'The fuckin' kid needs your help. So come on.'

An hour later, Gonzo was talking to Whopper about where he should go from a scrum on this side of the field; where he might go if, say, Ragwort was going to cut into midfield from his wing on that side. Ten minutes later, Gonzo said he would provide token opposition, to check Whopper's body position going into a ruck. Token opposition turned into a full-scale wrestle and all the other forwards piled in. Gonzo was back. They threw themselves at him. And then all the backs joined in. The session ended in a huge pile of wriggling bodies, with Capper standing on top, jumping up and down. There was the sound of applause from the stand and Capper turned round to see Max.

'Penalty against you for stamping, Capper 'Arris,' shouted the Frenchman.

Paris Max had qualified for the European Champions Cup as the lowliest of France's seven participating clubs. Even the process of making it to the start line had been arduous. They had had to win a play-off against Gloucester to take their place in the 20-team competition, and had done so largely because the English club ended the home tie with thirteen players on the field – one in the sin bin and one shown a straight red for a headbutt – and Paris Max had scraped through 28-27 on aggregate. But there they were, in the elite competition, keeping the company of the top clubs, provinces and regions of France, England, Ireland, Wales, Scotland and Italy. As the bottom-seeded French participant, they found themselves drawn in a pool containing Leinster of Ireland, Bath of England and the perennial giants of their own country, Toulouse. The media had been quick to point out that in such an illustrious group, Paris Max stood out like a hobo on millionaires' row – the patched-up bankrupts in a group of former European champions.

Of their three home games, they won two and lost to Leinster. They lost on the road in Toulouse and in Bath and went into their last game in Dublin knowing that it was mathematically possible to progress, but highly unlikely. On a day of bizarre results elsewhere – there were three drawn matches in a sport where the tied result was a rarity – the mathematical complexities were simplified. A victory for Paris Max against Leinster at the Royal Dublin Showgrounds would usher *Le Max* into the last eight. Leinster had already qualified – and in such convincing style that with this sixth round still to go, they were already guaranteed, as one of the teams with most points, home advantage in the quarter-finals. On a day of Irish rain and high winds off Dublin Bay, the French visitors won 6-5 in a game described by the *Irish Times* as 'the most unwatchable of all time'. One try, the result of a charged-down clearance, against two wobbling penalties. Other newspapers were even less generous with their praise. Since Paris Max's advance was at the expense of Harlequins of London, there was a suggestion in the English press of a Franco-Irish stitch-up. That Leinster had colluded in order to have a weaker foe in the last eight, rather than a serious contender.

Only in *L'Equipe* and *Midi Olympique* was their any real praise for the plucky spirit of the resurrected club. If the English thought there was a stitch-up, they should count the stitches in the Paris Max changing room. Noa Diawara had split open the wound he had suffered in Dubai and five other players had required sutures. Four more had reported unfit for duty two days after the Dublin encounter, with injuries ranging from heavy bruising to a hyper-extended knee. If this was collusion, then it was a very expensive way to cheat.

The knee injury was suffered by Didier Palmier, who was

already a stand-in at number 8 for Mike Newent, a veteran Australian who had broken his fibula in December. This meant that Paris Max were generally compromised and severely depleted in particular in the back row. The rules of the Champions' Cup allowed clubs that had qualified for the knockout stages of competition to nominate up to three supplementary players for registration. Such a player in English tended to be called simply 'additional'. In French he was *le joker médical* and Max was in Wales to see if Gonzo would agree to be this joker in the French pack, and to be reunited with himself and Noa – the Barbarian trio, together again.

Gonzo flatly refused. He crawled out of the bottom of the human waste tip on his village pitch and embraced Max and listened to what he had to say and thanked him. And said no. There was too much to do. There was Whopper to guide, there was work to do, there was an orphanage to run and a cottage to finish. He didn't say it but there was Grace to mourn. There was Martin …

One by one the players extracted themselves from their pile-up and they, too, listened. And one by one, led by Capper and then the Professor, they filed past Gonzo and told him to go. Go to Paris. On one last adventure. Gonzo's last mission. We're going nowhere; we'll be here when you get back. What would Grace say? Of course you must go. Only one player remained at the end.

'Whopper doesn't want you to go,' said Daff.

'No,' said Whopper, the last in line. 'That's not strictly true – not true at all – because I want you to go so that I can make you proud of me.' It was the longest sentence Whopper had strung together in all his time in South Wales. The players all looked at each other.

'Anybody else not get a fuckin' word of that?' asked Capper. 'What did he say, Max?' Max shook his head.

'He said what you all said,' said Gonzo.

'And so?' said Max.

'So, I'll go,' said Gonzo.

The Welsh press did not take kindly to this news item which they shaped into a paragraph or two on the inside back pages. Gonzo's desertion, they called it. They quoted the regional coaches who had half-heartedly courted him after his game against New Zealand and who now questioned Gonzo's loyalty to his homeland. Not just now, but over the years. Where had he been? No wonder they couldn't get youngsters to commit, if this was the sort of example set by an old dog of the game. A few letters to the same newspapers asked the rugby correspondents who had filed the quotes if they were for real, and the journalists, sensing that they had been manipulated by the coaches in an attempt to explain away another season of Welsh disappointment in Europe, ended up taking an ironic dig at themselves. Why would Gonzo Davies ever choose to go to Paris? Answer: it's Paris. They showed a picture of Max Ferry and his wife, Perrine, dressed up for a night out. It's Dior. They showed Noa Diawara in full flight. It's Noa. Better to play with him than against him.

The less bitter approach won the day and Gonzo was sent to the continent with a smattering of good wishes. He was back within a week. Paris Max required him solely as cover in the European Champions Cup whose knockout stages would not start until April. As the eighth-placed qualifier, they would play the number one team, Clermont Auvergne, in their Stade Marcel Michelin in Clermont-Ferrand. This team, packed not with mercenaries but with the meanest, hungriest trophy-seekers in the world game, a collective that had accumulated even more points than Leinster by consuming all in the qualification rounds, would be unleashed before their fanatical supporters in their mountain rugby fortress – against the team that had scraped through. Gonzo was a sort of fill-in on what looked very much like a one-match contract.

Paris Max were welcoming and appreciative, but they had to be realistic. They gave Gonzo a medical so cursory it hardly required a doctor. They said that he came with the endorsement of Max and Noa, and that would do. The coach, Jean Lalanne, shook his hand and the rest of the squad – or what remained of its 38 starters – introduced themselves and they all said they would do their best to integrate him within their systems. But not right now. Gonzo was told that with the Six Nations set to fill February and March, he did not have to report for duty with his new club until a fortnight before the Clermont game.

Perrine at least looked on the bright side. She promised him that she would find him a little apartment of his own by the time he returned. 'But not for one match, like they are all saying,' she said. 'But for three months. Two months of rugby and one month to live like a normal human being in the city of light.'

In the meantime, she insisted he stay with them in their flat in the 6th arrondissement – the old left-bank neighbourhood that was boisterous enough for her husband, she said, and quiet enough for her. She cooked for four and three did all the talking. Gonzo made Noa sound like a chatterbox, although he did eventually give them a brief account of his second trip to Dubai. Max wondered if the decision he had made – and it was very much his decision as club captain – to reach out to Gonzo had been wise.

He trained lightly with Paris Max for five days, an introduction to an alien rugby culture, but he was not included in the team routines. There were fixtures to play in France's Top 14 programme between January and April and the club would have to soldier on with their existing squad. Gonzo was not registered for domestic duty and Noa was resting his eye. Max alone of their trio played on, but he would soon be on duty with France in the Six Nations. On the last morning, as Gonzo was thanking Perrine for her hospitality, he made her a promise – that when he returned, he would be more like a normal human being.

He couldn't play in France and he couldn't play at home in Wales now. Paris Max were sorry but the retainer they were paying Gonzo came with a clause making him exclusive to them. For a club supposedly rising precariously from insolvency, the money was serious – enough for Gonzo to finish the cottage without using Grace's credit card again. He set about the task with determination, working there on Sundays and on midweek nights when there was no training. He worked until he slept, usually falling into the one-armed chair downstairs because he was not ready to breathe in the scent of Grace on either of the two mattresses upstairs.

On match days in the village, he stood with the Professor on the touchline and they shared observations on Ragwort and Whopper in particular. The team were doing well in the league, sometimes playing twice a week to overcome the backlog created by the inactivity before Christmas. Without exactly telling the electricity company the true extent of the extra load, Capper boosted the training lights at the ground to make these additional games playable at night. Like the luminosity of the bulbs, the club's name rose.

'Have you seen the league table?' said Buddleia after the second floodlit win of January. 'We'll be in danger of being promoted if we carry on like this.'

It was not a given that going up a division was in the village's interests. There were criteria applied to every next tier up in the Welsh rugby pyramid. Improved standards were expected in almost every aspect of a rugby club's life, especially when it came to the playing and medical facilities – but also relating to what the Welsh Rugby Union's handbook called 'norms of spectator behaviour'. Perhaps it was the thought of trying to gag Meg and Annie in the stand that made the club baulk at the thought of going to a higher place.

Doubts about their appropriate place in the league pyramid were put on hold in the last week of January. The village were to play on the final Sunday of the month – never a day set aside in their annals for action, but a place reserved now for them, and as the defending champions no less – in the first round proper of the Babcock Cup. They had an away draw against a team from six valleys over to the west. Ragwort was available but Whopper was cup-tied, having been registered to play with a lower-league Newport club, one of the official feeder clubs to the region, while on an earlier loan deal. It was a complicated system, especially since Whopper had never played for his loan club, and Capper was prepared to run the risk of selecting him and pleading ignorance should their selection of an ineligible player be exposed. The Professor was having none of it.

'Capper, we have to abide by the rules,' he said. 'It's the very essence of the game.'

'Not in my position, it's not,' said Capper. 'We cheat like fuck in the front row. Pardon my Welsh, Whopper.'

'I would be caught,' said Whopper. 'I come from a very unlucky family. It's not like you can hide me. I'm a big man. And the Professor is right. Or rather, it is wrong. I don't want to cheat.'

'This club is going to the dogs,' said Capper. 'Fair play will be the end of us.'

The game was to be televised live on S4C, who had bought the rights for the last Babcock Cup final and seemed to have taken an option for the entire competition for the next three seasons. The Welsh-language television service were slightly disappointed that Bendigeidfran Jones, the only mother-tongue Welsh-speaker in the village, was not allowed to play, but as a pre-match feature he was asked to give his impressions of his new club. Unleashed in his own language, Whopper was unstoppable. He introduced the team solely by their nicknames, translating all the Children – Y Plant – into Welsh. Moss was Mwsogl; Buddleia, Coed Mêl.

'You're young,' said Eleri Catrin, S4C's touchline reporter on match days and presenter of features. 'What are you called?'

'I imagine it would be something like Efwr Enfawr,' he said in Welsh. Eleri was standing on a crate but she was still a foot shorter than the player she was interviewing. She looked blank. 'Giant Hogweed,' he said in English. 'But I don't think that would roll off the tongue down here. They call me Whopper, Eleri.'

In the light of his performance in front of camera on the last night of training, he was asked if he would like to be the co-commentator for the match. Whopper declined, saying it was his duty to be with the team even if he could not play. He had known them only a short time, but they were his family – and Sunday was family day.

Without Gonzo and Whopper, it was also a day of defeat. The cup-holders went down defiantly – Tulip from the losing side was named the Babcock man of the match – but they were never allowed to flow. It was a scrappy, frustrating affair and during the live transmission the commentators had to apologise three times for any bad language that might cause offence. It wasn't always Capper to blame for imprecations captured on the referee's microphone. More often, the offensive language was picked up on the effects' microphones pointed at the crowd. In the highlights programme later that night there were twelve bleeps inserted into one eight-second tirade aimed by a screaming Meg at the referee. Half her words were censored, which the production team at S4C believed to be a record – at least in English. Meg didn't think it was even a personal best.

Far from dampening spirits for the remaining three months of the season, the defeat concentrated the minds of the club on the league. They decided to set aside their doubts about meeting all the promotion criteria and go for it. If they finished first and didn't have a defibrillator in the medical room, or if they couldn't persuade Capper to return the back-up generator to its rightful place in the stand, or if they couldn't promise to find stewards with the moral fibre to tell Meg and Annie to mind their language and show some respect for the referee, then they could always decline the invitation to go up and stay where they were. For the moment they would enjoy the ride.

February and March became a blend of improving their standing on the field and supporting Wales on the grand stage of the Six Nations. The village performed admirably on both fronts, going six league matches unbeaten home and away, and supplementing three trips – Owain Owens specials – to the Millennium Stadium in Cardiff with a trip to Lansdowne Road in Dublin. Wales were less successful on the field than the village were on tour. They lost in Dublin and they lost in Paris to France to finish in third place, one place above the French who had an equally taxing Six Nations campaign, during which they lost to England and Ireland and demoted Max Ferry to the bench for the last game in Italy.

On the village's return from Dublin, Ragwort took to his bed for three days and Cinnabar threatened to terminate his association with the club. After he staggered up to the door of the Orphanage on the Monday after the mini-tour to Ireland, missing an eyebrow and with a precisely measured half of his head of hair shaved off, she screamed at Capper: 'You're animals.'

'We'll take that as a compliment,' said Capper, quickly realising that Cinnabar was not in the mood. She pulled her Ragwort into the house. 'Mind the …' said Capper as she slammed the entrance to the Orphanage in his face, ' … door.'

Whopper came home with his entire face covered in an intricate lacework of henna. 'Celtic filigree,' said Capper as he delivered his next victim back to the Orphanage. Kitty stood at the door this time. She looked at Capper reprovingly as she gently closed the door on him and took Whopper to the bathroom. The tattoo would disappear, but not for a week. He declared himself unavailable for any work on S4C and was called Hiawhopper until the dye turned yellow and then faded altogether.

In that time, Gonzo kept him hard at work. The green light for construction and conversion had been given and the village was teeming with hard hats and heavy vehicles. Whopper laboured on site at the Institute by day, a huge insect clambering up and down the scaffolding that now covered the building, and went training with his mentor at lunchtime and again after work, a pair of tiny ants working their way up to the skyline. Gonzo did not go to Cardiff or Dublin to support Wales. He stayed at home and worked. And he ran. If he was about to be a one-game wonder in France then he was going to do everything he could to make it memorable. Besides, running and training made him tired and if he was tired he slept. And in the sleep of the exhausted he did not dream. He ran and he no longer fell into the chair downstairs but took to his bed – their bed. The bed whose scent he would make himself too tired to notice.

Our Marnie and John kept Gonzo and Whopper well nourished. They laughed at the sight of the painted giant running to the Gherkin off the moor, the young St Bernard, fully grown but still not entirely in control of his limbs, bounding after his master, and then sitting down at his side eating the same food, lapping up every word. They laughed, but every day that Whopper absorbed the advice and hardened his physique the better he became. Gonzo-Lite was fast becoming Gonzo the Second. And as for Gonzo the First, he too felt the benefits of the hard work, the satisfaction of teaching, of seeing words turn into thumping reality on the field as Whopper developed. At the same time, he felt the frustration of having to wait for his own turn. But at least he was feeling again. And feeling was something. Something could be multiplied, to make a life.

In his apartment in Dubai, Martin stared at the desert. He had stopped going to the coffee shop in the morning because there was no Ravi any more. He thought he had seen the Indian driving past one day, but he had not been sure. Ravi had perhaps gone back to Mumbai. Martin stared at the list of contacts on his mobile phone, found K for Kala and deleted the name and number. With the disappearance of the Indian, his list was half empty. And then fully empty. Martin paused. Fully empty – what an odd combination. Like Martin and Ravi. Like Martin and Frank. He'd tried to call Frank, but it seemed Frank's phone was out of service.

He found F in Favourites on his phone. Pressed Edit and Favourite Frank was gone.

He could start again. Drivers were two a penny. Would he ever need a car again? An associate? He could easily rescue another businessman being fleeced. Offer a bit of advice that would tease a deal towards a conclusion. He knew the best listening posts in the hotels where commerce was the small talk, the big talk – the only talk. He could sidle up to enough people of influence who might appreciate the view of a man removed from the heat of the debate, a man a step back. He could help. He didn't want to help. He wanted to know how Gonzo Davies was suffering. He thought about going to the Red Square, but he knew that to present oneself as a member without a token – to be a member that had given away his membership, as Martin had to Gonzo – was to be condemned to being abandoned to those that waited in the shadows of Sonapur. There was only one way to return the red square with honour …

Martin thought about entering Sonapur as a shadow in his own right. He could lurk with the shadiest of them. But he would not find Gonzo Davies there. And no other fuel would do. Martin stared over the sands of the desert and thought about oil and burning and how badly he needed to know that Gonzo Davies was still suffering.

16

Before he went to France, Gonzo attended a meeting with the Professor, Capper and half a dozen senior representatives of the company responsible for the ground works at the mine. Spring was in the air, the schedule was tight and there was a need to press on, said the men in suits in the Shard. Would the rugby club be agreeable to site-clearance being initiated – as with immediate effect? The cycling circuit could be cleared first and the Lewises of the Graig Club had already said that they were prepared to make the sacrifice for the long-term reward. Would the rugby club be equally amenable? There was an additional pressure on the time frame since another group of engineers, coincidentally surveying the deserted buildings up on West Street, had decided that although the subsidence itself had not worsened, the housing stock was beyond repair and increasingly unsafe. In their estimation, the sooner a general programme of clearance could be ordered, the better for all concerned. Capper and Our Marnie were to be evicted from the old clubhouse. Bulldozed from their bed. The engineers in the Shard explained that as luck would have it – and this use of the word 'luck' made Gonzo suspect a stitch-up – the West Street rubble would serve as hard core on the site of the mine, where it was anticipated all sorts of problems – to do with levels and workings not clearly marked on their historical site-plans – would soon be exposed beneath the crust of grey waste. In short, everybody with a big machine wanted to start clearing as soon as possible.

Gonzo waited for Capper to raise an objection to his eviction. The compensation for the rugby club – where 'luck' applied to them and the Graig cyclists – was that they were going to end up with a brand new linked arena at the mine and a shared clubhouse at the Institute, all for nothing. Somehow they had ended up as a 'planning gain' from all the negotiations that had gone into making the village a guinea pig in 'multi-faceted regeneration', as the engineers put it. But it would leave Capper and Our Marnie homeless, a prospect that seemed not to have struck him yet. He was staring out of the window of the Shard at the nearby rugby stand.

'You know on our trip to Dublin, Professor …'

'I wasn't there, Capper.'

'Right. But you know Dublin … you being the Professor an' all … '

'Well, I suppose … '

'Well, before we went to the Aviva, Mystic and Blossom and me, we went to the other one. Croke Park. Just to have a look. And there's a terrace there … what's it called?

'Hill 16.'

'That's it. Built from the rubble of the Easter Uprising in 1916.'

'Very good, Capper,' said Gonzo, conscious that the engineers were looking a little worried. 'But …?'

'Well,' continued Capper, 'if we build the new stand on the rubble of West Street, can we call it the West Stand?'

'Strictly speaking,' said the head engineer, 'it'll be a North Stand.'

'See, that's what I was thinking. So, tell me … if we twist the pitch a bit – you know, like they did with the Millennium Stadium – only not so far, 'cos obviously we wouldn't want to be copy-cats or anything, like … but if we move it a bit and stick the stand down the new side, it could be the North-West Stand?'

The engineers looked at him in bemusement. Capper suddenly slapped the table. 'Only joking, lads,' he said. 'I say we go for it. We'll kip down at the Orphanage till the flat in the Institute is ready. Aye, let's do it. As I've been trying to tell this lot for ages, this place is long overdue some multi-fuckin'-faceted regeneration.'

There was a problem at the Orphanage with space. Four bedrooms were already occupied by Dario, Ragwort and Cinnabar, John and the Professor, and Kitty. Whopper had already overflowed into the living room. The problem was solved when Dario went to watch the machines preparing to start work at the mine. He realised that the very first act was to remove the Shard and the Gherkin. With a cry of anguish he hobbled in and out of the heavy plant and their diesel fumes and pressed himself up against his beloved caravan. Before a prong of a mechanical digger had penetrated the grey crust, before a bucket of waste had been raised, work was brought to a halt. By lunchtime, the Gherkin had been patiently taken by low-loader and repositioned on the driveway of the Orphanage. One rounded end protruded, like Whopper's feet off his mattress, into the street. By tea-time, the long-suffering engineers from the utility companies had made power and water connections, and by midnight, Dario was back in his old home, curled up on the sofa, out of earshot of Cinnabar. Now, within range of her ongoing interrogation of Ragwort, who had not been able to furnish her with an explanation of how the only two players with any sort of future in the game had been subjected to such humiliation, was Whopper. His painted face lay easy on his pillow and even more of his giant feet and white ankles hung over the end of the bed in Dario's old room.

For half the following day, the Professor toyed with the idea of offering the Shard to Our Marnie and Capper. It too had to go. Fortunately, the matter of re-housing the tenants of the old clubhouse was already in hand. Our Marnie, hearing of their imminent homelessness, had struck a deal with the demolition squad of West Street and the refurbishers of the Institute. If those engaged in bringing down one section of the village started at the far end, she reckoned that with a concentrated burst by those rebuilding another part of it, they would be able to go from West Street to the Miner's Institute without having to expose Kitty's pristine home to Capper's strange habits. She wouldn't have to ask Gonzo to let them be the first to sleep in the cottage, to which he was putting, with an obsessive attention to detail, the finishing touches. Even Capper thought it would be too weird for words to move into the house that Gonzo was still building for Grace.

The demolition crew on West Street also ran into a protest that brought their machinery to a halt. Job-shy Capaldi sat on the remains of his collapsed front wall at number 13 and refused to budge. In the end he was persuaded to come down and meet the overall project manager, who for the umpteenth time explained about compensation and appeals procedures that had been observed and compulsory orders that were binding and told Job-shy that the Capaldis would be far from destitute. Job-shy knew all this. He was just fully-paid-up awkward. The manager asked him what it would take for him to leave, to which Job-shy gave a simple answer. 'This place,' he said. 'I loves it.'

And so the Shard was relocated, too, to a flat patch of ground on the edge of the moor, just beyond the subsidence exclusion zone. Without having to be asked, the power and water engineers sighed and made their connections and the Shard lived on, its walls still tilting slightly one way and its stovepipe chimney leaning the other. By day, Job-shy helped his wife, Francesca, make the Shard their home on the inside. By night he returned to West Street, salvaging and reclaiming. Soon he had a new front wall, a completed project to welcome in a new spring. And then three more walls. And within these four walls he grew a garden – or transplanted one, selecting the most verdant and thriving of the shrubs and plants from all the abandoned back gardens of West Street. He relocated the best bits of the decking laid only last summer by the Williamses at number 18 with the fancier design of the Evanses in 17 around the Joneses' pond from 16, and from his new vantage point overlooking the wilderness, Job-shy could watch the streets being pounded by heavy vehicles going up and down between the mine and West Street. The whole village was vanishing into giant clouds of dust. From below, rose the fine grey particles of mine waste, and into them sank the heavy brown powder from demolished bricks and mortar. In Job-shy's eyes – that saw only burgeoning beauty in his haven – the village, this experiment in post-industrial regeneration, had never been dirtier.

*

Gonzo caught a plane from Cardiff to Charles de Gaulle Airport in Paris. Following emailed instructions from Perrine, he dared put some euros into a ticket machine for the RER train to Saint Michel-Notre Dame. He had his kit and enough clothes for four days, folded not very carefully into a single bag. On board the Line B train, he watched the Stade de France go past and felt memories stir – of the Game of the Century, which now seemed like a full century ago. A quarter of an hour later, he stepped up into the warm late-March air of central Paris. He stood on the pavement for a few seconds, assailed by sounds familiar to a player that had once lived in a city, and yet so different from anything he had ever heard. The traffic din was different, the sirens were different, the language was different. He felt a lurch into futility. What did he think he was trying to be or do? And then he stood his ground. This was home, he told himself, somewhere around here, off the Boulevard Saint-Michel. Be brave. Take the plunge. He stood for only a few seconds, because Capper, who viewed life in a big French city through Welsh eyes narrowed against the glare, had told him that if he dawdled he would be robbed of everything in seconds flat.

On his first visit to Paris, he had been driven by car to Max and Perrine's flat, but now he set out to find it on foot and by phone. It didn't take long and he was surprised how quickly the sound of the city faded with even a single turn off the main streets. Two lefts and a right after the Jardin du Luxembourg and he was on his own, Paris reduced to a background rumble. He found number 58, climbed the stairs to the second floor and rang the bell of apartment 4.

'Good directions,' he said when Perrine opened the door.

She had known he was coming and hadn't gone to lengths that she would have described as great to greet him. Those were reserved for her star-nights out with Max, occasions when she entered, despite her frequent denials that she would ever stoop to such a thing, the competitive world of not being upstaged by the wives and girlfriends of other players. Perrine was a bit older than Max, who was 28. He had had a tough time playing for France in the Six Nations, too conspicuous with his blonde hair to go unnoticed through a campaign that had been by their own analysis insipid. The hunt was on for a scapegoat. Noa was absolved of any blame, universally decreed 'noble' in every game; Max was described as 'worn out' by *Midi Olympique*, and 'bedraggled' by *L'Equipe*. Noa had been the complete player; Max was a little bit of this and a little bit of that and not much to shout about. He had been put on the bench for the last game in Italy, but instead of emerging rested from the demotion, he looked careworn. The Clermont forward, Brice Moreau, who took his place, had played outstandingly in Rome and both the press and Perrine wondered how many more star-nights in high Parisian society there would be for Max Ferry and his wife.

But if Perrine hadn't gone through a full routine, she had made an effort for Gonzo, if only to try to disguise what she saw in the mirror as chronic fatigue. And she wished she had done more.

'My God,' she said. 'You look fabulous, Gonzo Davies.'

She showed him to his small flat three streets away and ordered him to open his bag and reveal its contents. With a snort of disgust she pushed him back out of the flat and took him to the shops. They emerged two hours later with a wardrobe that would at least, according to Perrine, not have him 'arrested as a vagrant.' They went back to her flat and waited, the gaps in their conversation growing longer as the evening progressed and there was no sign of Max.

'Now you know why I look like shit,' said Perrine eventually. 'For one month he has been doing this to me. I don't …'

The doorbell rang. It was Noa. Gonzo caught him shaking his head at Perrine before he smiled and embraced Gonzo. 'Hey,' he said, squeezing Gonzo's shoulders, 'you are ready for battle, I can tell.'

'Do you know where he is?' asked Perrine. Noa hesitated. He looked at Gonzo and nodded. 'Let's go and get him,' said Gonzo.

Noa walked quickly to the doorway of a club five minutes away and stopped. There were two heavies under a flimsy porch, guardians beneath illuminated letters that should have told them that they were at La Crimée Club. The worn letters and missing lightbulbs made it look more like Crime Club. The bouncers would not let Noa in. It seemed they had had this conversation before and Gonzo was surprised at how the noble Noa was strangely cowed by this overt discrimination. Gonzo was permitted to enter, although he was patted down first and told to pay one hundred euros. He went down into a cellar bar of velvet and shadows. Max was draped between two women who turned out, after Gonzo gave him a slap and told him they were leaving, to be men carrying knives. Gonzo held up his hands and backed away.

He ran up the stairs and went to Noa who was waiting on the opposite side of the street, twenty paces away.

'The reunion starts here, Noa,' he said and turned back towards the heavies. They knew what was coming and gave themselves a little elbow room under the awning. Gonzo burst into a run ten metres from them, aiming first for the one whose hand was slipping inside his jacket. He jabbed him in the eye with his left index finger and kicked the second heavy as hard as he could between the legs. The first squealed and the second doubled over. Gonzo pulled him upright and headbutted him, throwing him against the first whose hand was again reaching inside his jacket. He then banged their heads together and ran down the steps and into the bar where Noa, with grave distaste, was picking up the knives dropped by the now unconscious escorts. He stuck them in the tabletop. They picked Max off the floor and Noa slung him over his shoulder, allowing Gonzo to lead the way up the stairs, check on the doormen and take back his hundred euros.

Max could remember nothing of the incident the next day. And Noa was not going to say anything. And Gonzo would not have known how to begin to tell the rest of the squad in their own tongue about the state and the rescue of their captain. But there was something about the respect in which Noa in particular held the ancient *Gallois* that seemed to rub off on everybody. Jaded by two defeats away from home in March and hurt by the sneers that so often came their way from all corners of France – and with Max's recent travails on the field seemingly doubled – they were in need of a more loving boost. And Gonzo, fresh and rested, seemed to bring a new energy. It was a start. Jean Lalanne was wise enough to let the recovery be player-led. There was little the coach could do in April, the ninth month of the French season, to introduce new tricks that might outfox Clermont Auvergne. If Paris Max stood a chance – and it would never be anything more than a slim chance – it would be because a desire to play for each other would make them courageously defiant.

Max woke from his stupor. Over lunch that day he sat Noa down and ordered him to tell him what had happened. That night he visited Gonzo in his new flat. 'Gonzo, I …'

It was as far as his apology was allowed to go. 'Max,' interrupted Gonzo. 'We've all been there. To the dark side. It goes with the job. I'd tell you how many rugby players are bi-polar, but it would only … depress you, and I think we need … we need the real Max back.'

'OK. I am going to spend an early night with Perrine and tell her she has very bad taste in men's clothing. But before I go, two words: thank you.'

Coach Jean asked Gonzo to sit with him in the dug-out for the last Top 14 game before the Champions Cup quarter final against Clermont Auvergne. It was a home game against La Rochelle, two mid-table teams squelching through a pitch that had been over-watered on Jean's instructions. He wanted Paris Max to play on a soft cushion. He had picked a team containing as many reserves as possible. He spent a large part of the game talking to Gonzo through Max as interpreter.

'Jean is asking himself this question over and over,' said Max. 'Does he start with you? You do not know the plays.

You do not know the players. He does not know you. You do not know him.' Jean looked at Gonzo and then at Max. Max spoke rapidly in French. 'I have replied for you,' he said to Gonzo. 'I've told him you insist. You will start.' Jean was nodding his head. He spoke again, intensely to Max. 'Jean says this confirms everything he is feeling in his stomach. He says you have made the right decision.' The Paris Max reserves won the game 9-7. 'We are champions of one thing already,' said Max. 'Nobody plays unwatchable rugby like us.'

No sooner had Gonzo started to acclimatise to the hustle and bustle of Paris – of living on the Left Bank and training less glamorously in a tatty concrete bowl in the southern suburbs beyond the Périphérique – than he was on his way back to the mountains. Not the mountains of home, but the volcanic Puys of the Massif Central. Clermont Auvergne sold themselves as the club of the mountains, of clogs and cowbells. Rugby was the chosen sport of the *Auvergnats*, the people of the high plateau. They expected their representatives to play hard everywhere, but they insisted absolutely that the home they shared as players and supporters together – their fortress, their citadel – be defended with unrivalled ferocity. Their record of twenty-six European games without defeat at the Stade Marcel Michelin spoke for itself – but it was about how they won, more than how many. Clermont liked to destroy opponents by subjecting them to unrelenting waves of runners who charged in short bursts and passed as soon as they felt their momentum slacken. Slackening was not generally an approved option at the club, but it was tolerated in this context because it contrasted with – and thus enhanced – the aggression of the next player on the charge. Visiting the tyre city of Clermont-Ferrand as a rugby player was also about surviving the vocal storm of support. To play here was to suffer assaults to the ear and the body.

In the second minute, the ball came to Brice Moreau. The Clermont player who had taken over from Max in the French team was the most dynamic ball-carrier in the team of pumped-up chargers. His first run was always a statement and it always went accompanied by a rising wall of sound – a choral roar with cow-bell accompaniment. Brice took the ball and ran. And Noa, thinking of how he had cowered across the street from La Crimée club, ran by way of repentance at Brice. He ran like Gonzo had run at the doormen. And if Noa could only remember that he could not jab anyone in the eye or kick them between the legs or headbutt them, then his collision was going to be a legitimate counter-statement. Noa's shoulder hit Brice in the solar plexus and his thick arms swept in a scything arc around the ball-carrier's back.

A photo of the moment was printed in the following week's *L'Equipe* magazine. It showed Noa with his feet just off the ground and his ramrod-straight body at a forty-five degree angle, spearing himself into Brice, who was buckling in the middle. Brice's legs were straight and exactly parallel to Noa's body, the studs of his boots visible as he was lifted off the ground. His arms were straight out in front of him too. Four helpless limbs perfectly framed Noa's diagonal thrust. Noa's face was invisible but a look of horror filled Brice's. His gumshield was flying out of his mouth and the ball out of his hands.

The picture editor at *L'Equipe* thought about cropping the picture, to take out the hand of a third party that was reaching for the ball. But he liked his rugby and he remembered the words of Noa after the game. The television commentary team had been reluctant to give the man of the match award to Noa Diawara because he had a history of giving monosyllabic answers in post-match interviews, but he could not be denied and on this occasion he spoke effusively. He told the watching world not about himself, but about the player who had come to Paris Max and made such a victory possible, who had taken a team without confidence and given them hope; a player who himself had been forgotten but who was now making his new club do unforgettable things. Had they never thought they could beat Clermont – and so convincingly in the end? 'Not until he came,' said Noa. What had he done? 'He put us back together,' said Noa. Wasn't it Noa's tackle that was the turning point, the moment when Paris Max found self-belief? 'You must listen to me,' said Noa, his eyes blazing. 'I am nothing. He made us strong. He made us believe.'

The picture editor checked the video footage until he found the exact moment that matched Noa's tackle. He wanted to know who was reaching out for the ball. He edged the footage forward, frame by frame. He did not crop the photo but scribbled a captioning note: 'Suggestion: leave in the hand of Gonzo Davies.'

17

When the coalmine in the village shut half a century ago, it was merely one of so many closures. There was little sentiment attached to the process; the end of work sparked no great search for keepsakes, bar the odd lamp. The pithead winding gear wasn't so much dismantled as pushed over and buried. The price of scrap – with so much available across the South Wales coalfield – did not prompt salvage operations. Recycling wasn't in fashion yet. The mine was gone. Best to shove it over and be done with it.

Gonzo and Capper in their youth had begun to stockpile bits and pieces they found on the site. In fact, what they accumulated became the pile with which they began to build – but they saw themselves as scavengers rather than progressive re-users of materials. And they could only scratch at the surface. When the heavy plant now set about clearing the site for redevelopment, all sorts of relics of the old days were brought to the surface. So much twisted metal came up that it formed a huge pile and the engineers knew they would need every ounce of the rubble and hard core of West Street to fill in the holes and pack the ground. One of the objects that caused a stir was the pithead wheel. Word spread fast that it was on its way out of the grave and the village came down in force, led by the Widowers for whom it was the clearest reminder of what they had been in their prime, to see the disinterment.

At the same time as the past was rising, the Graig cyclists were starting to reappear in force. Their winter lull was over and, with the advance of spring and the lengthening of the days, they were back on the trails and doing the Blaenavon-Brynmawr Flying Five and generally taking to altitude again. The one element to have been removed from their portfolio of events was their speedway. CycleCity had disappeared beneath the diggers. The clearance work seemed however to spur them on to take a greater interest in the village, and each day they assembled, first in small groups and then by the score, simply to stand and watch, waiting for the day when all this would be theirs to enjoy. They all dressed for the occasion, having added a bandana to their list of essential items. The air at the bottom of the village was thick with dust. Capper's Bulldog Bowser had given up the ghost and was back in Beaufort Street, nursing a broken axle. The dust rose and fell, unwatered and untamed. The cyclists all stood and watched with their colourful bandanas covering their mouths. Capper reckoned that if they'd had a bank to rob in the village the police would have about a hundred ready-made suspects. 'Suspicious-looking lot, you cyclists,' he told the Lewises, who were still keeping the rugby changing rooms immaculate. 'Especially you three, the Unrelateds.'

The Unrelated Lewises became very animated at the excavation of the pithead wheel. They dismounted and rushed into the machinery, causing another hold-up. After a lot of arm-waving, the engineers ordered the digger driver to deposit the find not on the great pile of scrap that would soon be bound for China, but on its own on the edge of the site. Capper saw an old bit of mining machinery, rusted and a bit buckled; the Unrelateds saw a bicycle wheel. Within a week it had been taken down to Coleg Gwent, where it became a student project. A fortnight later it reappeared, not perfectly unbuckled – that was not the Lewises' intention – but definitely and very reverentially reworked as a giant rear bike wheel, complete with an abstract set of gears and a length of chain. What had been the symbol of work would now stand as a welcome sign to all cyclists coming to the village. The Widowers were booked to perform a ribbon-cutting opening ceremony when the time was ripe.

Paris Max were to go on the road again, the European Champions Cup semi-final draw having been made before they played Clermont – before they beat Clermont. The 18-9 victory took a bit of time to sink in, not that they had much in which to dwell on the best moment by far in their short history, since they were due to travel to Dublin to play against Munster only a fortnight after defying expectations and reaching the last four. Munster would be travelling up from the south-west of Ireland to the capital, but to play at the Aviva was still country-advantage in their favour – if not quite the same as enjoying true home advantage at Thomond Park, a stadium that would give the Marcel Michelin a run for its money as a rugby madhouse. Dublin wasn't Limerick – or Cork for that matter – but it would still be far enough and loud enough for any French club.

Gonzo travelled meanwhile with the team to Brive for the Top 14 game before the semi-final. Once again, Jean picked as many of his reserves as he could and sat Gonzo by his side and asked him through Max if he should be in the starting team next week against Munster. They all laughed, but it wasn't so funny on the pitch, where Paris Max lost by 20 points. Noa had to play because of an injury crisis in the back row and five minutes after half-time he limped off. Gonzo's heart sank, and sank again because within ten minutes, Max, who had gone on to replace Noa, was also coming off. Max went straight down into the changing rooms where Noa had gone. Jean pointed after them, indicating to Gonzo that he should go the same way. Gonzo found the pair with their feet up and not an ice-pack in sight.

'There are Irish spies here,' said Max. 'Our own spies, that we have sent to Limerick, tell us this.' He slapped Noa on his supposedly bad knee. Noa did not flinch. 'We thought it would be good to give them something to report.'

The village were to play their last home game of the season on the same day as the European Champions Cup semi-final would be played in Dublin. The village would play as usual in the afternoon of this Saturday and Paris Max would kick off in the evening. There were two league rounds to go for the village but such had been their run since Christmas that they could clinch the league title with a game to spare. That is, if they won on the Saturday, they could throw a celebration party. But where? The Gherkin and Shard – the Sherkin – were gone and all the surrounding ground, that had until very recently been large enough to accommodate both CycleCity and the barbecue area, was covered in machinery and mounds of metal and filth, and Keep Out signs. The Miners' Institute would be ready to receive Capper and Our Marnie into their top-floor flat any day, but the new social hub downstairs was weeks away from completion. The Colliers' Arms wasn't a quarter big enough. The old clubhouse stood on its own now on West Street, a double-house bookend with no books to support and a plywood gable-end wall that banged in the wind. The diggers were lined up before it, arms raised, at the ready, a few jabs, a few shoves away from sending it into oblivion, or at least into the holes at the mine.

Capper checked the forecast, which promised dry if not warm weather. He resurrected the barbecues that had been thrown on the scrap pile for China and put them on stand-by around the pitch, which was the only uncluttered area on the whole site. It stood out for its emptiness, not because it was an oasis of green in the midst of all the churned grey. It no longer was, but had turned the colour of all the dust that had floated or been blown its way. A huge order was placed with the micro-brewery that had been opened by two of the Graig cyclists in the old furniture workshop that marked the start – or the end – of the Flying Five in Blaenavon. Finally, Capper had a word with John and the Professor, who had a word with the Leisure and Recreation Officer on the council, who had a word with a cousin of his in Barry. And the day before the final home encounter, a large van snaked its way across the site and a big screen was erected behind the posts at the far end of the ground. The village would be able to watch Gonzo in action live. They wished him luck, prayed the weather would hold and hoped they hadn't been a bit premature in organising a victory party.

Almost as a premonition of what self-control would be required in the league above, first Meg and than Annie received a formal warning from the referee. They were both then red-carded, unable to stop themselves before half-time screaming abuse at him, and sent from the stand. They stood behind the scrap heap – the Chinese takeaway, they called it – and watched in silence as the village nervously edged their way to the title. Standpipe was playing in the back row, a replacement for Buddleia who had been trodden on – accidentally – by Whopper in training. In every position he had played recently, Standpipe had adopted the identity of his Paris Max counterpart. 'Today, I am Noa Diawara,' he had proclaimed when the team was announced. To make sure the opposition were fully alerted to his new persona, Standpipe ran at full speed into a tackle, shouting: 'I am Noa.' Picking up the crumpled heap that was all that was left of the village wing forward, three paces back from where he had made contact, Capper said: 'You're Standpipe fuckin' Dodds, Standpipe, so let's go easy, eh?'

Whopper saved the day by stretching out for a try with an arm that seemed to go from Blaenavon to Brynmawr, and putting the village in the lead for the first time with seven minutes to go. Ragwort, who had had a slightly unfortunate afternoon trying to catch balls coming at him out of the dusty sun, then added a little sheen to the performance by setting off on a solo run in overtime. The rest of his teammates were shouting at him to kick the ball off the park, but he heard only Cinnabar. 'Show them, Ragwort … go on … that's it … show the fuckers,' she screamed. She then froze in her seat, went the colour of the dust off West Street and buried her head in Kitty's shoulder. Kitty stroked her hair and politely applauded Ragwort's effort.

They drank copious amounts of Pedallers Ale from the micro-brewery and settled down to watch Munster-Paris Max on the big screen. The weather over the Aviva Stadium was not good and Capper wondered if the Radio Wales forecast might not have been a little optimistic. He stoked all the barbecue fires and placed them closer together, so that the party would stay warm.

Never before had they seen Gonzo on the receiving end of such treatment, and not just him, but Max and Noa too – perhaps especially Noa. 'You weren't so far off, after all, Standpipe,' said Mystic as Noa painfully got back to his feet after being projected towards his own line. Munster had done their homework. They'd not only worked out that everything without exception in the Parisians' armoury started with the back row, but also how to stop it. They doubled up on the 6, 7 and 8 and hit them wherever they went: on the ball, off the ball, in the air and on the ground. Even when Conor Browne was sin-binned for standing on Max's fingers – not stamping, said the referee, for that would have been a straight red card – Munster imported another player to keep their hit-squad of six fully manned. For fifteen minutes the three victims took their punishment, reeling backward and floundering. And then Gonzo suggested that if three were attracting the attention of half a dozen, it had to mean that elsewhere a full dozen Paris Max players were being looked after by nine of Munster. There had to be room for somebody else. At the very first attempt to relieve the pressure, Arnaud Champs in the centre eased through a gaping hole and scored. Five minutes after that, Georges Sandry scored on the wing.

Munster recalculated and redeployed their markers.

Paris Max's new playmakers were shut down. Not that there was any chance for Max, Noa and Gonzo to retake their customary places in the control seat. To be in control they had to have the ball, but it appeared to have disappeared. Munster swarmed and Paris had no possession and the question of adding to what they had on the board became largely academic. The only question was whether they could hold out with the fourteen points they had managed to accumulate. Munster cranked up the pressure, nibbling away at the lead. They scored three points in the second quarter; seven in the third; three in the first ten minutes of the fourth and last. 14-13 said the scoreboard. Noa made 28 tackles, Max 24 and Gonzo 22. Between them, they made 35 tackles in the last fifteen minutes. There was nothing any of them could do, however, to stop Slab O'Brien working his way into drop-goal range. It was a Munster speciality and Slab – so called by his teammates because they reckoned that if you took his core temperature at the time of greatest tension, he would be no warmer than a body on the slab of the Cork morgue – was its ace practitioner. On countless occasions – the man himself knew it was precisely sixteen – the outside-half had settled a tight game such as this with the last kick, a winning drop goal. He prowled his way from one side of the zone behind the forwards to the other, calmly keeping one eye on the clock and one on his scrum-half and the pack. He waved them onward. He was not ready yet.

Such patience demanded discipline from his forwards, too – not to lose control of the ball, not to let an opponent anywhere near it. But it also had its effect on the Paris Max players, who didn't dare put a toenail out of line for fear of giving away the penalty that would have been even more straightforward for Slab to land than the drop goal. Gonzo buried himself in the throng of forwards, wrestling, pushing but knowing he was helpless. Noa and Max stood on either side of the main clump, inching backwards, not straying offside, waiting to run one more time at Slab and try to charge down his kick. They would go as fast as they could, but they felt helpless too.

Slab suddenly dropped back. He was ready. Little Billy O'Reardan, as he had done on sixteen occasions, prepared to give him the seventeenth pass that would allow him to win another game – a long flat pass, slightly to Slab's right so that he could drop it all the more smoothly onto his right boot. Out went Billy's pass into Slab's hands. He paused for the merest fraction of a second, just to be perfectly balanced. Noa and Max were in full flight but they never got near the ball. It was up and away before they were halfway to their target. Slab struck the ball cleanly. He always did. He turned away, knowing it was good.

It was, until it hit one of the freak swirls of wind in the stadium. The bad weather Capper feared would ruin the celebration in the village came to Gonzo's rescue in Dublin. Slab was still looking away when he heard the unmistakable sound of a rugby ball hitting a steel post. It was a hard bounce and the ball flew back into play. Gonzo was staggering from the maul when it came at him. He caught it with a slight juggle, and as furious hands and arms sought to tear it from him, he dropped it on to his big right boot and thumped it inelegantly straight back at the posts, praying it would not hit them. The ball sailed through the middle and over the dead-ball line. Gonzo could not score with a punt against his own team. The referee blew his whistle and Paris Max were in the final.

A huge cheer went up at the village. *Le Village.* They were all French. The first drops of rain began to fall. There was a huge flash above them and the overloaded floodlights went out, quickly followed by the big screen. Capper tried to remember where he'd put the back-up generator after the supply to Gonzo's cottage had been connected, but the Pedallers seemed to have slowed down his processes.

'Oi, Professor,' he shouted, changing the subject in his head. 'Where's Gonzo's final going to be played? His final fuckin' final fling, like.'

'The Millennium Stadium,' said the Professor. He and John had tears running down their cheeks, so did Our Marnie. The beer had gone down well all round. Kitty was doing a can-can between Meg and Annie on the halfway line. 'He's coming home.'

18

Paris absorbed the news that its one top rugby club had made it to the final of the European Champions Cup without over-excitement. Rugby was a niche sport in the capital, which partly explained why a city so large had been unable to sustain two professional outfits. The victory over Munster was fêted on the Sunday in the media and followed up on the Monday, but after that brief stay in the spotlight, Paris Max were due to slip out of the news and be left to their own preparations for a week. In the days before the final in Cardiff there would no doubt be renewed interest, especially as the encounter pitched Paris against London – *Le Max* against Saracens – but for the moment their plan was to be allowed to go about their business of finishing the domestic season in peace.

The first part of the plan went quite well – to finish the Top 14 without fuss. The club won one of their famously unwatchable games at home to Bayonne and snuffed out the last fear that they might yet end up in the bottom-two drop zone. To go to the elite European final and be relegated from the Top 14 in the same breath – now that would have been news. But the club scraped through on reserve power and there was nothing sensational to report. The second part – that this conclusion to the season be negotiated in peace – proved a little more elusive.

Paris Max were nowhere to be found on the news pages, or even the sports pages, but five days after the semi-final in Dublin, *Le Parisien* published a whole-page feature on the home village of Gonzo Davies, the player memorably identified by Noa as the one that had made everything in their European odyssey possible. Jacques Bonnot, the photo-journalist and author of the piece, called Gonzo '*la bétonnière*' of Paris Max. The cement mixer. It didn't seem a particularly flattering start but Jacques then produced a portrait of Gonzo's home in Wales, an affectionate sketch that put the village on the French map.

The story was set on the mid-morning of the Monday after the semi in Dublin and the village's promotion-party. Having flown into Cardiff Airport and picked up a hire car, Jacques arrived in time to witness and record the demolition of the rugby stand. He assumed it to be evidence of yet more decline in what was obviously a pitifully deprived village. He saw nothing but scrap and waste and dust. He couldn't understand a word of what anybody was saying, or shouting. But then he met the Widowers, who were leaning against the railing on the far touchline from the stand, watching the latest chapter in the clearance work. Patiently and in language Jacques could understand, they became his guides for the day, explaining everything about the village and the redevelopment. They took him to the café and he treated them to lunch. They showed him the Miners' Institute and they hobbled on their sticks up the moorland path to West Street and the old clubhouse. There, Jacques lined up the Widowers under the collapsed letters of 'RFC' and produced the shot of the day, the old miners' pride and defiance shining through the isolation and poverty.

Included in the spread was a shot of the Graig Bike, the former pithead wheel. If rugby in Paris was of limited popularity, cycling was of more universal appeal. A television producer who was enjoying a rest after covering the Paris-Roubaix race in early April happened to be reading *Le Parisien* and noticed the photo and Jacques' short section on the Graig Club. He contacted a stringer in London, who reluctantly made the long trip into Wales and found, much to his surprise, that cycling there was a boom sport and that the Graig was the fastest-growing club in the United Kingdom and that they were planning a special event to coincide with the arrival of summer and the start of construction work, after the end of the demolition process, on their brand new cycling centre. The Graig were also teaming up with their partners in renovation – the rugby club – who were celebrating their own promotion and looking forward to the participation of their most famous son, Gonzo Davies, in the Champions Cup Final.

The rugby final in Cardiff was scheduled to kick off in the evening of the first Saturday in May. That left plenty of daylight hours for the Graig extravaganza in the village. The Unrelated Lewises were working flat-out on the finishing touches to a grand race that would go up, over and down the Blorenge. The race would start in Abergavenny and aim at the mountain – but at its quiet eastern side. Between Llanfoist and Llanellen, the riders would turn right, away from the River Usk, and take the narrow road to the top, the theory being that the incline was so severe that congestion would soon not be an issue. Once at the top of the extreme climb, they would cross the domed moorland and, just before the Keeper's Pond, turn right and hit the great descent. They would within seconds pass the spot where Grace had left the road and plunged to her death, and they would speed down to the bends before Govilon, dash into Llanfoist and back to Abergavenny to complete a lap and start all over again. The race would be three-and-a-half laps long – the final half comprising a fourth ascent of the eastern escarpment, a left turn – not a fourth right – at the Keeper's Pond, a burst down half the Flying Five from Blaenavon and a dash after Garn-yr-Erw across the wilderness into the village for the finish.

In their haste and in their delight at being inundated with requests to take part from all over Wales – and increasingly from further afield – the Lewises had failed to come up with anything better as a name than the Blorenge Challenge.

Somehow, the encouraging but concise report from the stringer became an expression of serious interest from the French television company, FranceSeize. They couldn't organise multi-camera coverage in time or in budget, but they were prepared to send a couple of camera bikes and a couple of self-shoot producers to this unlikely cycling hotspot. The edited package would form part of a special feature to be shown the following day. Inspired by the piece by Jacques Bonnot in *Le Parisen*, it now had the working title: 'La Journée du Village'. The rugby adventure of Paris Max's Gonzo Davies would be the main storyline, but it was the cycling that clinched the programme's commission. FranceSeize also came up with a name for the race: 'Le Tour du Mont Blorenge'. Posters began to appear in shops and on-line, showing the converted pithead wheel and the shortened name which caught on: 'Le Mont Blorenge'.

Max was so bruised after the Munster game that he could not move for three days. He was in no shape to play in the Bayonne game and the only place he went was the physiotherapist's. He lay on his couch at home and he lay on a couch at work. He seriously began to doubt that he could be patched up in time for the final, although there were two weeks between Dublin and Cardiff. Coach Jean ordered him to take the entire first week off.

Perhaps it was inside his head that Max couldn't heal. He

felt down. Noa was the hero as usual and Gonzo was the miracle man, and Max was simply the third man. Not even a musketeer any more; he was the third of three. For two days he shooed Perrine out of the flat, knowing that he was feeling sorry for himself. She came back and told him where she had been with Gonzo, what she had shown him of the Paris that she and Max adored.

'Come on, Max. Why don't you come too?' she said. He showed her the bruises to his ribs and the swelling to his ankle and declined, and the next day she went out again. Noa came to see Max and they sat in silence for hours. Noa never minded. He said he would come back the next day after training and an early lunch there, but instead of letting him stretch out on his favourite sofa, where he would soon fall into a deep sleep – into 'Noa's world', as he called it – Max told him to go and have lunch with Gonzo and Perrine in the Jardin du Luxembourg.

'But I've eaten,' said Noa.

'Go and find them,' said Max. Noa still raised an eyebrow. 'Just do as I say.'

Perrine knew what Max was thinking and she didn't care. Sober, drunk … when he was like this she couldn't take it. At least when he was drunk he was absent. She knew about his excesses; she knew where he went. Paris was a huge city, but it was a village. People talked and word spread and Perrine heard. All that she heard of her slumped husband aboard the carousel of his moral compass, slewing in the direction of the first whore to catch his bleary eye, she normally kept to herself. Because to talk was to reveal, and to reveal was to spread the word, and that would make her just another leak in the sewers of gossip that flowed under her beautiful Paris.

As the sun of midday appeared from behind a high white cloud, she eased off her light cashmere cardigan. Gonzo couldn't help but notice how toned her arms were. She may have been older than Max but she was still a lot younger than Gonzo. Perrine knew that Gonzo noticed her. While Max lounged in self-pity, she worked to stay in shape. She leant back against the bench in the Jardin du Luxembourg.

'Do you know why he is the way he is?' she asked. Gonzo knew what Max did. He hadn't needed to spend long in Paris to see Max Ferry at play, to recognise the rapid slide from Max at full throttle, the life and soul of a party, quick of wit, to the stalled Max who took verbal swipes at anyone within earshot. Mostly the slump came through alcohol; sometimes Max turned boorish for no good reason.

'What we do is not natural,' he said. 'Rugby. We have to will monsters to run at us at full speed, so that we can knock them over. Only Noa can do this without having to give himself a boost. Rugby players are adrenaline junkies. And as with any addiction, there can be side-effects … or a craving for that feeling – that you can stop anything coming your way. That nobody can stop you.'

'And you, Monsieur Gonzo? Do you have a craving?'

'I overdosed a long time ago on all that stuff,' he replied. 'No, no craving – at least, not through rugby any more.'

'What then?'

Gonzo thought of the Orphanage. 'I seem to be collecting people,' he said. And then he thought of Grace. 'And I don't want to lose anyone else.' He looked Perrine squarely in her eyes. 'I've always thought that He – you know, him – and I were going to have it out, settle the score one way or the other. But sitting here, I'm not so sure. I said to Grace that I seemed to be hitting the buffers. It's true.'

'You have your grand finale,' said Perrine, thinking that if she touched his elbow and he didn't flinch, if she placed a finger on that strong forearm and he didn't recoil, she would lean forward and kiss him.

'Yes, I do – but then we'll see.'

Perrine thought about that. And then seemed to snap out of her reverie. 'Tell me,' she said. 'When you were playing for Wales ...'

'Long time ago ...'

'Even so, when you were playing, did you sing the Welsh hymn?'

'The anthem? Mae Hen Wlad fy Nhadau?'

'If you say so ... did you sing it?'

'No. I used to shut my eyes and listen. There's no sound like it. Hell, that was a drug on its own.'

'And will you sing ours? La Marseillaise?'

'Just one problem ... it's in French, isn't it?' They laughed and she did touch him on the arm, but only fleetingly. She did brush his forearm but her hand was already moving away.

'You sing, you win ... and then ...' she said, '*Gonzo fait ses adieux au rugby*. And then, after your goodbye, you have a month here in your Paris flat, living the life of a normal human being. Not a rugby junkie.' Perrine could feel her fingers stirring, her hand creeping towards Gonzo.

'Hey, Noa,' said Gonzo as the sun was suddenly blotted out. 'How's the prince of darkness? Oh, shit, sorry, not you. Him. Max.'

In the week leading up to the first Saturday in May, S4C television came back to the village. Le Mont Blorenge and Gonzo's final had attracted the domestic media as well as the French. FranceSeize were intrigued by S4C's arrival and the making of a portrait of the village in the Welsh language became part of theirs in French. They were especially interested in the relationship between Eleri Catrin, standing on her crate, and Whopper Jones, who by popular demand was back as the guide to his village.

One of the French self-shooting producers was called Emil and although he had good English, he was nervous of the villagers, all of whom spoke with an accent he simply could not begin to understand. He was assured by one of the engineers on site – a Bob from Hereford – that what they were speaking was English not Welsh, but Emil was struggling. He knew that 'fuck' was a bad word and since he heard it inserted at least twice into every utterance from the mouths of most of the locals, he assumed they had taken against him. He approached them with extreme caution. But when he saw Eleri and Whopper side by side, he couldn't help but seek further information, and the first person he saw just happened to be Capper Harris.

'Excuse me,' said Emil.

'Ah,' said Capper, 'Bon fuckin' jour … Capper,' said Capper.

'Pardon?' said Emil.

'I'm Capper. Capper fuckin' 'Arris.'

'Ah,' said Emil, shaking his hand. 'I'm Emil. Emil fuckeen' Dubois.'

'You speak our language very well, Emil,' said Capper.

'May I?' said Emil pointing at his little hand-held camera.

'Of course. Everybody else's been ignoring me.'

'Thank you. Please, that man and woman, who are they?'

'That, butt, is a Welsh bird on a crate talking to our fuckin' Whopper.'

'What is Whopper?'

'Whopper is the name of our next fuckin' superstar from our dearly beloved fuckin' shit 'eap of a village. You 'eard it 'ere first, that that bloke will be boxing your French ears at the Stade de fuckin' France before you can say 'Bonjour effin' Fifi'. Pardon my French, Emil. By the way, what are you doing up 'ere, you lot?'

'We are making 'La Journée du Village'. The Day of the Village. And I was interested in … Whopper.'

'Big fucker, isn't he? The Day of the Village, eh? Aye, look at 'im. More like the Day of the Triffid.' And with that, Capper groaned and put his head in his hands. 'Oh no,' he wailed. 'Too fuckin' late, Emil. Too fuckin' late. He's one of the Plant, see. Triffid. Of course. Whopper's fuckin' Triffid.' He than recovered and looked at Emil, who was staring at him, wide-eyed, through the viewfinder. 'Come on, Emil old son. I'll show you round. Keep that little fuckin' thing on.' And they set off on Capper's guided tour, which was a little more colourful than the Widowers' and which ended at the Colliers' Arms, where Capper left Emil in the company of Meg and Annie. 'Could you make a porn movie with that camera, Emil, love?' he heard Meg ask as he left.

Martin no longer went to any of the finest hotels in Dubai. He didn't go anywhere. He sat in his apartment and watched the screen of his laptop. It was the only light he ever turned on. Sometimes, when he closed the lid and lay down on the mattress he could see its slowly beating glow and he thought it was the only thing in the room with a pulse. When he awoke, never more than a couple of hours later, he returned to keeping tabs on Gonzo Davies. He knew he was 'la bétonnière' of Paris Max and he knew he had been to Clermont-Ferrand and to Dublin. And he knew that Gonzo was going to play in Cardiff. It was after the Wales-England game in Cardiff many years earlier that Martin had commissioned Danny Mewson to maim him. That had been a good bit of business for Martin. Danny had soon afterwards stamped on the head of Gonzo Davies. Once, to slash it open; twice, to fracture his skull and nearly blind him in one eye. Good days. It gave Martin no pleasure now to see that Gonzo seemed to be feeling no pain. But who could he commission now? Who would do Martin's bidding? Where were the Mewson brothers now? Gone. Where were Ravi and Frank? There was always the Professor, on whom Martin had once always been able to rely. But no. Martin shook his head. Who would do it? Martin would have to do it himself.

19

Kitty went to Gonzo's cottage. She found the key under the stone where it always lived and opened up. She left the front door open, thinking the house needed some light and air. She hadn't heard from Gonzo, but in case he came home before the final, she wanted his home to be welcoming. It was immaculate inside. Capper had said he was worried Gonzo was building the cottage 'for Grace' and Kitty had been afraid that she would open the door on some sort of shrine. She was braced to find a hundred spent candles before an altar to the Sacred Grace, but instead found a finished kitchen on a slate floor and a living room with new furniture. If there was a reminder of the brief time Gonzo and Grace had spent together in the cottage it was the old armchair, still in pride of place in front of the latest television. It seemed Gonzo wasn't yet ready to park himself in dusty work trousers on anything but the old piece of salvaged furniture.

Against one wall was a pedestal desk. It wasn't new like the three-piece suite and wasn't as worn as the old armchair. It was an antique Gonzo had bought in Crickhowell. Kitty went round the house, plumping pillows on the main bed, generally dusting and tidying. Saving the desk to last. She tried the drawers – four half-drawers down either side of the leg-space and a shallow full-width drawer above it. They all opened smoothly. There wasn't much inside. The biggest item took up all the space in the full drawer – the photo Grace had taken at the entrance to the cave, in its frame with a single crack across the glass. Something in Kitty wanted to take it away and have it reframed and put it on wall, where Grace had planned for it to be hung, but she left it where it was and closed the drawer on 'Gonzo's Finest Hour II'. Something in her wanted to leave the front door unlocked, but she turned the key and put it back under the stone.

On Wednesday, the day before the Paris Max team left for Cardiff, Gonzo was in his flat. He'd been out to walk the streets whose sounds were no longer alien. He'd bought a baguette, more for the smell of the *boulangerie* than out of hunger. He'd had his *café crème* in the bar on the corner, no longer self-conscious about being so obviously non-French. He'd said 'Bonjour' and shaken hands with the *patron* as he did as a matter of course now, and sat and watched Paris go by. Once, when he'd killed time in the arcade cafés of Cardiff, he'd sat with a book. Grace had found him in Camacho's and soon there wasn't much time for reading. Here, in Paris, he'd spent the last week watching, not reading – but what he'd been doing was less important than what he wasn't doing, less important than the person with whom he wasn't doing that anything. Gonzo was very deliberately on his own, afraid of what might happen beyond the safety of training, of reducing life to the simplicity of preparing for the match. He needed to concentrate on that one goal, and yet he needed to keep it in context. It was to be his final fling, but it could only ever be a game – just another game – of rugby. An exclusive opportunity, but just another game. He needed a few more days without distractions. But they were everywhere, especially off the streets. In his flat he was unable to let the sounds and smells and routines of Paris protect him. He lay in the flat thinking of Grace. He couldn't help it. He thought of her with a yearning that made tears well in his eyes. The doorbell rang.

This time, Perrine had made the full Parisian fast-lane high-society effort. She'd watched Max, his blonde hair spilling from under his crash helmet, disappear on his beloved scooter, his super-cool darting Vespa that could weave him in and out of the densest of traffic jams and she'd sat down to make herself gorgeous. Soon she'd looked good enough to silence a reception at the Elysée Palace. But she'd then stripped herself of paintwork, unhappy with her appearance. For what she was going to do she needed to be mid-morning natural. She re-applied a minimum of make-up and a minimum of clothing over her lithe body and walked with her swinging gait the few streets to the flat of Gonzo Davies. He opened the door.

'I've come to teach you the "Marseillaise",' she said.

20

On the day of Le Mont Blorenge, there was a race within the race. Or several races within the race. The first was against the weather. The first Saturday of May dawned fresh and bright but a front was moving in off the Atlantic and was expected to hit West Wales by mid afternoon and Cardiff by the evening. The roof of the Millennium Stadium was going to be shut whatever the weather at the request of both Saracens and Paris Max, who both wanted the theatre to be as atmospheric as possible. The roof stayed open by day to ventilate the pitch but eyes kept looking at the sky in case the moment of closure had to be brought forward.

The other races within Le Mont Blorenge were to do with keeping the loop of the mountain clear for the elite cyclists. The Graig Club had reckoned, based on the requests to take part in the formal race, that they might have five thousand competitors. But they had to work out by how many that official start-list would be increased on the day by cyclists simply pitching up to give it a go. There was a fun element to the day, although the Graig had repeatedly stressed that this was not an event for the short of breath. The emphasis on the risks involved seemed to make the race more alluring. The Unrelateds didn't know what to expect – and this ignorance preyed on their organised minds – and so they were very relieved when the police, much to the annoyance of the traders of the town, insisted on closing the entire town centre between 9 and 11 o'clock in the morning. Twelve thousand cyclists, give or take the odd hundred, pedalled into Abergavenny for the start of Le Mont Blorenge.

The next problem, the organisers envisaged, would be to keep the wobblers and the walkers – those in danger of coming off their machine and those who already had – out of the way of the serious competitors on the uphill. On the day, the danger wasn't so great there because the speeds involved were not life-threatening, and there were stewards at every turn to keep the stragglers out of the way of the contenders. The real danger would come, they imagined, on the rush downhill from the Keeper's Pond to Govilon, when the best would be lapping the worst – and even some much better than that – on the second and third loops. By that time in reality, however, many of those who had pitched up to give it a go had gone. Almost all made it to the top once, but a great many then called it a day and sat down in the heather to rest their pounding hearts and enjoy the views. By lap three, the field in Le Mont Blorenge was down to a hundred or so cyclists, and even they were dreading the fourth and final pull up the mountain to the village.

The strain in the visitors' changing room at the Millennium Stadium, where a toss of the coin had placed Paris Max, was palpable. It was what changing rooms in international sporting venues were all about, a careful blending of the output of gland and brain, adrenaline and thinking. Heat and coolness. But there was an extra tension in the Paris Max ranks. Not everybody noticed it, since they all had their own routines and superstitions and would concentrate on these personal matters until they came together to remind themselves that they could achieve nothing – absolutely nothing – unless they sacrificed their individual selves for the good of the team. But Noa felt it, and coach Jean noticed it, and without resolution of it, Paris Max were doomed to fail. Unless Gonzo and Max sorted themselves out, there was going to be only one outcome. Although Paris Max were not expected to beat Saracens, to go down without the defiance born of trust and togetherness would break their hearts.

Having caught their breath, the short-course – the one- or two-lap – cyclists were faced with a choice. Either they could take the left turn at the Keeper's Pond and follow the

Graig Bike logo-signs and arrows pointing to the village, or they could turn right and freewheel off the mountain. Most opted to be back in Abergavenny for lunch, but it still meant that thousands of red-faced enthusiasts cycled down half the Flying Five between Blaenavon and Brymawr and turned left after Garn-yr-Erw to go and see what was arising out of the dust of the village. There, of course, and as long as the sun shone on this two-wheeled triumph of a day, they created a whirl of dust of their own. They had come prepared and up went the bandanas over their mouths. And so it was that Martin managed to ride into the village and sit and watch and listen without anybody seeing any more of him – between his cycling helmet and sunglasses and the bandana he'd bought while waiting his turn to start among the strictly uncompetitive – than his nose.

The Owain Owens bus was parked up at the highest point in the village, not outside the old clubhouse, where there was no room to squeeze past the diggers poised to strike, but at the junction of Upper Street and West Street. The old bus was pointing downhill and was at the ready to take the club down to Cardiff for the final. Capper had anticipated that the air around the rugby field would be clogged – 'And we wouldn't want anything to give us a fuckin' thirst, would we?' – and had ordered a departure from above the pollution line. Besides, there was no room anywhere down below to congregate. The village was overflowing with people, and bikes blocked every street. The Colliers' Arms and the café were serving non-stop and Jones the Other Builder had pulled down the boards over the windows of the old church and chapel, thrown open their doors and offered quick-release-energy replenishment more for the body than the soul.

The rugby field marked the end of the race and the diggers and other machinery at the mine had been lined up as a finishing corridor, a guard of honour. A giant crane had been assembled on site over the previous three days. Its first lift was the Graig Bike which was now suspended from its hook high over the far 22-metre line. Between the crane's lifting cable and the top of a cherry picker at full stretch a large banner announced: Finish – and Restart. It was a reference to Le Mont Blorenge and a signpost to the future.

The rugby club had done their bit to support the cycling club in the morning, but their desire to be on mini-tour to Cardiff was strong. As the cloud of dust thickened, they wound their way up the old familiar pathway from what was left of their ground to what was left of their old clubhouse. They all stared in wonder at the West Street that was no more. If they felt a pang for the old headquarters that stood on the brink of obliteration, it did not last long. They piled through the front door and went straight to the bar, dusted and polished for the first time in a year by Our Marnie, and bought pints of Pedallers, ordered for the second time in a month by Capper. Twin Tub took his place at the discordantly out-of-tune piano and struck up a song. The Widowers pulled up their chairs around their old table and sipped their halves and patiently waited for the moment they would have to go and rescue the men in Meg and Annie's company.

'Look what we found coming through the murk down there,' said the irrepressible pensioners, dragging Emil

Dubois and Alun, the recently retired Under Secretary on the Community Affairs Committee at the Senedd, into the club. The French television producer was holding his camera and Alun, Welsh civil servant, was in cycling gear. It was his 'something to do' in retirement. He hadn't imagined it could be as exhausting as this and was grateful to have been offered a lift back to Cardiff.

'You're more than welcome, Alun, love,' said Annie. 'There's plenty of room in the boot of the bus for your bike. You can ride with us all the way then. Emil can film us, can't you Emil, darling?'

Gonzo did not sing 'La Marseillaise'. He stood with his eyes shut and waited for it to end. Max, as captain, was at the end of the line, Noa by his side. Gonzo was towards the other end, the last player before the replacements. Before the Band of the Welsh Guards finished the last note of the French anthem and struck up with the first of 'God save the Queen', Gonzo strode down the line and forced his way between Max and Noa. Max would not move, but Noa gave the player to his left a nudge and the entire Paris Max line shuffled along to make room for Gonzo. As the singing finished and as the full house of 73,000 burst into applause and as the French section of supporters – tiny in comparison with the red and black of the Saracens – waved their flags and blasted their trumpets, Gonzo grabbed Max and held his head in two hands.

'I did not betray you, Max,' he shouted into his face. 'Do you hear? I never would.'

*

And he had not. It was one of the sacred tenets, one of the unbreakable taboos of rugby life. Not to take from another player. Gonzo had taken Grace from Martin, but Martin was not a fellow player. Grace had known that betraying Martin would have consequences, but they were not married. Gonzo had always felt a scratch of guilt about the start of their affair. He was not a good man, he had been reminded – but it was no more than that, a scratch. He was not a bad man, was he? Unlike him. Unlike Martin who did not require victimhood as the betrayed partner to reveal his true self. Martin was by essence in a different league. He satisfied all the criteria for promotion. Gonzo would resist. He would not be a reviled man, an outcast, a pariah. He would not do evil. He would not take Perrine, except by the arm and steer her out of the flat she had found for him Paris. 'I can't,' he had said to her. 'We can't.'

'Am I not good enough for you?'

'You are beautiful,' he had said. 'But you are Max's. You must not punish him like this. It's your turn to save him.'

She had nearly flared up at him, but the fight suddenly went out of her and she ran from the door, from the flat and into the street. She ran away from Gonzo, back to her empty flat.

In all the years of Max's stupors, in all his phases of being drunk, bitter, biting, cruel and morose, in all the long days of having his reason pulled out of shape by the irresistibly downward suction of his own sinking spirits, in all his dark nights of being slumped against a woman – any woman, any man-woman – and in all the times he had flown above the crowd as the raconteur, the wit, the star turn without whom a party could not come to life, he had never once cheated on Perrine. He had sobbed in the arms of hookers and paid them for it, he had talked beautiful women to the point of ecstasy until they realised he was not talking about them, but his true love.

Max thought he had lost Perrine to Gonzo, and now he was being told it was not so. Most of the players thought it was a little one-on-one huddle, a last moment before kick-off between Gonzo on his home patch and his friend who had invited him out of the wilderness to walk tall again. Gonzo still held Max's face but he turned it away from his own and pointed it up, high into the stands where Perrine stood. Where Grace had once stood. Perrine looked at them – no, at Max – and painted an M in the air with her finger.

The occupants of the Orphanage arrived at the old clubhouse in the Kittymobile. Whopper was in the front seat, with the Professor and John, Cinnabar and Ragwort in the back. It was a tight squeeze in the pick-up, but the situation was slightly eased when Cinnabar said: 'Put your arm around me, John. We'll have more room then.'

Cinnabar wanted to go down to Cardiff with Kitty, but Kitty told her it was an Owain Owens special and perhaps it needed Emma to ride shotgun, to ensure that eyebrows were left as brows above eyes. Cinnabar nodded. She would take her place in the bus, and heaven help anybody that dared even look at her Ragwort. She'd scratch their eyes out. Kitty told her she was sure there would be no need to go quite that far. Only Kitty could reserve the right to say – and strictly to herself – that she felt a little too respectable for coach outings. Kitty wanted to go to the final, but she did not want to feel Pedallers washing over her feet and she did not want to linger in Cardiff. She had told the Orphanage she'd prefer to be back early and have some food ready for them when they came home. The last of her orphans to arrive in West Street was Dario. He'd not been in the Gherkin on the drive when the Kittymobile left and everybody assumed he'd done the sums and decided that he would be the one passenger too many. He appeared at the gate to the moor, hobbling on his crutches, which made everyone in the Kittymobile feel guilty.

'Sorry, Dario,' said Whopper, his North Wales tongue rolling the 'r'. 'I would willingly …'

'It's OK, Whopper,' said Dario. 'I wasn't at home …' He hauled himself, slightly preoccupied, inside the club and looked for Kitty, who was being shown round the building she had never been in before by Capper. 'I'm like the village fuckin' tour guide, Kitty,' said Capper.

'Language,' she said. 'Hello, Dario. Sorry, we couldn't find you …'

'No …' said Dario.

'Anything the matter?' asked Kitty.

'I dunno. It's just … no, I don't know … just … I don't think I'll go to the game, that's all.'

'Come on, Dario,' said Capper. 'Gonzo's last last last big one. We've got to be there.'

'I suppose,' said Dario.

An hour later, with the Pedallers all gone, Kitty counted the orphans aboard the bus. Dario was the last to go up the steps.

'Dario,' said Kitty. 'Are you sure you're all right?'

He looked back down at her and then looked over her head at the village, where sunlight still shone on the cloud of dust. The tall crane rose out of the swirl. 'It's all change, I know,' he said. 'But there's something not quite right ...'

'Go on,' said Kitty and she climbed the steps and planted a kiss on his cheek. 'Enjoy the game.'

The Owain Owens bus set off, not in its customary cloud of smoke since it was pointing downhill, but with a clunk from the hold, where Alun the Under Secretary's bike shifted and settled, a bit like Alun between Meg and Annie.

Kitty watched the bus depart and then went to her pick-up truck. She didn't set off immediately after the bus, but sat watching the village for a few moments. Finally, she started the engine and eased her way down Upper Street.

Saracens had reached the final without distress. They were recognised as the most clinical takers of opportunities earned through persistence and doggedness. They were not the biggest physical specimens in a world of giants but they more than made up for their lack of height with an aerobic fitness second to none and a collective will of iron. Stamina and tenacity were their watchwords. They gave nothing away and they expected little in return. But when the little somethings came their way, they grabbed them unerringly. They had not scored many points, but they had never looked in danger of losing in the two knockout rounds. Unwatchable Paris against miserly Saracens – nobody was expecting a feast of scoring.

Max played like a cork released from the bottle of his

favourite and very expensive champagne. On the one occasion in the first half when Saracens tried to move the ball towards their left wing, he made three tackles in a row, knocking one player down after another and bouncing back to his feet in between until the ball was dropped over the touchline, with the throw-in to Paris Max. Even the unflappable Saracens felt buffeted by the whirlwind and yielded a couple of penalties to trail 3-6 at half-time.

Capper had conveniently forgotten to off-hire the big screen at the rugby ground in the village. The Unrelateds thought it might be in the way of their finish area, but had eventually decided they could work around it. They tried to turn it on and reported to one of the engineers that the electricity supply seemed to have been cut off. For the very last time, the engineers set about repairing the connection to the stand that no longer existed and the extension – about which they knew nothing – to the big screen. Two hours after the last of the hundred-odd top cyclists finished Le Mont Blorenge, the banner between the crane and the cherry picker was taken down and the Graig turned on the big screen for the rugby final.

Martin had moved in and out of the village with the myriad cyclists all day. He had checked on the lie of the land to the cottage. He knew exactly where it was through reports from Frank and Danny in the past. He had even dared go back to the spot where he had walked into the path of Land Rover. The moment of his life. Step out. Click.

He needed to wait for darkness now and he joined the small crowd at the rugby pitch for the final. To see Gonzo

Davies in close-up during the French national anthem chilled him. And thrilled him. Enjoy the moment. Your time is coming. The crowd thinned in the village as the first half drew to a close. A long day was coming to an end, and the approach of night was hastened by storm clouds gathering to the west. The wind picked up and the big screen began to shake. Martin slipped into the last group of riders making their way out of the village. He became this peloton's rear-gunner, sheltering behind them as they battled through the side wind. Instead of following them towards the Keeper's Pond and the long run for home, though, he slipped back and turned off his lights. He stopped until their tail-end red glow had gone and he waited another minute for his eyes to adjust. And then slowly – there was no race now – he made his way to the cottage. He tried the front door. He turned his headlight back on, using one hand to reduce its beam to a thin shaft, and lowered himself to his hands and knees. Strange thing, it struck him – to be worshipping on the doorstep of Gonzo Davies. He found the hiding place for the key. A stone. So obvious. He unlocked the door and turned off his light. He wanted no deviant inbred of the mountain to see a dancing beam of light in this of all places. Darkness was best. He turned into the living room and felt his way towards a chair. He lifted it and turned it silently to face the way he had come. He sat down and opened his backpack. He put the extinguished light on the end of the armrest. Behind it, nearer his right hand, he carefully placed the Glock pistol he'd bought in Cardiff – from a place once recommended by Frank. Frank who might have once become a friend. Frank – the now treacherous, disloyal Frank. Martin settled down to wait, no matter how long it took, for Gonzo Davies to come home.

Paris Max scored a try at the beginning of the second half. It wasn't quite the dance of the dervishes revisited because Max was still such a wriggling eel that he could not stay glued to Noa and Gonzo. But their combined work over five metres allowed Max to slip free and cover the last two metres on his own. The conversion was missed but it still gave Paris Max an eight-point advantage. In a low-scoring match, eight points stood for easy living. And a third penalty made it even easier. 14-3. Saracens would have to score at least twice. For twenty minutes the final was plunged into the unwatchable as the orthodox systems of the London club ran into the resolute defence of Paris's. Nothing went ten metres beyond the halfway line in either direction. The final was dying on its feet for the television audience; it couldn't have been going better for Paris.

And then Max blew up. Exhaustion seized his fevered body and mind and he collapsed, as if shot. He was one second moving into a routine tackle and the next he was grovelling on the ground, easily thrust out of the way. He lay there, without the energy to raise his head to watch. Saracens had the quickest player on the field, Spikes Yarling, and he sprinted away to score in the corner. The conversion missed and le Max led 14-8. The player who had missed the tackle could go not another metre. The French would have to finish the job without their captain. '*Le Max sans son Max*,' they said on FranceSeize.

It didn't matter. Paris controlled the last eight minutes

of the game. They made the game even more unwatchable, declining to pass or kick at all. They did not give the ball air to breathe, but buried it, slipping it invisibly from forward to forward, from strong arm to strong arm. On the stroke of overtime – when the clock turned red at 80 minutes – they set up a maul five metres from the Saracens line and against every command from their coach Jean Lalanne's mouth and against every wish in his heart, the entire Paris Max set of backs, from scrum-half to full back, joined the forwards' maul. It was a well-tried, relatively risk-free drive for the line, a quirky but not unfamiliar flourish to kill the game off – a fourteen-man maul. But not fifteen. Gonzo did not join it. He was spent, with just enough strength to take a step back and watch his French team finish the job.

It was relatively risk-free, but not entirely. The giant maul was already over the line when the ball slipped out of the clutches of players a tiny bit too greedy in their desire to score the victory-sealing try. Noa snaked out a hand to try to regain control and to touch the ball down, but his hand bumped against one of the twenty-eight Parisian legs and the ball bobbled two inches into open air. Little Naps – short for Napoleon, as in small and intent on world domination – Hargreaves, the Saracens scrum-half, ablaze with frustration, aimed a wild boot at it and caught it flush in the sweet spot. The ball flew high towards the halfway line and Spikes Yarling, who had gone nowhere near the hairy mammoths in their ugly maul, hared off after it. And Gonzo turned and ran too, the only Paris Max player between the Saracens goal-line at one end and the one he was suddenly defending on his own in the far distance.

The little button clicked and light shone on Martin in the armchair. He could see nothing but the dazzling glare. There was no sound and Martin did not make a move for the Glock.

'Who are you?' he said calmly.

The infuriating thing about an oval rugby ball, as Gonzo had been taught at every stage of his life in the sport, was that it was impossible to read its bounce. Sometimes he could gauge when a ball bouncing end over end would rear up, or when a spiralling torpedo kick would start to curve in the air. But this ball he was chasing was going over and over and round and round. And Spikes was already past him, the Commonwealth Games sprinter against the exhausted Welsh has-been. A second wave of Saracens three-quarters was bearing down on the halfway line. Gonzo was surrounded and being overhauled. The crowd groaned when he slowed. Go out with some dignity, old man.

But as the thoroughbred runners of the chasing pack kept their eyes fixed on a point in front of them and as they concentrated on their sprinting technique – knees high, arms driving and heads still – Gonzo never stopped looking up. He slowed again. The ball came down and bounced in front of Spikes and flew backwards, over the head of the winger, over the heads of the second wave and into his large, safe hands. He headed for the touchline, only for Spikes to turn and come for him. Gonzo stopped again, this time to hand off the winger with an open palm. He then bunched his fingers together to lift Spikes off the ground by his shirt. They crossed the touchline and before the referee even blew for the end of the match, Gonzo had put Sparks gently on the ground and carried on down the tunnel with the ball, followed all the way by one of FranceSeize's little cameras. He went into the Away changing room, pulled the oxygen mask off Max with an apology to the team doctor and carried the victorious captain back to the playing arena.

'I am the woman,' said Kitty, 'who's been dying to fire this for ages.' And into the beam of light from Gonzo's head torch was raised the Browning pistol, that Kitty had found in the second drawer down on the left-hand side of his desk against the wall, on top of the picture of the foetus in Grace's womb. Kitty had not gone to the final after all, but had felt Dario's tremor of fear and had taken it upon herself in his absence – the brief relief from his vigil, the outing on which she had sent him with a kiss – that she, Kitty, should be the guardian of the village. Its defender. She squeezed the trigger.

They partied late into the night. The evening kick-off meant that the players did not emerge from the changing rooms until nearly midnight. There were speeches in the Presidential Lounge at the stadium and there was quite good champagne and there was noise. And there was love. Max collapsed into the arms of the beautiful Perrine, who had made the effort of her life and truly stopped the show when she later entered the ballroom of the Sir Tasker Hotel in Cardiff Bay. Max cried and Perrine cried and she had to go out and start her effort all over again. When she returned, Max, Noa and Gonzo swept her up and they went out into what was left of the night to sit on a bench overlooking the water with a couple of bottles of the very best champagne

Max could find in the Sir Tasker cellar. Gonzo told them about where he and Grace had met, where he had lived, how he had lowered her gently so that she could be with Martin and live a different life. What had happened to his head and eye. His vacuum years. His recovery years. How Grace had come back to him. Where the bomb went off. How the Babcock Cup final, played a week after the explosion, had become this, the last play.

'This Martin,' said Noa. 'What are you going to do?'

'I don't know,' said Gonzo. 'I thought I did, but I'm not so sure now.'

They sat and said nothing for a moment. Perrine reached out and touched Gonzo's arm. And then she stroked Max's cheek. 'And you, my Max, *mon Max,*' she said. 'How are you?'

'I am … stable,' he said. 'I am with you. All of you. And the others. Come on, I have responsibilities, you know.' And he pulled Perrine to her feet and kissed her. And as the wind began to whip up waves in the waters of the Bay and the slanting rain began to lash into Cardiff, they all went back into the Sir Tasker.

Whopper had recorded the final and Capper, the Professor, Ragwort and he sat down in the Orphanage to watch it again. Our Marnie wanted to check on Kitty, who had not been seen at the game. There was no sign of her in the house and no food had been made. John set about putting that right in the kitchen. Cinnabar went upstairs to put on her zebra-striped pyjamas and Dario paced up and down in the Gherkin until Our Marnie sent him to watch the game with the others. She went to help John.

'So, Whopper, what d'you reckon?' asked Capper forty-five minutes later. They had fast-forwarded through the bits of inactivity between play and through half-time, and were analysing the final moment. 'The bounce of Gonzo Davies. Was it luck, like the commentator said? Or did he read it?'

'That was not luck, Capper,' said Whopper firmly. 'Not luck at all. Na, na, not at all. That was the master at work.'

'The blind faith of the pupil,' said the Professor. He wanted to see the low-angle replay from one of the corner cameras at the end Gonzo was defending – and running towards. 'Look at him,' he said to Capper, Whopper, Ragwort and Dario. 'Never takes his eyes off the ball. And he slows … because he knows.'

'He slows … because he knows,' they all recited.

In the minute fraction of a second when he knew he was going to be shot, Martin flinched and in doing so made the old arm of his chair collapse. The bullet fired by Kitty did not miss as he fell to one side, but caught him in the shoulder, rather than plum in the middle of his chest, where she was aiming. It meant his heart did not stop. He began to bleed over the armchair and floor. And his brain did not shut down. He reached for the Glock, but not in time. Kitty fired again. And again, and again. Martin lay on the floor, taking his last breaths, thinking his last thoughts. If there had been a click – just one click - he might have stood a chance. He had been dazzled by a light. Who was this woman in the house of Gonzo Davies?

*

When Gonzo saw the ball spinning end over end and also turning with sidespin off the boot of Naps Hargreaves, up into the air of the Millennium Stadium, a blur of white through the glare of the lights and then set clean against the latticework of the closed roof, he knew that this was the end. It was no longer a question of hitting the buffers; he was simply running out of steam and would roll to a halt, making the softest of contacts against the finish line. But he also knew he had to finish this last task. In the extremes of exhaustion, forcing his legs to restart and take him from his observation post – from which he could admire and applaud Paris Max's try of their own mass making, bar him – was agony. His brain ordered an instantaneous reaction to the ball suddenly propelled high into the air, but his shaking, aching legs responded only sluggishly. Even in the full flush of youth he would not have been able to keep up with the runners closing him down, going past him. It was hard to think of anything but the strain of it all, the futility of all this – why bother? It was just another silly game. The functions of his body on the brink of closing down – his heart pounding and his lungs screaming for air fresher and in greater volume than this indoor, methane-tainted bubble could provide – came before the workings of his mind, the calculation of which spin was prevailing, the curvature of swerve and the rate of descent and above all the destiny of the ball once it struck the ground. Only his eyes, their steadiness undermined by the jarring vibrations of his ragged running, and their clearness of vision threatened by the beads of salty sweat only temporarily diverted by the hairs of his eyebrows and their underlying ridges of scar tissue, did not waver. Eyes in front of which a twilight world had once swum in double now fixed a single tracking beam on the ball. And it fell to earth and behaved precisely according to his will. He caught it and he made it safe and he went into the changing room and brought Max back on stage so that they could take their bow. So that he could take his bow. Adieu, Gonzo Davies.

Kitty stumbled through the wind and the rain from the cottage to the outskirts of the village. She knew she had to observe the rules of darkness – do not be seen, murderer. She found the pick-up where she had left it, at the bottom of Upper Street. She drove home and went into the kitchen.

'Ah, there you …' began Our Marnie, but then took in the sight before her.

'I have done something,' said Kitty and began to topple. John caught her before her head hit the worktop. Our Marnie shouted for Capper. Everybody congregated in a flash in the kitchen, all talking at once. John took control, ordering Capper to carry Kitty back to the pick-up, to take her to hospital. 'Not there,' said Kitty, opening her eyes. 'The cottage.' And she wriggled with surprising strength out of John's supporting arms and said: 'I have killed a man.'

It was as if the Professor had pressed Pause on the remote again. The Orphanage stopped. And nobody made a sound.

'I have killed a man,' repeated Kitty.

'Who?' said Our Marnie. 'Who, Kitty?'

'Him.' Kitty took a deep breath. 'I should go to the pol …'

'No way,' said Dario.

'Tell us what to do, Kitty,' said John.

'I must go to the pol …'

'You must not,' said the Professor. 'Tell us what to do.'

'It will make you …'

'Tell us what to do,' said Whopper.

Cinnabar and Ragwort found Arkle emerging from his usual hollow. Cinnabar fed him the apple she had taken from the bowl Kitty restocked every day in the Orphanage, and he nuzzled the pocket of the coat that flapped in the wind, looking for more. She was about to tell Ragwort that they might have to coax and push him, but the horse turned and led the way across the moor to the cottage. When he reached it he did not head for his shelter but waited at the gate, as if he knew his work was not yet done. Perhaps he sensed there was another apple. Capper and Our Marnie were inside, staring at Martin on the floor, illuminated by the table lamp they had dared turn on. They had to see. They wanted to see him. John and the Professor were in the kitchen, looking under the sink. They reappeared, the Professor with a bucket of water and cloths, John wearing an incongruous pair of yellow rubber gloves. Our Marnie could not see Gonzo in rubber gloves. The cleaners stopped in front of Martin and John gave a little cough.

'Oh,' said Capper. 'Righto.' He still hesitated. 'Can't say I've ever done this before. Better treat it like a fuckin' bag o' sand, I suppose … think of it as a ruck that's got to be cleared out … or …'

'Capper,' said Our Marnie. 'We haven't got all night.'

Capper decided that there was no point in being delicate. He grabbed Martin and with a grunt picked him up, slung him over his shoulder and carried him outside. Cinnabar couldn't watch and, as she withdrew, Arkle turned with her and Ragwort had to calm the horse. Arkle tossed his head but stood still as Capper unloaded Martin on his broad back. Cinnabar gave him a pat and led him back to the moor, into the wind and the rain – a young woman in zebra-striped pyjamas beneath her coat, leading an old horse, with a corpse draped over him and a cortège of Capper, Our Marnie and Ragwort close behind. A few paces further back came Whopper Jones, pushing Martin's bicycle. Inside the cottage, John and the Professor scrubbed and dabbed and wiped and rinsed. Kitty sat in the kitchen of the cottage, feeling the colour returning to her cheeks. More than colour. She felt alive. She felt strong. And high on the mountainside, little Dario, panting and soaked, threw down his crutches and leaned against the rock wall of one of his natural shelters and kept watch, making sure his were the only eyes on the wilderness, that he alone saw the faint light from the cottage as the stains left by Martin Guest were made to disappear.

Gonzo sat in the Sir Tasker with Noa and Perrine. Max was rallying the team for one more burst of celebration before they fell into their beds and slept for what remained of the night – before they made their weary, joyous way back home. Gonzo would not be going with them. There would be no extra month in Paris. He had not broken the great taboo, and Perrine had snapped out of her daze of the scorned. For now. Gonzo did not know what he might do as a normal human being in the world beyond his final, final whistle. Or how long Max could keep swimming against the downward pull, keep striking for the surface, not surrendering to free-fall into the deep, the pit that beckoned to the thrill junkie. When next Gonzo opened the door to Perrine, would he be able to push her away – gently, gently touch her arm and turn her and steer her back to a Max that could not put her before the demons that reached out to him?

The body of Martin Guest disappeared down the hole into Capper's cave. Capper and Whopper tipped him off Arkle and he was gone without a sound. With a shudder, Capper climbed down the rope he had brought and made sure the corpse went to the side of the spike of rock that had broken his own fall. Once on the edge of the chamber of horrors, he kicked Martin without ceremony into the blackness and heard him land. He clambered back to the surface and pulled the rope up for the last time.

The bike was a little too wide to go all the way down the hole. They noticed that the first light of day was appearing. They needed to be off the mountain. They left the bike where it was, caught at the bend where the vertical drop levelled out. Capper pulled the rock back over the hole against the boulder. Whopper was amazed at the natural hinging of the rock and pushed it back and forth. He was also worried that it might be too easily re-opened in the future. He bent his long frame and put his shoulder to the rock and signalled to Capper that they should push to one side. They heaved – heads up, backs straight – and the rock slowly tilted out of the ground. Whopper told Capper to stop before it toppled. He put his huge hands under the exposed bottom of the rock and he lifted and twisted with all his might and the rock came back down into a new position, flat over the hole, another slab of immoveable limestone on the mountainside, a tombstone that would soon be hidden by the bracken that grew on the sheltered side of the domed top of the Blorenge.

Gonzo stood and wandered towards the toilets off the foyer of the Sir Tasker. As he left, Max came back to the table where Noa and Perrine were sitting. They watched Gonzo walk stiffly, wearily out of the room. Max sat between them and took the small pale hand of his wife, with its two expensive rings, and then he took the huge black bare hand of Noa.

'Were you tempted?' he asked Perrine. She didn't look at him, but gave a brisk nod of her head.

'And you?' Max asked Noa. And Noa's head gave one slow nod.

From the foyer Gonzo noticed it was light outside. He had his kit bag in his room, containing his medal and the ball he had caught. He had most of the clothes Perrine had bought with him in Paris in a separate case. He was wearing the dinner suit that the players had found hanging on their pegs when they finally came in off the field, after several laps of honour. Paris Max had gone, it seemed, from being buried in debt to designer-label chic overnight. The bow-tie was long removed, the top button of his dress shirt long undone. Gonzo's new shoes were pinching him a bit. He thought about going to his room to change them, but instead he walked out of the hotel and stood under the portico, looking across the Bay at the Senedd. He remembered hearing from Brian Griffiths, the President of the Welsh Rugby Union, about his selection for the Barbarians at the reception there, the party to which the village had been invited. Gonzo of the

Barbarians, a bit of gossip that slipped out. He remembered his chat in the Siambr with Carole Williams about not uncovering the real story behind the bomb. The Chamber with its secrets.

'No secrets in our shit-heap,' Capper had said to the Presiding Officer of his country.

Gonzo put his head down and walked out into weather, driven by the wind at his back up the long straight mile of Bute Street towards Cardiff Central Station. He was going home, to his cottage on the moorland just outside his village, where new life was coming out of the wilderness, where buildings would soon be cutting through the crust of filth and rising into the mountain air, cleared of its dust by the rain and the wind off the Atlantic, a cleansing storm coming up the valley, heading for the top of the Blorenge.